SWORD
OF
POWER

SWORD
OF
POWER

THE BLACK MUSKETEERS

Oliver Pötzsch

Translated by Jaime McGill

amazon crossing ⊙

Previously published as *Die Schwarzen Musketiere—Das Schwert der Macht* by bloomoon in Germany in 2016. Translated from German by Jaime McGill. First published in English by AmazonCrossing in 2018.

Published by AmazonCrossing, Seattle

www.apub.com

Amazon, the Amazon logo, and AmazonCrossing are trademarks of Amazon.com, Inc., or its affiliates.

ISBN-13: 9781503904415
ISBN-10: 1503904415

Cover design by Mike Heath | Magnus Creative

Printed in the United States of America

*In memory of Ulrich Kiesow, inventor of the German
fantasy roleplaying game* The Dark Eye.

Through that game, I became a storyteller.

Thanks, Ulli!

PROLOGUE

July Eighth in the Year of Our Lord 1633, near Hamelin in the German Empire, during the Thirty Years' War

Count Leopold von Torgau stared out at the swords clashing all around him, thrusting, piercing—and at that moment, he knew the battle was lost.

Men were gasping and shrieking in mortal fear. A twenty-pounder cannon thundered not far away, shaking the ground. Shortly thereafter, clumps of earth sprayed into the air and rained down on those few imperial-camp tents still standing.

Torgau's charger whinnied and reared up when a second cannonball hit just a few paces away. The explosion was so powerful that at first Torgau thought it had deafened him. He was thrown off balance for the briefest of moments. The reins slipped out of his hands, and he tumbled to the ground as his horse fled in terror. He crawled into one of the abandoned trenches and immediately found himself stuck knee deep in mud. He crossed himself and prayed silently.

Help me, O gracious God! Let this nightmare end . . .

The long-serving and highly decorated officer had already fought in many other battles of this German war. He was certainly no coward—he was a Black Musketeer, a member of General Wallenstein's legendary elite troop. Duke Albrecht von Wallenstein was the German Kaiser's most important general, and the Black Musketeers were known as the finest soldiers in the entire Reich. However, this battle was the bloodiest and most horrific Torgau had ever experienced, and even he was beginning to think the Devil himself had a hand in it all. How else could it be that every one of his men had been either killed, injured, or driven to desertion?

That their mission was on the brink of failure?

The German Reich had been at war for many years now: Catholics against Protestants, imperial troops against the princes' soldiers—even Swedes, Danes, and Saxons against Bavarians and Spaniards. There was no end in sight to the war, and each fighter hoped to make off with the greatest spoils. Through the thick fog of gunpowder, Leopold von Torgau saw the enemy men-at-arms storming the imperial camp with pikes, short swords, and long knives, bellowing and shrieking. A musket ball whizzed past, mere inches from Torgau's helmet. He ducked and loaded the only remaining shot into his pistol.

I'm the last, he thought. *I must not fail!*

The Kaiser had sent a good twelve thousand men here, near the town of Hamelin, to defeat the accursed Swedes. But the terrain was rough, full of treacherous rocks and hills, and soon riders had encircled the army, thrusting sabers and firing pistols at the foot soldiers from atop their horses. Even Torgau's Black Musketeers, normally so brave, had scarcely put up any resistance. Their courage had vanished—mainly because of unnerving rumors that had been spreading through the camp since the night before.

The enemy, the rumors said, was in league with the Devil.

There were whispers of invincible spirits, so-called frozen ones, soulless creatures who brought death and destruction wherever they went. Word had it that a wizard of black magic fighting on the Protestants' side had given them eternal life: neither bullets nor sword blows could kill them. Indeed, Leopold von Torgau had already witnessed a few eerie sights in this battle—a bolt of flame tearing through three tents, for example, or men walking upright even after numerous swords had pierced them. Perhaps Torgau had simply imagined it all; he wasn't entirely sure.

Cautiously, the old officer poked his head out of the trench and glanced around. To his relief, he discovered that the enemy forces had moved on without noticing him. He stuck his loaded pistol back into his belt and hoisted himself out of the trench. It was time to secure the powerful artifact that the Kaiser himself had entrusted Torgau to retrieve.

Torgau's Musketeers had been tasked with bringing the object back to Nürnberg. But they had all failed, and failed miserably. Now Leopold von Torgau could only hope that the enemy had not beaten him to it.

He hastened past the many wounded and dying men around him, toward a nearby hill, where a nondescript tent sat hidden amid a dense shield of trees and bushes. Torgau climbed the hill and stumbled into the abandoned tent, where he swept aside a table full of maps and battle plans, revealing a wooden panel in the ground, covered by grass and leaves. With anxious anticipation, Torgau pushed the panel to one side and reached into the hollow underneath. He felt damp wood and the cold iron of a padlock. The old warrior breathed a sigh of relief.

Thank God, it's still there!

Torgau withdrew a fine, polished walnut chest the length of his arm. He ran his fingers over the wood, tracing the silver fittings and ornamentation. The chest was old, but what it contained was far older: an artifact that, together with a few other objects, could seal the destiny of the German Reich. And now, at last, it was to be returned to Nürnberg, where—

A sudden noise made Torgau freeze.

He turned around and, to his horror, saw the point of a saber boring through the tent canvas. It sliced the cloth from top to bottom, creating a slit the length of a man.

The Devil stepped through it.

Gasping, Leopold von Torgau stumbled backward a few steps, still clutching the chest in both hands. The man who had just entered the tent through the tear in the fabric was towering and broad shouldered, with long, oily black hair. He wore a helmet, a cuirass, and pantaloons—a typical mercenary, probably from the southern Spanish lands. But what shocked Torgau was not the soldier's size, but the look in his eyes.

These were the eyes of a dead man.

Now that the man was close, Torgau saw the many gaping wounds on his body as well—each one surely a fatal blow, yet none of them stopping him from closing in on Torgau. The soldier with the dead eyes growled.

"Stop, you monster!" Torgau commanded. With grim determination, he clamped the chest under one arm and aimed his pistol at his adversary. He only had this one shot; he had to make it count. His mission was too important! If this chest fell into the wrong hands, all was lost. "Not another step or I'll shoot!" Torgau gasped. He cocked the gun, ready to fire at any moment.

The huge man with the dead eyes grinned. "Try . . . it," the mercenary said in a strangely sluggish, creaky voice, as though dragging each word from the depths of a grave. "You . . . can't . . . kill . . . me."

"Nonsense, of course I can! See for yourself!"

There was a loud bang; the weapon's recoil sent Torgau tumbling back. He stared, dumbfounded. The mercenary was still standing there grinning at him, a fresh hole in his breastplate.

Right at the level of his heart.

"As I . . . said," the mercenary creaked. "You . . . can't kill me. *I'm . . . already . . . dead.*"

The giant lurched slowly toward Leopold von Torgau, who could only stand there gaping, awaiting his fate. His hands trembled so violently that the chest crashed to the ground.

Ghosts! So these frozen ones really do exist! My men were right. Black magic, the Devil . . . The count tried to wrap his mind around this realization.

Then the man with the dead eyes reached him.

I

Two Weeks Later
Near Heidelberg in the Palatinate

The old buck stood peacefully at the edge of the clearing, perfectly unaware of its imminent death. It was a magnificent twelve-pointer with sharp antlers and powerful flanks. Lukas lay on his stomach about thirty paces away, holding his breath. From behind the cover of a blackberry bush, he aimed his crossbow at the beautiful, noble animal.

Lukas hesitated for a moment, but he knew he could not allow himself to feel pity. He and his comrades had caught only a couple of small rabbits and partridges in the past few days—not nearly enough to feed all the residents of Lohenfels Castle. The war had brought poverty and hunger to the Palatinate; the fields had been trampled or scorched in the summer heat, and the people desperately needed something to eat. Lukas said a short prayer of thanks and then curled his fingers around the trigger.

Just as he was about to fire, the buck collapsed as though it had been struck by lightning.

"What the hell?"

Lukas stared at his crossbow, baffled. The bolt was still in the groove. So what had brought the buck down so suddenly? Was there another hunter hiding somewhere in the clearing? Perhaps even some malicious assassin? Mercenaries were always wandering through the woods, robbing and murdering without pity—even here, near Lohenfels Castle, Lukas's home. He glanced around cautiously as he reached for the dagger on his belt. A twig snapped somewhere in the dim light of the forest, birds fluttered up, and a jay screeched over his head.

All at once, peals of laughter rang out like bells, and Lukas exhaled in relief.

"Elsa!" he sighed, sheathing his weapon again. "Damn, I should have known you'd be snooping around."

His younger sister stepped out into the clearing, just a few paces away. Elsa had flaxen hair that contrasted sharply with Lukas's black mane, and now, in the summer, she had more freckles than there were stars in the sky. At eleven years old, she was impudent at times, precocious at others. Both often got on Lukas's nerves.

"You didn't see me!" she giggled. "Admit it, I scared you!"

"Ha ha, very funny!" Lukas gestured at the motionless buck. "I swear, Elsa, if you had anything to do with that, then—"

"You should have seen your face!" she interrupted, laughing. "That alone was worth the spell."

"Spell?" Lukas gave a start. "You . . . you mean you used magic again?" He straightened up and gave his younger sister a stern look. "Didn't you promise me you would only use magic in emergencies?" Lukas still couldn't get used to the fact that Elsa could actually do magic. Not cheap village-fair tricks, but real magic. She'd apparently inherited the ability from their mother, Countess Sophia von Lohenfels, who had practiced white magic and had been a healer.

Elsa shrugged, pouting. "I do have to practice. What if a real emergency happens and I can't defend myself, hm? What if Spanish mercenaries suddenly show up, or frozen ones, or even Waldemar von Schönborn—"

"Be quiet, Elsa!" Lukas broke in. "We agreed we would never mention his name again."

Finding out that Elsa was only his half sister, and that the dark inquisitor and magician Waldemar von Schönborn was Elsa's father, had come as a shock to both siblings. Even though Elsa hated her father, Lukas feared she was more like him than she would admit.

Especially when she used her magic.

"Not talking about him doesn't put us any less in danger," Elsa spat. She turned completely serious; the sneering look vanished from her eyes. "Lukas, you know we aren't safe here at Lohenfels. Not as long as we have no idea what *he's* planning. He'll seek revenge, one of these days!"

They both lapsed into sullen silence, and Lukas found himself thinking back on the past two years, which had changed him and his younger sister so much. It had been two summers since Inquisitor Waldemar von Schönborn and his battalion of Spanish mercenaries had descended upon their home, Castle Lohenfels. Lukas's father, Count von Lohenfels, had been killed in the attack; their mother had been burned at the stake as a witch in Heidelberg, and Elsa had been abducted by Schönborn. It had taken Lukas over a year to find his sister again—and to discover a secret long kept by their mother.

It was the secret of the *Grimorium Nocturnum*, the *Book of the Night*, the most powerful magic book in the world.

That book was now in Elsa's possession—which was why she was able to perform real magic. The *Grimorium* and Elsa's powers had driven Inquisitor Schönborn away, but Lukas suspected that he would one day return to recover the book.

"You mean you have the *Grimorium* with you now?" Lukas asked quietly. "If you're right about us being unsafe at Lohenfels, then we're even less safe here in the woods! We agreed the book would remain in the castle library."

"Don't worry." Elsa shrugged. "I no longer need the *Grimorium* to do magic. At least, not the smaller spells. I've already memorized quite a few."

"I was afraid of that," Lukas murmured, mostly to himself. The very thought of the *Grimorium* sometimes robbed him of sleep. He was afraid that *any* spells might draw Schönborn's attention. But that didn't stop Elsa from spending nearly every evening paging through the book and occasionally using the spells.

"Not knowing what our enemy is planning is all the more reason to be cautious," Lukas admonished his sister. "Magic is no game, Elsa!"

"Fine, then, we'll just remove the spell, since young Master Lohenfels prefers it that way. EVIGILIA ACUTUM!" Elsa clapped her hands, and the buck got back to its feet again, wobbling a little, as though just awakening from a deep sleep. Before Lukas could reach for his crossbow, the animal bounded off into the woods.

"Damn it, Elsa, I didn't mean it like that!" he exclaimed. "You know how badly we needed that meat. You finally cast a useful spell for once, and then you go and do this!"

"So *do* you want me to use magic, or *don't* you?" Furious tears sprang to Elsa's eyes. "I only wanted to help, but there's no pleasing you! You're . . . you're just jealous that I can do magic and you can't!"

Lukas rolled his eyes. "Elsa, that's not true. It's just that . . ."

But Elsa had already turned and run off into the forest. Lukas wanted to hurry after her, but decided to let her go. Even though he was fourteen now, nearly a young man, Elsa rarely listened to what he had to say anymore. He decided to abandon his hunt for today and go back to the castle. He was sure Elsa would show up again once she was finished pouting.

He uncocked his crossbow, slung it over his shoulder, and set off for home. The late-afternoon sun shone pleasantly warm though the dense foliage; birds twittered, and a rushing stream gurgled somewhere nearby—but Lukas was still uneasy.

Again and again, he found himself thinking of the evil Waldemar von Schönborn and his black magic.

Lukas left the forest behind him and hastened up toward the castle. Lohenfels sat enthroned atop a rocky promontory, a hundred paces above the Neckar, the broad, languid river flowing toward Heidelberg. Several fields and farmhouses to the west of the castle walls belonged to the estate as well. It still amazed Lukas how quickly they had managed to rebuild his parents' property. When he'd returned here with Elsa six months ago, they'd found Lohenfels almost completely destroyed at the hands of the Swedes. But thanks to the help of the rest of the castle denizens and many other farmers in the area, the castle now stood above the river once more, nearly as proud and mighty as it had been back when Lukas's parents were still alive. Lohenfels was a small, humble manor—nothing like the Kaiser's huge castle in Vienna—but Lukas had always been proud of his home.

He strode quickly across the broad ramp leading up to the open castle gate. Beyond it was a courtyard surrounded by several stone buildings. Completing the scene were a tall tower, the servants' quarters, and the main building itself, which looked more like a defiant fortress than an actual palace.

Two farmers in tattered garments were unloading a sack from a cart and carrying it over to the storehouse. Standing beside them was an older gray-haired man. It was Eberhart, the castellan, who was managing castle affairs until Lukas came of age.

Eberhart gestured sadly to the two small sacks remaining on the cart. "This is all the barley the farmers were able to reap this year," he explained. "The hailstorm a couple of weeks ago destroyed almost everything."

"And now we're taking part of this meager harvest away from them," Lukas replied, scowling. "Is that fair?"

Eberhart shrugged. "This has been the custom for ages. The church receives one portion, the castle another."

"Leaving the farmers to starve?" Lukas protested.

"My young lord," Eberhart sighed. They'd discussed this topic many times before. "The servants at the castle need to eat, too. And we have expenses. Restoring the castle costs money, and now a summer storm has ruined our vineyard in the Palatinate as well." The old man shook his head. "I'll have to travel there tomorrow and look into the situation myself. And I pray to God that—"

"Good Lord, is this worrywart talking your ears off again?" a bear-like voice growled behind him. "Come on over here instead, and help us get this monster ready for dinner."

Lukas glanced toward the castle gate. It was tall, broad-shouldered Paulus, standing there grinning at him along with Lukas's other friends, Giovanni and Jerome. The three of them were carrying a massive wild boar tied to a rod, its tongue lolling out of its mouth.

"Feel free to help," Giovanni groaned as they hefted the burden off their shoulders for a moment. "This beast weighs at least as much as the fat innkeeper at the village tavern. We carried it all the way up from the river."

"You mean *I* carried it," Paulus growled, flexing his powerful biceps. "You two held the ears at best."

Seeing his friends lifted Lukas's spirits a little. They'd met two years ago and performed as fencers in a group of traveling artists. The four of them had survived quite a few adventures since then, and had even joined the ranks of the legendary Black Musketeers, an elite troop under the command of General Wallenstein. Lukas's friends had been living here at Castle Lohenfels for a good six months now and had become like brothers to Lukas—not least because they occasionally quarreled and scuffled like brothers.

"*We* found this fine specimen down at the ford," Jerome said in his French accent. He laughed. "I suppose it was looking to buy passage to

Heidelberg!" As always, Jerome was wearing the finest clothes—in his red velvet doublet, he looked like he was headed to a ball rather than returning from a hunt. A long ash bow dangled from his shoulder. "And you?" He winked at Lukas as they carried the heavy animal to one corner of the courtyard. "Catch any rabbits? From the look on your face, I'm guessing not."

"I nearly shot a fine buck," Lukas snapped. Then he lowered his voice so that Castellan Eberhart couldn't hear. "But Elsa cast a spell on it."

"A spell?" Giovanni looked up, sounding annoyed. "*Malissimo!* We expressly forbade her to do that." Although he was already fifteen, Giovanni was scarcely any larger than Lukas. What he did have, though, was the mind of a learned man, and he sometimes used such prim language that they all had trouble understanding him, especially their strong friend Paulus. "Upon my soul, if Elsa persists, every farmer in the region will soon know that a witch resides at Lohenfels again," Giovanni whispered. "And I need not quote the infamous *Book of the Inquisition* to make you understand what they do with witches around here."

"I think you know as well as I do that forbidding Elsa to do something doesn't stop her," Lukas replied. "What am I supposed to do, tie her up in the library?"

"Maybe not such a bad idea." Jerome whistled through his teeth. "*Mon dieu,* your sister can really drive a person crazy sometimes. You know I like girls, but she can sure be an intolerable, know-it-all beast."

"An intolerable beast that can do magic, unfortunately," Paulus added grumpily. "So watch what you all say, or she'll make our noses grow, and shrink another important part of ours."

The others laughed, and even Lukas forced himself to smile. "It's true," he admitted. "Elsa is truly insufferable sometimes. But she's still my younger sister. I'm responsible for making sure that nothing happens to her." His face grew serious. "Giovanni is right. What if other people find out that she can do magic? Just think about what happened to my mother! They'd burn Elsa at the stake." He clenched his hands into fists. "Damned witchcraft. If only we'd never found that book."

"I'm starving," Paulus grunted, pulling out his knife. "Let's forget about Elsa and witchcraft for a moment and take care of this boar, or we'll be having dinner at midnight."

◆ ◆ ◆

The four friends ate in the great hall, which was always cool and damp. There was a small fire burning in the fireplace, though it was giving off more smoke than actual heat. Elsa didn't join them. The castellan had informed Lukas that his sister had returned to Lohenfels some time ago and had shut herself away in the library.

The castle library was Elsa's favorite place. She went there to flip through the *Grimorium* and read the many books that had once belonged to their mother. Elsa had always been a bookworm—unlike Lukas, who preferred a good fencing match over a book any day. Besides, his Latin was awful, and most of the books in the library were written in that ancient, hideously boring language.

Paulus bit into his leg of boar with visible relish. It was already his second. Sometimes Lukas could scarcely believe how much food sixteen-year-old Paulus could put away. Of course, Paulus also had the strength of three men. He washed down the boar with a swallow of beer and belched loudly. "God knows what Elsa spends all that time doing up there," he muttered, pointing up at the ceiling. "Well, let her eat her books, then, if she's got such an appetite for them. More boar left for us and the servants."

"All you think about is eating and fighting, fat man." Giovanni smirked. "Books really can be filling, though. Back when I was a novitiate, I once read for two days and nights without stopping to eat." Giovanni was the third son of a minor noble from the Verona area. His parents had shipped him off to a monastery, which he fled. But he still had the wealth of knowledge he'd acquired in the monastery library—and had helped his friends many times with it.

"A scrawny little herring like you can manage that, maybe," Paulus retorted, grinning, as he took another steaming slice of meat from the platter. "People like us need something more solid."

"Eat while it's there." Jerome dabbed his lips with his lace handkerchief and glanced around solemnly at his friends. "It might be our last piece of meat for some time."

"What do you mean?" Lukas asked.

Jerome shrugged. "Word has it that war is returning to the Palatinate. Just two weeks ago, there was another large battle in the North, somewhere near Hamelin. I imagine we'll soon see towns and villages burning again around here. *Merde!*"

Jerome had fled Alsace as a child; his parents, traveling jugglers, had been murdered by mercenaries. He often sought comfort in the arms of beautiful girls, who seemed to fall for his good looks by the dozen.

"The war is still far away," Paulus assured him.

"Not far enough." Jerome furrowed his brow. "You all know how quickly an army like that can march. The mercenaries could be here in a couple of weeks. And the castle isn't sufficiently fortified yet."

All at once, Lukas's appetite vanished. Jerome's news made him uneasy. It was more or less peaceful here at the edge of the Odenwald Mountains, but that could change from one day to the next. Practically the entire Reich had been in flames since Lukas's birth. Everyone was fighting—it seemed like half the world had been battling on German soil for an eternity. People were freezing to death in the hard winters, starving from the poor harvests, and succumbing to the plague. More than a few regions were so thoroughly deserted that only wolves and bears wandered through the desolate villages.

And then, somewhere out there, there was an evil magician who had sworn eternal vengeance upon them.

"Where do you suppose that rat Schönborn has crawled off to?" Paulus asked, as though reading Lukas's thoughts. "To be honest, I'm more worried about him than about a few Swedes."

Giovanni pushed his plate aside, having apparently lost his appetite as well. "The last we heard was that he had gone to Rome to collect his strength again, and that he was likely to be named a cardinal there." He shook his head. "A magician as cardinal. If only the Pope knew! Alas, Schönborn is an adept pretender and has him fooled."

"Somehow, I have the feeling that we'll be hearing from him again soon," Lukas said quietly.

After what became a very monosyllabic meal, Lukas took a couple of pieces of cold roast boar, a jug of cider, and half a loaf of bread upstairs to the library. He knocked softly on the door.

"Elsa? I know you're in there. Open up."

"I don't want to see any of you idiots!" Elsa called from inside. "Go back to your stupid friends with their stupid swords and crossbows!"

"I brought you something to eat. Meat and bread and . . ."

Abruptly, the lock clicked, and the door opened a crack, revealing Elsa's face. She winked at her brother. "Well, that's a different story. I . . . ah, I actually am a little hungry." She accepted the food eagerly, hurried over to a table piled high with books, and began stuffing her mouth with roast.

Lukas grinned. Their earlier argument had apparently been forgotten. "A *little* hungry?" he echoed teasingly. "You're eating like a starving wolf!" Then he looked down at a plain little book on top of one of the piles. It was bound in worn black leather, with no title or decorations. "That's it, isn't it?" he whispered, as though someone could hear them. "It's been a long time since I've seen it."

Until a few months ago, the *Grimorium* had been safely tucked away in a box in the cellar, but then his sister had insisted upon hiding it here in the library.

Elsa nodded to the door. "Better lock that," she said between bites. "Just to be safe."

"Why?" Lukas asked, laughing. "Are you afraid the *Grimorium* will fly out and attack Paulus?"

"Who knows? I don't know enough about its power yet. But you've seen yourself what the *Grimorium* is capable of, so best just to lock the door." Elsa's tone was absolutely serious, and suddenly Lukas wasn't in the mood for jokes anymore, either.

He slid the bolt into place, and then sat back down at the table and stared at the book.

The *Grimorium Nocturnum* was the most powerful magic book in the world. After remaining well hidden for centuries, it had come into their mother's possession. Inquisitor Waldemar von Schönborn had tortured the countess in an effort to seize the book for himself, but Sophia von Lohenfels had kept her silence until the end, never revealing its hiding place. Lukas, Elsa, and Lukas's friends had been the ones who ultimately found it.

Lukas shivered in the dark, cold library. This book lying unassumingly on the table before him was the most dangerous object he knew— more lethal than any sword, more destructive than any cannon.

And it had made his sister into a sorceress.

Lukas had often toyed with the idea of destroying the *Grimorium*, of simply burning it or tearing it into a thousand pieces. But he knew Elsa would never forgive him. "Listen," Lukas said. "I know you were only trying to help me hunt earlier, but I really feel like you shouldn't use the book's power too often. Not only because people will start spreading rumors about a possible new witch at Lohenfels, but also . . ." He hesitated.

"Also what?" Elsa wiped her greasy mouth.

"Because the book is changing you."

Elsa laughed. "How do you mean? Because it's making me older? Wiser, more mature?" She shook her head. "How often have I used this to help you in the past few months? Just think about those robbers I drove away."

"You set two of the men's hair on fire," Lukas replied quietly. "One of them didn't make it to the river in time and died miserably."

"Rightful punishment." Elsa nodded, looking dour. "They would have killed us like they killed the chickens, otherwise."

"And the kitchen maid with the red pustules on her face?"

"She was rude to me. I thought the pustules suited her." Elsa giggled, taking another piece of cold roast.

"She was crying when she left the castle. We have no idea what she told people in Heidelberg. Besides, it was unnecessary," Lukas said. "What next?" He gestured to the book. "Are you going to turn the cook into a slimy toad for burning the barley porridge?"

"Idiot. You know I couldn't do that, even if I wanted to. I haven't studied the *Grimorium* long enough. All the signs and runes in there—sometimes they speak to me, like little black angels." Elsa abruptly went completely still. After a moment, she shook herself as though clearing a bad dream from her mind. "You're right, I should be more careful with the book." She rose to her feet and lifted the tome with two fingers, as though handling a sachet of explosive gunpowder, and carried it over to a heavy, iron-studded box on a shelf. She locked the book inside the box using a key that hung on a chain around her neck. "I sense that *he* still wants it," she whispered. "And he wants me, too"—her voice cracked—"because I'm his daughter."

Lukas drew her in and hugged her tightly. Elsa hated Schönborn—but he was still her father. She was the child of a white-magic witch and a wizard of black magic, a discovery that now made her seem far older than eleven sometimes. She was only his little sister, but at those moments, Lukas felt like he was looking into the eyes of an old woman.

"Let's forget the book for a while," he said, comforting her. "What do you say we go up to the tower and look at the stars? The way we used to, when our parents were still alive."

Elsa smiled gratefully. "Yes, like before. Let's just be brother and sister again. That's what we are, aren't we?" She gave him a tight squeeze, and then the two of them tiptoed out into the hall, sneaking across the courtyard and up the stairs to the top of the tower—like two perfectly normal children on a nighttime excursion.

But Lukas knew that they were no normal children.

Neither of them was normal.

II

"Keep your guard up, damn it! Otherwise the enemy will bore holes in you like sacks of flour. Wrath cut, feint, lunge, thwart cut! God in heaven, I said *thwart*, not stroke and tickle!" Paulus was sitting on the edge of the well in the courtyard, his broad arms propped to either side of him as he watched two dozen farm boys laboriously practice stick fighting. It was early the following morning, and although the sun was just coming up behind the keep, it was already as hot as an oven outside.

The boys were standing in two rows, facing each other. Lukas, Giovanni, and Jerome had interspersed themselves among the young fighters. Lukas stood across from a skinny twelve-year-old named Jonathan from the neighboring village. The boy trembled in awe as he held his ash stick in the air. Lukas had developed a reputation as a fencing legend, particularly over the past few months.

"You need to pay more attention to your legs," he told his scrawny training partner. "Your legs are just as important as your arms. Every fight is like a dance. See? Like this." Lukas took a few steps forward and then to the side as the boy followed his lead. Then Lukas feinted to the right with his sword hand, before swiftly lunging left. The boy's stick clattered to the ground.

"S-sorry, my lord," the farmer's boy stammered, lowering his eyes. "I'll probably never be a good fencer."

"Sure you will! It's all a matter of practice. Practice, practice, practice, every day! And stop calling me 'lord,' or next time I'll smack you in the fingers so hard that you can't hold a spoon for two weeks." Lukas winked. "And now, retrieve thy sword, noble squire," he said, gesturing at the stick. "The battle against the dragon continues. Into position!"

They returned to their starting stances, and the fight began again. This time, the boy made more of an effort. He danced back and forth, prancing nimbly and carefully watching Lukas's movements. Finally, he went for a lunge of his own.

At the last second, Lukas stepped aside, dodging the attack.

"Much better already," Lukas praised the panting boy, clapping him on the shoulder. He thought back to how his father had practiced with him every day. Lukas's hands had often been black and blue afterward.

Paulus interrupted Lukas's thoughts. "Damn it, if you keep fighting like that, we can only hope that the Swedes will die laughing," he thundered from the edge of the well. As the son of a Cologne weaponsmith, he was the one in their group who most knew his way around weapons. Paulus leapt to the ground, snatched up a cudgel, and began thrashing two of the boys with it at the same time, until they nearly fell into the well. "Ox, low cut, follow after . . . like that!"

"Stop it, Paulus!" Giovanni scolded. "You're going to beat them to a pulp, and then the Swedes will be victorious for sure."

Paulus lowered the cudgel, grinning, and wiped the sweat from his brow. He had been practicing nearly every day with the farm boys for a good two months now. A few of them were genuinely gifted, but most could barely tell a mace from a pitchfork. Even so, the four friends had made it their goal to turn the boys into a regiment fit for battle, so that if the Swedes or some other band of mercenaries attacked Lohenfels and its villages again, they would be in for a nasty surprise this time around. With the battle up near Hamelin, however, they were in danger of running out of time.

"When I think back to how we fought with the Black Musketeers," Paulus snarled. "Commander Zoltan and his men would have eaten these whelps for breakfast!"

"The Black Musketeers are trained soldiers, they've been practicing for years," Lukas said sternly. "These are farmers, and I think they're doing pretty well, considering."

"Pretty well isn't enough. They need to be better. Better than the Swedes, the Danes, the Spaniards, or whatever other brood of vipers shows up here in the Odenwald." Paulus clapped his hands. "Back to work! Everyone find a new sparring partner!"

The boys took their places again, and Lukas watched them get a tiny bit better with every blow.

One more year! he thought. *Then we'll have a properly trained regiment here.* But he knew that they wouldn't have a whole year. Maybe not even a whole month.

Lukas glanced up toward the castle battlements and saw Elsa sitting on the platform of the keep tower, engrossed in a book. Though her legs dangled a good fifteen paces above the ground, she was clearly unafraid—but then, suddenly, something seemed to unnerve her. She straightened up and stared eastward, toward the Heidelberg road leading up to the castle.

"What is it?" Lukas called to her. "Did you see something?"

Elsa nodded. She disappeared down the trapdoor, and a few moments later she joined the others down in the courtyard. "A lone rider!" she panted, out of breath from running. "He's still pretty far away, but it looked like he was wearing clerical robes." She hesitated. "Maybe even those of a cardinal. I couldn't see whether any other riders were following him."

"Schönborn!" Lukas gasped. "I knew it! He probably has a whole battalion of papal soldiers with him." He turned to his friends. "Tell the castle guards and the farm boys to be at the ready! If it *is* the inquisitor, he won't find us defenseless."

"You bet your ass he won't. The bastard won't escape me this time!" Paulus reached for his broad, freshly sharpened saber, which was sitting on the edge of the well. The four friends exchanged grim looks. Lukas, Giovanni, and Jerome all girded their rapiers.

"To hell!" Lukas called.

"And beyond!" the others shouted back in chorus, completing the Black Musketeers' old battle cry.

Together, they stormed toward the portcullis.

The rider approached slowly, still alone. From the parapet above the gate they could see that he sat atop an elegant black horse. His attire was similar to clerical robes, but rather than a red cardinal's cassock, the man wore a strange blue cloak that almost seemed to glow, as though swallowing up the sunlight and then casting it out again.

Lukas blinked. "I think we can relax," he said hesitantly. "It isn't Schönborn. If I could just see his face in the sun, I . . ." He stopped short, realizing who was riding toward them.

"Senno!" Elsa cried in surprise. "It's Senno!" She let out a relieved laugh—but then her expression darkened again. "He's probably here for the *Grimorium*, but he can forget about that. It's mine!"

Senno was General Wallenstein's court astrologer, a shady reader of the stars. He had helped the friends find the *Grimorium* during their last adventure. Paulus, Giovanni, and Jerome didn't trust him, but Lukas treasured his knowledge and his wisdom. Senno was Schönborn's greatest adversary; he had seen through the inquisitor before anyone else had. Of course, Lukas could not be sure that Senno wasn't after the *Grimorium*, just as Schönborn was.

Lukas stared down at Senno, who had now stopped in front of the castle gate. The astrologer had hardly changed since Lukas had last seen him, six months before. He wore a simple priest's cap, and his twirled goatee was as neatly groomed as ever. Peering closer, Lukas could make out several strange symbols on the blue cloak. A few of the castle guards and farm boys began murmuring to one another and crossing themselves.

"Greetings, my young friends!" Senno called up to them. He gestured to the castle. "I see you've done quite a bit of work," he added. "The last time I was here, not a stone was left standing."

"What do you want, astro-babbler?" Paulus snapped at him. "If you want to tell the future, you're better off performing at the Heidelberg fair."

"How about you all start by letting your old friend in?" Senno asked in his usual bright, clear voice. "Before your superstitious guards shoot me full of arrows?"

Lukas opened the gate himself. Senno dismounted and led his horse into the courtyard, where he handed the reins to a servant and came toward Lukas and Elsa with open arms. "The Lohenfels siblings," he cried. "How wonderful to see you two happily reunited!"

Lukas bowed, but Elsa held back, seeming to withdraw into herself. Apparently she was still afraid Senno was going to try to steal her *Grimorium*.

"It is a great honor for us to welcome General Wallenstein's court astrologer here to our castle," Lukas said in a formal tone. "Do make yourself at home."

Senno raised an eyebrow. "Oho, he already talks like a real count! Your parents would be proud of you, Lukas." He glanced around at the farmer boys, who were still eyeing him suspiciously. "I'm sure you'll make a fine lord to your subjects one day."

"Ever the old sweet-talker," Giovanni whispered to Lukas. "My opinion is the same as ever. I only trust him as far as I can spit."

"Well, let's just see what he wants first," Lukas replied quietly.

They all sat down together around the fireplace in the great hall. The narrow windows let in only a little sun, so Senno's face was masked in shadows. The eerie blue cloak looked almost black in the dim light. The astrologer left the bread and cheese on the table untouched, but he did ask for a large carafe of wine.

"Mm, that's a fine red wine you have here," Senno said after taking a deep swallow from his goblet. He wiped his mouth and nodded with pleasure. "From your own Palatinate vineyards, I assume—for which your esteemed castellan set off just this morning." He sighed. "Pity that I won't have a chance to meet him."

"Something tells me that you chose this exact moment to visit us here," Giovanni retorted. "Is that not so?"

"Let's say I . . . uh, wanted to speak with you all undisturbed." Senno looked around. "And are we? Undisturbed here, I mean?"

"We've sent the farm boys home, and the servants are over in the kitchen," Lukas said. "So talk already! What brings you here?"

"Let's not be impatient, young count." Senno took another deep drink of wine. His expression turned very serious, and Lukas sensed that they were done with polite small talk. "Do you all remember how I told you about Emperor Charlemagne's sword the last time I visited you?"

"You said it had disappeared," Lukas recalled. "Dark forces stole it."

"Indeed, dark forces." The astrologer nodded grimly. "And they succeeded even though the sword is part of the venerated Imperial Regalia."

"The imperial . . . what?" Jerome gave him a blank look. *"Je ne comprends pas."*

Giovanni rolled his eyes. "Don't they teach you anything in France apart from wine, women, and song? The Imperial Regalia are the most sacred objects in the entire German Reich! They need them in order to crown a new German king. What were they again?" Giovanni began counting on his fingers. "The sword, the crown, the scepter, the holy lance, the cross, the orb . . . and a dozen others at least. As far as I know, they're all safely stored away in Nürnberg."

"Well, I guess they're not anymore, you know-it-all," Paulus broke in as he poured himself a tankard of beer—a drink he quite enjoyed, unlike Lukas and the others. "If I understand the astro-driveler here correctly, the sword is gone."

Senno raised his eyebrows, looking annoyed. "That is correct. Only no one has noticed yet. There is a convincing counterfeit in Nürnberg, and it has been a while since the last coronation. Unfortunately, more Regalia have disappeared without a trace as well."

"Disappeared without a trace?" Elsa echoed, giving Senno a skeptical look. "Priceless objects like those don't vanish into thin air. Weren't they locked away safely?"

"Well, the imperial sword was stolen from the Hospital of the Holy Spirit in Nürnberg a long time ago. No one knows how." Senno furrowed his brow. "The imperial crown went missing while in Vienna. It was there for the Kaiser's formal ceremony. Now the imperial scepter has been lost as well! The Kaiser himself gave it to his generals, hoping that it would aid them to victory—a foolish idea, if you ask me." He shook his head. "A certain Leopold von Torgau, of the Black Musketeers, was charged with looking after the scepter."

"Torgau!" Giovanni cried. "Commander Zoltan mentioned him quite a bit. Old comrade of his, I think."

Lukas, too, recalled Torgau's name having come up in conversation with Zoltan. Lukas had always had a particularly close relationship with the commander of the Black Musketeers; Zoltan had known his father well.

Senno nodded and took another sip of wine. "Leopold von Torgau was one of the Black Musketeers' best fighters, but even he could not prevent the scepter from being stolen during the battle near Hamelin."

"We heard about that battle," Paulus said. "Does anyone know who stole the scepter?"

"Unfortunately, dear old Torgau can no longer tell us who the thief was. God rest his soul." Senno cleared his throat. "But I have suspicions about who was behind it. You all know him."

Lukas jumped up from his stool, his heart hammering in his chest. "You mean . . ."

"Indeed." Senno nodded. "Everything points to Waldemar von Schönborn. His accursed frozen ones were spotted at the battle near Hamelin. Word has it that there was something unnatural about the other two thefts as well."

"But what would Schönborn want with the Imperial Regalia?" Elsa still looked skeptical. "I don't expect he's trying to make himself king of Germany?"

Senno let out his high, crystalline laugh. "Not exactly, no. But having three of the most important parts of the Regalia means he can blackmail the Reich. Emperor Ferdinand is old and feeble now; the next coronation is likely not far off. With the Regalia in Schönborn's grasp, he can make whatever demands he likes of the German princes." Senno lowered his voice. "He's already a cardinal in Rome. If he decides he wants to become confessor to the new emperor as well, the entire Reich will be at the mercy of his black magic. And in such terrible times, too!"

"A truly tragic story," Jerome replied, shrugging. "*C'est horrible.* But what does it have to do with us?"

"With you four, nothing. But with her . . ." Senno pointed a thin finger at Elsa, who flinched. "If anyone can . . . dispossess Schönborn of the Regalia again, it's this girl. Elsa is the only one capable of it!"

No one said anything for a while.

Finally, Lukas cleared his throat. "Give me one reason why Elsa should leave Lohenfels and put herself in such danger." He regarded Senno, arms crossed. "Just one."

"Perhaps because this is about the fate of the entire German Reich, and Elsa Schönborn is the only one capable of mounting any real resistance?" Senno retorted. "Don't forget, now that her mother is dead, she's the last of the white witches."

Lukas bit his lip. Senno had been the one who first explained white and black magic to him. Both came from the druids who had lived in remote valleys and impenetrable forests long ago. The Romans had driven them there, and had killed many of them as well. The white-magic druids had devoted themselves to the healing arts and other helpful spells, whereas the black-magic druids pursued revenge and destruction. Sophia von Lohenfels had apparently been the last white witch, and her powers had passed to Elsa.

"If we want to defeat Schönborn and retrieve the Regalia from him, we need Elsa," Senno insisted, jolting Lukas out of his brooding. "No one else can do it."

"You mean you need the *Grimorium*," Jerome remarked, scowling.

Senno sighed. "Believe me, if I could use the book alone, I wouldn't need to go begging you for it. I would just come to Lohenfels with a company of soldiers and take it from you. A few farm children could hardly stop me."

"You treacherous little . . ." Paulus jumped out of his chair, but Lukas held him back.

"I'm not going to do that, of course." Senno smiled. "As the past has unfortunately shown, the *Grimorium Nocturnum* has already chosen its young owner. Taking it away from Elsa would be suicide." He leaned forward with interest. "Naturally, I'd love to see it again. Just for a moment."

"Forget it!" Elsa spat. "And you can forget about me coming with you, too." She hesitated. "Where are these Regalia things supposed to be, anyway?"

Senno ran a finger around the edge of his glass goblet until it began to hum quietly. "They're in Prague," he said at last. "The old imperial city in Bohemia. I managed to find out that much—Schönborn has hidden them there somewhere."

"Prague! Well, if that's all it takes . . ." Giovanni said sarcastically, shaking his head. "Prague is hundreds of miles away. It would take you and Elsa weeks to get there—likely even months, with the war going on! What would we tell the castellan? That Elsa has gone off to Heidelberg to purchase herself a few nice dresses? Or that she flew off on a broomstick?"

Senno winked at them. "The good master castellan would never find out, because we would be back before his return. I doubt we would need longer than a week."

"Goddamn nonsense!" Paulus banged his tankard down onto the table, causing the beer to foam up. "Heidelberg to Prague and back within a week? That would take . . ." He stopped short.

"Magic, yes," Senno said, nodding in agreement. "The *Grimorium* could bring us there. Remember, it transported you to another place once before. Why shouldn't it work again?"

"That's madness!" Lukas broke in. "We were extremely lucky that one time. A second time would never—"

"Yes, it would work," Elsa said. She spoke softly, but her words were enough to silence the entire hall. "It would," she repeated. "I've studied the spell. I think I could transport myself to Prague. Myself, Senno . . ." She raised her head. "And everyone else here."

"Elsa!" Jerome barked at her. "Nobody's forcing you to go there. Not you, and not us!"

"Oh, so the rest of you would rather stick-fight with the farm children some more while *he* takes control over the entire Reich? Is that what you're saying?" Elsa's voice was loud and angry. She turned to Lukas. "I've thought it over. You said yourself, we can't hide from Schönborn forever. So let's beat him to it, before he grows so powerful that we have no hope of defeating him."

"Watch what you say, Elsa." Lukas gave her a pleading look. "I beg you."

"If you won't come with me, then I'll go alone," she replied stubbornly. "Waldemar von Schönborn is my father, and I refuse to run from him any longer. In fact, I think I've been hiding for far too long already."

Something told Lukas that this wasn't just about her father. Elsa probably also liked the prospect of taking on a truly great sorcerer. She was right, though. They couldn't evade Schönborn forever. Sooner or later, they would meet again, one way or another.

Better it happens now, when he's not suspecting it, Lukas thought.

"You know we would never let you travel alone," Giovanni said solemnly, turning to Elsa. "We all consider you our younger sister." He gestured around at the others. "We swore to Lukas that we would watch out for you. One for all and all for one—it includes you, too."

"And I'll be with you all," Senno added. "And not just me, either." He winked. "We won't be completely unprotected in the city. I've asked a few old friends of yours to join us."

"Friends we can trust?" Lukas added, eyeing Senno suspiciously.

"Just wait and see," Senno replied. "Anyway, with the book in your hands and me at your side, you'll already be as safe in Prague as you are here at Castle Lohenfels, believe me. If everything goes well, we'll be back in a few days with the Imperial Regalia."

"It's settled, then." Elsa rose to her feet with a gleam in her eyes that Lukas didn't like at all. "I think I'll retire to the library now and prepare the ritual. When the moon is high above the castle, we'll set off on this long, yet short, journey."

Lukas stared at her, flabbergasted. *"Tonight?"*

"Full moon tonight—the night of the witches." Elsa shrugged. "We won't find a better night than this one. *Samsara al mantaya!"* With those strange words, she left the hall.

For a while they all stared glumly into the fire, not saying a word.

"What did she mean with that spell thing?" Paulus asked at last. "Samsara whatever, you know."

"It means 'Let the spell begin.'" Senno smiled and took a last long gulp of wine, licking his lips appreciatively. Then his expression turned thoughtful. "That girl really does have extraordinary powers," he said quietly. "In every respect. We need to keep a close eye on her."

III

Everyone met in the library when the bell in the castle chapel struck ten.

The four friends had spent the day getting their weapons into top condition and making final preparations for their trip. Lukas was sure Castellan Eberhart would remain at the small Palatinate vineyard for a few more days, so he told the servants that they would be setting off very early for the cattle market in Heidelberg to look for a breeding bull.

Besides, Eberhart couldn't possibly suspect that we're heading to Prague to search for the most powerful objects in the German Reich, Lukas thought. *The Imperial Regalia!*

Lukas still thought using the *Grimorium Nocturnum* to travel to the proverbial lion's den was absolutely insane, and he had spent hours wrestling with Elsa's decision to go along with the plan. In these uncertain times, it would be dangerous to leave the castle in the hands of the servants and a few guards, but Lukas knew that once his sister had gotten an idea in her head, nothing and no one could stop her. Senno had promised they would be back in just a few days, so perhaps everything would be fine.

The fact that the Imperial Regalia items were hidden in Prague, of all places, helped Lukas feel more comfortable with the idea. His mother had lived in a Prague cloister as a young nun before returning to the

Palatinate to marry Lukas's father, the knight Friedrich von Lohenfels. Their mother had described the old imperial city to him and Elsa many times. In her stories, Prague had been a place where dreams came true, populated by good spirits, water sprites, ancient churches, and crumbling palaces. Lukas had always wanted to visit it.

Now they were all sitting at the worn round table in the library. Senno was the only one who seemed to be genuinely looking forward to the trip. He drummed his fingers on the tabletop excitedly as he watched Elsa light a candle for each person and arrange them in a circle around the table. Then she set out several wooden objects that looked like cheap toys. Lukas peered closer and saw a tiny castle, a bridge, and a roughly carved church.

"What's this supposed to be?" Paulus asked. "Are we playing with blocks now?"

Elsa smiled. "Not exactly. I borrowed these toys from the son of the smith." She gestured to each object in turn. "This is Pražský hrad, Prague Castle. This one is the famous stone bridge over the Vltava River, and that's Saint Vitus Cathedral."

"How do you know all this?" Jerome asked, reaching for the toy castle. "What's this thing called again? Pesky rod?"

Giovanni slapped his fingers. "She knows it because she reads, instead of merely amusing herself in shady taverns," he said sternly. "The question isn't where she got the information, but why we need it."

"I explained it to you already," Elsa replied. "Magic actually happens only inside our heads. These are just tools designed to help us cast the spell—they help us all concentrate on our destination, on Prague."

"And that works?" Paulus looked skeptical.

"Your little friend is right," Senno chimed in. "I've read about this method. It is only part of the magic ceremony, though. What we need is the book." He glanced around, searching. "It *is* here, isn't it?"

Without a word, Elsa turned away and went to the iron-studded box on the shelf. She opened it with the key on her necklace, and then returned to the table carrying the plain little book.

Senno's eyes widened. "The *Grimorium Nocturnum*," he whispered reverently. "Could I perhaps just—"

"Have a peek inside?" Elsa gave him a look of contempt. "The last person who tried that was Waldemar von Schönborn, and then a hellstorm blew him away."

Senno sighed. "You're right, little one. Well, then, let's begin the ceremony."

"Ah, actually . . . what happens if the spell only half works?" Jerome asked nervously. "Say, we're transported to Prague, but high up in the air? Or, worse, deep underground—buried alive?"

"Then I'm afraid our trip will come to an inglorious end fairly quickly," Senno said in a dry tone. "But I'd say we ought to trust Elsa." The astrologer rubbed his hands. "I can't wait another moment to feel the power of the *Grimorium* for myself. *Samsara al mantaya*," he added quietly. "Let the spell begin."

Elsa sank down onto the last free stool beside Lukas and flipped through the book before finally opening it to a specific page. "Now, all of you, focus completely on the objects within the ring of candles," she ordered.

After a moment, her lips parted and she began murmuring. Her voice was almost inaudible at first, but gradually it swelled to a torrent of words that sounded to Lukas like they were from another world.

"JAVA AL BARIVIA, CON MARTATEM SORAYA, LUMEN IN NOCTIS . . ."

They sat there motionless, staring at the carved wooden toys.

Elsa continued murmuring the incantation. "LUMEN EST OMNIS, TELEPORTIA IN LOCA ORIENTIS . . ."

Suddenly a gust of wind blew through the library, causing the candles to flicker. The pages of the book rustled quietly and then began moving back and forth on their own, as though the *Grimorium* itself were searching for the lines needed to complete the spell.

Elsa's voice grew louder with every word.

"IN LOCA ORIENTIS . . . IN LOCA MATERIA . . . IN LOCA PORTABILIS . . . NUNC MANIFESTA!"

"I don't think it's working," Jerome whispered to Paulus.

"If it doesn't work," Paulus hissed back, "then it's probably because you can only concentrate on three things: wine, dancing, and pretty girls."

"Ah, *quelle bonne idée*! At least that would bring us somewhere nice . . ."

"Shh!" Giovanni gave the other two a severe look.

A powerful blast of wind whipped through the room, extinguishing the candles and plunging them all into sudden darkness.

"*Merde!*" Jerome whined. "How am I supposed to concentrate on those wooden things here in the dark? I can't even see Paulus's fat nose."

"One more word and—" Paulus was interrupted by a sound like tearing cloth—only much, much louder.

"My God," Senno breathed. "It's working. It's actually working!"

Lukas couldn't believe his eyes. The table was split down the middle, and crimson fog was rising from the crack in the wood! As the gap widened, the vague contours of a city began to take shape on the other side. A river snaked through it, and Lukas could just make out a large castle with high walls in the background.

There was a deafening bang, and then something knocked Lukas to the floor and dragged him by the legs toward the crack.

"SAMSARA AL MANTAYA!"

Elsa's loud voice was the last thing he heard before the red fog swallowed him.

IV

Lukas drifted through the thick fog, weightless. Occasionally he thought he could just make out his friends' silhouettes, or felt his arms and legs brushing against them. He heard shouts and cries, but everything was masked beneath a powerful rushing sound, as though they were tumbling down a gigantic waterfall.

Then everything went silent.

The next thing Lukas became aware of was a musty, slightly sweet smell that he couldn't identify at first. He opened his eyes and found himself staring up at the low ceiling of a small room. He was lying on a cold stone floor, shivering as though feverish. A narrow window above him let in a little sunlight—just enough for him to make out the beer barrels stacked against the wall by the door.

"Oh, my head!" someone moaned beside him. It was Giovanni. "It's throbbing as though I spent the whole night drinking."

"Hm, strangely, it smells that way in here too," Paulus muttered from somewhere nearby. "You'd almost think we were in . . ."

"A beer cellar," Lukas said, blinking as he pulled himself to a sitting position. "Looks like the spell actually did bring us somewhere else."

"Hm, the time isn't right, either." Giovanni pointed through the tiny window. "It's daytime out now—the journey must have taken longer than we expected."

"Well, at any rate, this isn't the Castle Lohenfels cellar," Lukas said. "So the spell *did* work. The question is whether Elsa actually brought us to Prague." Lukas stopped and glanced around. "Elsa? Elsa, are you around here somewhere?"

To Lukas's great relief, his sister was lying beside him, just a few paces away. Exhausted, he crawled over to her and brushed her hair out of her face. She was breathing heavily and looked extremely pale.

"Everything all right?" he asked quietly.

Elsa nodded, but without opening her eyes. "The spell . . ." she murmured. "Took almost all . . . my strength. Need . . . sleep. The *Grimorium* . . ."

"It's right here beside you on the floor," Lukas said, inspecting the book. "Looks like it got singed in a couple of spots somehow, but it's still in better condition than a couple of us." He glanced over at Paulus, who was just staggering to his feet. Giovanni and Jerome looked completely wrung out as well, but at least they were uninjured. Only then, as he peered around the dim cellar, did Lukas realize that someone was missing.

"Senno!" he cried. "Senno isn't here!"

"Damn it!" Paulus grunted. "I knew there was no trusting that quack. Maybe this is all a trap, and he wanted to get rid of us?"

"By leaving us here with Elsa and the book he so desperately wants?" Lukas shook his head. "I doubt that. Something must have gone wrong with the spell." He glanced behind the barrels and squinted into the dark corners of the room, wondering if Senno was lying unconscious somewhere. But the astrologer was nowhere to be found.

"Maybe he was simply transported a little farther away," Lukas surmised. "Out onto the street or into the building next door, or—"

"Five feet underground," Jerome finished, shuddering.

"At any rate, we're on our own now," Giovanni said. "Wherever we are. Who knows if this accursed cellar is even in Prague? And anyway, why a beer cellar?" He glanced at Jerome skeptically.

Jerome shrugged sheepishly and looked down at his feet. "Ah, I admit that I may have thought about a tavern for *just* a teensy moment when that red fog came," he mumbled. "And about dancing and pretty barmaids. Paulus was the one who put the thought into my head."

"Oh, fantastic," Paulus groaned. "Thanks to you, we've landed underneath some drinking hole. God knows where you last amused yourself with your women. We are probably in Frankfurt or Heidelberg, not Prague. Nicely done, Jerome."

"Well, it should be easy enough to check." Giovanni hurried up to the cellar door, opened it, and disappeared through it. The others followed him, Lukas supporting Elsa, who was still very weak.

On the other side of the door, they found a steep, wobbly set of wooden stairs leading up to another door. This one was a trapdoor in the ceiling. Giovanni pushed it open, and the sound of clinking tankards, laughter, and music washed over them. A moment later, everything fell silent. When Lukas climbed the last few stairs, he found himself in a tavern, surrounded by two dozen or so men and women in simple garb, seated at rough-hewn tables. They were holding foamy tankards and staring at the new arrivals as if they were ghosts.

From behind the counter, the bald-headed barkeep shouted, *"Jste zlodji?"* He barked at Lukas and his friends, *"Zlodji, hä?"* But Lukas didn't understand what the man was saying.

"Ah, good man, I fear we do not speak your language," Giovanni said with a bow. "But please be assured that we would never—"

"Zlodji!" Infuriated, the barman withdrew a club from beneath the counter. Several of the men jumped from their chairs and came toward the friends, bearing tankards and knives. One particularly large, clearly drunk, pockmarked man threw his tankard at Lukas, who was barely able to duck out of the way. The man charged toward him, but Lukas

moved quickly, stuck out his leg, and tripped the man. A moment later, the other revelers attacked as well.

"Let's get out of here!" Paulus shouted, drawing his huge, powerful broadsword. He used the flat of the blade to smack the cudgel out of the barkeep's hand, while Jerome and Giovanni used their rapiers to defend themselves against chair legs and tankards. Lukas grabbed Elsa by the hand, and they all ran through the front door and out into a narrow, foul-smelling alley. The angry mob remained in hot pursuit.

"We need to shake them!" Giovanni called. "This way!"

After a moment of hesitation, they turned onto a small side street. Lukas prayed it wasn't a dead end. They ran past a line of hunched, sorry-looking half-timbered houses with peeling plaster. The cobblestones were knuckle-deep in filth, and grunting swine briefly blocked their path. They narrowly dodged a cart carrying bundles of rags. Lukas kept helping Elsa along as they sprinted through the labyrinth of winding alleyways.

Gradually, the screams of their pursuers grew fainter, eventually fading away entirely. Panting, the group stopped in a small, junk-packed courtyard surrounded by shabby little houses. Apart from the black cat staring at them from a windowsill, it seemed they were alone—for the moment, anyway.

"We need to figure out where we are," Giovanni wheezed, out of breath. "The barkeep didn't speak any German, so we know we've at least left the country. Too bad everything in this accursed labyrinth looks the same. We could be anywhere in the world!"

"Give me a moment." Lukas stacked a couple of rotting boxes atop one another and climbed to the roof of one of the squat little houses. From his perch, he was able to see more of the city.

The view took his breath away.

Beyond the sea of rooftops, he saw a stone bridge with numerous arches spanning a broad river. There were several more districts on the far side of the river, and a massive castle—far larger than even the one in Heidelberg—overlooked the whole city. The castle grounds were so expansive that an entire cathedral would have fit behind those high walls. He recognized it.

The stone bridge over the Vltava, the castle, and the cathedral—they'd actually made it.

"Prague!" he called down to the others. "It's really Prague! I can see the Hradschin!"

Giovanni laughed. "Then I suppose the barkeep back there was speaking Bohemian. Fortunately, from what I understand, there are quite a few German speakers here in Prague as well. That should make things a bit easier."

"Things are still plenty complicated," Paulus muttered. "Without Senno, we have no idea where to go. We're supposed to find these Imperial Regalia things, but where and how? We can just as easily start looking for three needles in a haystack."

"Senno said we would have friends here," Lukas said after climbing down from the roof. "Who could they be?"

"They must have something to do with our time in Wallenstein's army," Giovanni mused aloud. "So who . . ." He stopped short, and his expression brightened. "Well, I don't know who it is, but I have an idea where we might start looking. I heard once that Wallenstein built himself a house here, a summer residence of sorts. Senno is Wallenstein's astrologer, so perhaps the spell sent him there." He gave Jerome a severe look. "And maybe we would all have ended up there, if *someone* hadn't had his mind *elsewhere* as the spell was cast."

"Well, then, let's go find this summerhouse!" Paulus clapped his hands. "If Senno is really there, Jerome owes us all a large tankard of beer."

They wandered through the narrow streets, stopping periodically so Elsa could rest. After a while, they came to a small church with a pair of street urchins playing marbles out front. Giovanni approached them and exchanged a few words; fortunately, these boys seemed to understand him. They gestured to the west, laughing and shaking their heads again and again.

"What did they say?" Lukas asked when Giovanni returned.

"I started by asking them what day it was," Giovanni replied, grinning. "I was worried that we'd been transported not only to another place, but to another time as well. But it really is the day after the full moon in July of 1633."

"And where do we find Wallenstein's house?" Jerome asked.

"The boys said it was on the other side of the river, directly beneath Castle Hill." Giovanni furrowed his brow. "Those obnoxious brats kept laughing when I referred to it as a house. But at least now we know where we need to go."

After a while, they reached the wide, rushing Vltava River and the stone bridge Lukas had seen from the rooftop. It was the longest, most beautiful bridge he had ever laid eyes upon, with tall gate towers and massive stone support arches. An endless stream of people crossed it in both directions: peddlers with their back-baskets, nobility wrapped in expensive scarves, knights in gleaming armor. Though the war had laid waste to the Reich, it seemed to have largely spared Prague thus far—or, at least, Lukas didn't see any major damage to the bridge and surrounding houses.

What he did notice was a row of sun-bleached human skulls on pikes, up on the bridge tower.

As he and his friends crossed the bridge, Lukas pointed out the gruesome scene. "Must be criminals of some sort, put on display here as a deterrent."

Giovanni knitted his brow. "I've heard that after the Bohemian uprising, the Kaiser had all of their leaders beheaded. I suppose the skulls are there to remind the people of Prague what happens to those who take up arms against the German Kaiser."

Lukas shivered a little as he passed the bridge tower. Now, on the far side of the bridge, they could also see a rectangular palatial property a stone's throw away, at the foot of Castle Hill. The estate seemed to stretch across an entire neighborhood, and was bordered by other magnificent residences.

"Well, it isn't Prague Castle—that's up on the hill," Jerome mused aloud. "But this looks like a castle, too."

Giovanni groaned and smacked his forehead. "That must be Wallenstein's palace. No wonder those boys were laughing when I called it a house. This 'summer residence' is practically a town in itself! How will we ever find anyone in there?"

"I'm sure people around here know of the astrologer and his drivel," Paulus growled. "So let's just go up to the gate and ask for Senno. Maybe he's been there all along. And then we'll be able to find out what went wrong with the spell."

They circled around the property until they discovered a broad main gate guarded by half a dozen soldiers bearing swords and halberds. The watchmen peered down at them mistrustfully as they approached.

"What do you boys want?" one of them snapped in German. "Get over to the new part of town with the rest of the servants!"

"Good day to you, gentlemen!" Lukas stepped forward, raising a hand in greeting. "We're looking for the honorable Senno, Wallenstein's astrologer. Would you happen to kn—"

The watchman laughed derisively. "Who do you think you are, boy? The chamberlain? Get out of here before I drive you off."

"We were just asking for information," Lukas tried again. "So please—"

The soldier smashed the pommel of his sword into Lukas's chest, sending him flying to the filthy ground. "Like I said, get out of here, farm whelp. Otherwise I'll hang you upside down by your feet until you learn your manners."

That was too much for Lukas—his old rage, which had caused problems many times in the past, got the better of him once again. He'd never had any patience for being treated unfairly. He leapt up, reached for his rapier, and disarmed the watchman with a single movement. The soldier's sword clattered to the ground. "I'm no farm whelp, I'm Lukas von Lohenfels!" he hissed. "Son of the Count von Lohenfels!"

Almost immediately, Lukas regretted his impulsiveness—but it was too late.

The soldier took a step back, baffled. Now the other guards were coming nearer, swords drawn. Lukas's friends, who had been hanging back with Elsa, rushed to help Lukas.

"Well, this won't get us into the palace, but at least there'll be a proper fight," Paulus muttered, swinging his broadsword. Giovanni and Jerome positioned themselves back to back, rapiers in hand.

"One for all and all for one!" Jerome cried. *"En voilà un, en voilà un deuxième, et terminé!"* Resolutely, he deflected blows from two soldiers and then disarmed a third with an elegant twist.

Paulus, meanwhile, kicked a barrel over from one corner of the forecourt and rolled it at the guards, who stumbled over it and fell flat on their faces. Lukas found himself fighting two men at once. Out of the corner of his eye, he saw to his horror that more guards were running out through the gate. Several of them were holding crossbows.

Damn my pride! Lukas berated himself inwardly. *How could I be so stupid? We'll never win this fight!*

As he parried the next blow, he turned briefly toward Elsa, who was cowering on the ground, clutching the *Grimorium*, looking exhausted. He remembered how that buck had suddenly collapsed, that morning in the woods—could that magic work on people as well?

Elsa, help us! Lukas thought, but his sister still looked like she might pass out at any moment.

One of the soldiers took advantage of Lukas's distraction, aiming the point of his sword at Lukas's neck. Lukas dodged it, but the blade caught his upper arm. The stinging pain caused his rage to flare up all over again. He'd let himself be duped by a simple lunge—merely because he'd put his faith in Elsa's magic instead of his own abilities!

"Together against death and the Devil!" he shouted, preparing for a quick lunge of his own. Feint, riposte, counter, attack. Just as Lukas was about to put his blade at the astonished soldier's throat, a powerful voice thundered across the square.

"Upon my soul! Who dares abuse the battle cries of the Black Musketeers! You scum deserve the gallows a hundred times over for that alone!"

Lukas glanced up and saw a tall, broad-shouldered figure directly above the gate. He was dressed all in black, except for a red feather in his cap. His knee-high jackboots were waxed until they gleamed, and he was carrying a broad-handled bastard sword with a serrated edge.

Lukas was so alarmed that his rapier nearly fell out of his hand. He knew this man, and he would never have dared raise a hand against him, not for all the money in the world.

The man before them was none other than Zoltan, the commander of the Black Musketeers.

V

Zoltan appeared just as astonished at the encounter as Lukas and his friends were. When he recognized Lukas, he gave a visible start. But after a moment, he collected himself again and gave the watchmen a sign. "These boys are mine!" he barked. "Lower your weapons; I'll handle them."

"But sir—" one of the soldiers protested.

"Weapons down, I said," Zoltan broke in, silencing the soldier with an imperious gesture. "Now!"

The guards obeyed, and Zoltan strode menacingly toward the four companions. The expression on his face was dark and inscrutable. "Surrender! We have a deep hole here to help upstarts like you remember their place. Or should I have you all hanged right here?"

"*Monsieur le commandant . . .*" Jerome whispered. "If we had known . . ."

Zoltan put a finger to his lips and gave the boys a penetrating stare. "Surrender, I said!" he continued in a loud voice. "Or all of you are dead where you stand!"

Meekly, they all lowered their weapons, and Zoltan led them and Elsa through the gate into the palace's hedge-framed interior courtyard.

As soon as the watchmen were out of view, the commander hissed, "Lord, have you all lost your minds completely? Follow me, but keep your eyes down!"

He turned to the right. They hurried past the hedges and through a low, narrow gate leading back out into a small side street. From there, they made their way through a confusion of cramped alleys, past other stately palaces, until they finally arrived in a poorer quarter upriver. The houses here were small and plain. The streets stank of human waste and the putrid water around a nearby pier. Lukas gritted his teeth. The wound on his arm was hurting worse with every passing moment—perhaps it was deeper than he'd originally thought.

Zoltan stopped in front of a tavern door with a metal sign showing a black boar dangling above it. He knocked three times short and twice long, and then the door opened a crack. A strawberry-blond giant with a wild beard stared down at the boys suspiciously. The massive sword he was holding was nearly as long as Lukas was tall.

"I do not think anyone followed us," Zoltan said quietly. "You can let us in, Bernhard."

The giant nodded and held the door open for them. Together, they stepped into a tavern that was empty except for one man at the door and two at the bar. All three were armed. One, a short, sinewy young man, was playing with a long knife. He had a patch over one eye, and he squinted at the boys sullenly, almost hatefully, with the other. The man beside him had a much friendlier look about him. Dozens of pearls and other glittery things were knotted into his long black hair. Leaning against the table beside him was an enormous crossbow with a strange wooden box over the groove. The man nodded to Lukas as he bit into an apple with relish.

"Bernhard, Jurek, and Matthias," Zoltan said, gesturing to each of the men in turn. "My best mercenaries. I selected them myself from my regiment. So behave, or they'll eat you alive."

"From your regiment?" Jerome whistled through his teeth. *"Mon dieu,* that means they're—"

"Black Musketeers, just like you," Zoltan interrupted. "These men, however, are quite a bit stronger, better skilled, and more experienced. They've spent the past several years serving as Wallenstein's personal guards and out on various missions. Unlike some," he added darkly, "they actually came *back* as expected from those missions."

Lukas looked at the floor in shame. He and his friends had fought tirelessly alongside the Black Musketeers. They had started as drummers, but soon they'd joined the ranks of the legendary warriors. In the end, they'd fled back to Lukas's home after they successfully found and rescued Elsa. Zoltan had never quite forgiven them for going to the Lohenfels residence rather than returning to duty.

"Senno summoned us to Prague to assist you in a delicate matter," Zoltan continued with a sigh. "Not that I trust that charlatan, but he does have Wallenstein's ear, so we obeyed. We were told you would show up here in Prague with him and then report to us at the tavern." He eyed the boys sharply. "So where is Senno? What happened?"

"We'd like to know that, too," Lukas replied. Hesitantly, he told Zoltan about their magical journey and the events that had followed.

"So you all thought you'd just march on over to Wallenstein's palace and assault the watchmen there, is that it?" the commander mused after listening. "You're very lucky I happened to have business at the palace, otherwise you'd already be swinging from the gallows." The commander cursed and kicked a chair, sending it flying into the corner.

Lukas flinched. When Zoltan got angry, there was usually no stopping him. People feared his violent temper nearly as much as his fighting skill.

"Do the words 'secret mission' not mean anything to you?" the commander shouted. "We *already* can't be certain whether or not Schönborn knows something is going on. Now half of Prague knows that four urchins and a little girl are looking for Wallenstein's court astrologer!"

"I'm sorry," Lukas said ruefully. "It's all my fault. I shouldn't have done that."

Zoltan waved dismissively. He took a deep breath, which seemed to help him get control of himself again. "Water under the bridge. Now our only concern is finding these three articles of Imperial Regalia before Schönborn returns to Prague and uses them for something wicked. As far as we know, he is still in Rome." Zoltan shrugged. "I would rather have had my men do all this alone, but supposedly this girl here"—his gaze flitted to Elsa, who was still leaning heavily on Lukas for support— "has magic that we will need in the fight against the powers of evil."

Zoltan shook his head. "Until very recently, I never would have believed in such superstitious nonsense. But the battle near Hamelin and the death of my old comrade-at-arms Leopold von Torgau forced me to admit I was wrong. Black magic! Dead soldiers that return as invincible war machines. What sort of age are we living in?" He regarded Elsa skeptically. "To be honest, this little brat doesn't look anything like how I'd imagined a witch would look. Does she at least have this book Senno was talking about?"

Lukas nodded. "Without it, we would never have made it to Prague. But the spell that brought us here weakened my sister a great deal."

"And you seem to have taken a lick or two fighting the palace guards," the friendly man with the pearls in his hair—Matthias— remarked, gesturing to Lukas's bleeding arm. "Let me take a look. I'm something of a feldsher for the Black Musketeers, an army surgeon."

"A goddamn quack is what he is, that's all," strawberry-blond Bernhard broke in, laughing. "But he can probably manage a little wasp sting like that," he added with a grin, leaning against his long broadsword.

Matthias examined Lukas's arm, cleaned the wound, and dressed it with a few scraps of cloth. In the meantime, the one-eyed man Zoltan had called Jurek put bread, barley soup, and a jug of small beer out onto the table.

Paulus lunged for it hungrily. "Nice inn you have here," he said with his mouth full. "Cook seems a bit grouchy, though." He gestured to Jurek, who was back to playing with his knife.

Jurek regarded Paulus with a disdainful sneer, but Zoltan waved him off. "The inn actually belongs to a cousin of Jurek's," the commander said. "He's marching in the imperial army, so this place is empty for the moment. We're using it as a meeting point—less conspicuous than Wallenstein's palace." Zoltan chuckled. "The neighbors avoid the place; they think we're all smugglers and assassins."

The soot-smeared walls were decorated with bearskins and threadbare tapestries; the beer-stained tables were scratched and weathered. By all appearances, the straw covering the floor hadn't been changed since before the war. A moth-eaten boar's head, the tavern's namesake, hung above the counter.

It's true, Lukas thought. *Nobody would ever suspect that an elite troop of Wallenstein's men was in here.*

"So do you all know where we can find the Imperial Regalia?" Jerome asked, picking a few slices of dried apple from a bowl and chewing them appreciatively. "Senno said Schönborn had hidden them somewhere in Prague. Not exactly precise."

"All of the pieces—the scepter, crown, and sword—are all supposedly hidden in different places," Zoltan said, counting them off on his fingers as he spoke. "We do have a clue regarding the scepter, at least." Grinning, he pulled a crumpled note out from his doublet. It was written on the finest handmade paper, the type only the well-to-do used for their correspondence. "We received this message just three days ago—it was pushed under the door. According to this, the scepter is located within Marquis de LaSalle's palace."

"And who would that be?" Lukas asked.

"The French ambassador in Prague, and a good friend of Waldemar von Schönborn. He lives in a manor beside the Vltava River. I have no idea how our mysterious friend acquired this information, nor why he passed it to us, but it seems to be authentic.

"Hmm." Giovanni tilted his head from side to side uncertainly. "A secret helper? I don't like it."

"Neither do I," Matthias said as he polished his large crossbow. "But it's our only lead so far, so we should definitely pursue it."

"With five children?" Jurek spat on the floor contemptuously. "I thought we'd at least have Senno on our side. But now?"

"We aren't children," Paulus retorted angrily. "I'd be happy to prove it if you like, One Eye."

"Sure, Fat Boy, if you're that desperate to lose an ear." Jurek reached for his knife, but Zoltan held him back.

"No fighting within the troop, or I'll throw you in the cellar. Is that clear?" The commander banged his fist on the table. "We don't know where Senno is. Perhaps the spell simply blew him to the other side of the Vltava and he'll join us tomorrow. Or perhaps he's halfway around the world. Maybe he's dead. We don't have time to find out. We need to act now."

"Elsa is still very weak," Lukas pointed out, giving his sister a look of concern. He pushed her a cup of milk that Matthias had given him. "Maybe we should wait a bit."

"Zoltan is right," Elsa broke in haltingly. "We don't have time. I sense that something terrible will happen soon—very soon—unless we retrieve the Regalia." She was now clutching the *Grimorium*, which she had been hiding beneath her cloak. "The book gives me the strength I need. At least for the moment." She turned to Zoltan. "So, what's your plan?"

"The marquis hosts a large event every year—a masked ball," Zoltan replied. "That will be our chance to walk around his palace unnoticed and search for the scepter. But they will be checking each guest thoroughly at the entrance. Can you all swim?"

The young comrades nodded.

"We will need to strike from the other side, from the Vltava," Zoltan continued. "There's a small riverside pier on his property used for receiving goods, and a door beside it that leads into the palace. If we can just distract the pier guards for a moment, we should be able to make it inside."

Elsa looked thoughtful and shrugged. "My powers should still suffice for a little distraction. When is this masked ball?"

"This very evening." Zoltan grinned, pulling a handful of masks and some colorful clothing from beneath the counter. "You have just enough time to pick out your costumes."

VI

They waited until nightfall.

Zoltan walked in front, carrying a lantern to guide them through the labyrinth of deserted alleys. Lukas was just happy that the wound on his upper arm hardly hurt at all anymore. Matthias, it seemed, was a better doctor than Bernhard the bearded giant had suggested.

Now, at the height of summer, it was warm and humid even after sundown. Lukas's clothing was soon clinging to his skin. The heat also amplified the terrible stench of trash and human excrement hanging in the air. He had pictured this fairy-tale city from his mother's stories somewhat differently—certainly with fewer of these disgusting piles in the middle of the street.

Lukas could still scarcely believe that they were actually in Prague. Until now, most of the magic he'd seen Elsa do had been little conjuring tricks: the wet wood in the fireplace suddenly bursting into flame, a gust of wind that blew the leaves from a tree, the red pustules on the maid's face. This magical journey was something else entirely. Lukas wondered what else the book made Elsa capable of.

And will it be enough against a black magician as powerful as Waldemar von Schönborn? he wondered.

Zoltan turned another corner, and the rotten stench of the Vltava hit Lukas once more. Each of them was carrying a small bundle wrapped in waxed cloth. The bundles contained their costumes and masks, and the waxed cloth would keep them from getting wet in the river. Lukas hoped no one would see through their disguises at the ball or try to engage them in conversation—especially in Bohemian, like the angry barkeep. To make matters more uneasy, they were only able to arm themselves with knives and small cudgels.

The river shimmered before them between the buildings, black as night. The large bridge was just a stone's throw away.

"The marquis's palace." Zoltan pointed to a magnificent two-story building right on the bank of the river, separated from the rest of the city beyond it by a small stream. Light shone out through the windows, and the soft sounds of flutes and shawms floated over to them on the breeze. "Looks like the ball is well under way," he added quietly. "Not a sound from any of you, starting now!"

Together, they crept toward a flight of stone steps, slick with algae, leading down to the river. Lukas stared, shivering, at the black swells splashing softly against the quay. When he'd told Zoltan he could swim, he hadn't known how deep and sinister the river would seem at night.

As dark as hell, Lukas thought.

Bernhard and Matthias disappeared into the water with their waxed-cloth bundles. Zoltan gave the others a sign and then dove down as well. Now, of the four grown men, only Jurek was left on the shore.

"Aw, are the little babies scared of the cold water?" he sneered. "I hear there are whales the size of boats in the Vltava, and small children are their favorite food."

"But they like one-eyed windbags even better," Paulus replied. "I'll let them know you're coming." Without another word, he leapt into the water from the top step with a huge splash.

"Damn it, not so loud!" Jurek hissed. "All right, now the rest of you." He signaled to the other boys and Elsa. "I'll take the rear guard." He clamped his long knife between his teeth and sat down on the steps.

Lukas glanced over at him suspiciously. He didn't like Jurek at all. He could only hope that Zoltan's trust in his people wasn't misplaced. Lukas shut his eyes for a moment and then slid into the dark water with Elsa. It was surprisingly cold, and the current tore at his legs. The palace was about a hundred paces away upstream. Suddenly, Lukas was grateful to his father for having taught them both to swim in the Neckar, even if he—unlike Elsa—wasn't much of a water rat.

He held his breath and dove beneath the surface. The bundle on his back hindered him as he swam, so his progress was slow. He tried to avoid looking down into the water. Dark as it was, he thought he could make out a shadow here and there, and once something soft and slimy brushed his leg. He could only pray that it was some kind of climbing plant, rather than a huge fish.

After what felt like an eternity, Lukas finally reached the stone pier of the palace, where the others were already waiting for him in the water. Another flight of steps led up to dry land. A few paces from the stairs, two watchmen were standing guard near the manor's small back door. A manned boat was bobbing in the current half a stone's throw away, in the middle of the river.

"Damn it," Zoltan whispered. Like the others, he was clinging to one of the slimy ropes dangling into the water from the pier above. "I wasn't expecting that! We might be able to take down the two guards at the door, but then the ones in the boat will spot us."

"Not if I cast a spell," said Elsa, shivering in the cold.

"How would that work?" Zoltan asked. "You can't turn us all invisible, can you? Don't play at being some great sorceress, girl."

Elsa didn't let the commander intimidate her. "Not invisible, but something like it. If it works, the men in the boat won't notice us. Promise."

"I suppose we'll have to trust the girl," Bernhard said. "We don't have any other options."

Zoltan cursed softly under his breath. "Damn it, I don't like this witchcraft nonsense. But try if you want. I doubt it will work, anyway." He turned to Elsa. "Do you need your book for that?"

Elsa shook her head. "I know this spell by heart. I tried it once before. Just having the book nearby is enough." She drew her waxed-cloth bundle to her chest, and then Elsa's gaze seemed to turn inward, so that only the whites of her eyes were visible. She spoke a few words that to Lukas's ears sounded terribly sinister, and as old as the world itself.

"INVISOR JAMEN AL INSPECTIS . . . NUNC!"

A gray cloud seemed to descend upon the group. Everything was hazy and slightly distorted, as though viewed through thick glass.

Elsa started trembling more and more; deep concentration was etched into her face.

"What the hell?" Zoltan began.

"Quickly!" Elsa commanded them, her voice breaking. "I don't know how long the spell will hold."

Zoltan spent another moment regarding the gray cloud in amazement. Then he and Bernhard clambered up the pier using the ropes hanging from either side. The cloud enveloped the two men like a plume of smoke.

Lukas prayed this would work. The soldiers remained calm, even though they simply *had* to have seen Zoltan and Bernhard. Lukas thought he saw two of the men in the boat staring straight at them, yet they sounded no alarm.

Zoltan and Bernhard lunged at the guards near the door, their movements almost perfectly synchronous. There was a brief struggle followed by two dull thumps, and then the soldiers were lying at the foot of the pier. Zoltan tossed his cloth-wrapped cudgel aside and waved Jurek over. "You're up!" he ordered.

Jurek climbed up onto the pier, which was now completely enveloped in the hazy gray cloud. The short one-eyed man fished around beneath his wet doublet and finally withdrew a ring of lockpicks. He quickly set to work at the palace's back door, but he appeared to be having trouble. His movements grew increasingly anxious as time went on.

"What's wrong?" Matthias hissed from where he was waiting with Lukas and his friends. "Jurek, you said this lock would be no problem for you!"

"I don't know," Jurek replied, breathing heavily. "Must be rusted."

"Hurry," Elsa wheezed, her eyes still rolled strangely back into her head. "Can't . . . hold . . . the spell . . . much longer . . ."

The gray veil surrounding them was already beginning to tear. Lukas saw one of the watchmen in the boat lean in over the railing, appearing curious about something.

"Damn, damn, damn!" Jurek growled. He switched to a different lockpick, but that one didn't seem to fit, either.

Elsa's head was slowly beginning to sag forward, and the gray cloud began to dissipate. Just then Jurek let out a soft whoop of victory, and the door swung inward with a squeak.

"Hurry!" Zoltan commanded, and the rest of them scrambled up the ropes. But Elsa seemed too weak already—her hands could barely grip the rope.

"Don't worry, I'll get her," Matthias said to Lukas, who was waiting hesitantly up on the pier. "Go on!"

As the last tendrils of fog began to evaporate, Lukas and Matthias, with Elsa in his arms, rushed toward the entrance. Lukas stumbled forward, feeling himself land on a thick, soft rug as the door closed behind them with a quiet click.

They were inside.

Lukas heard his own ragged breathing, along with soft music and laughter coming from somewhere above them. There were no sounds from outside—no shouts, no knocking. Apparently, they really had slipped away unnoticed at the last second.

Zoltan leaned against the wall, wiping his face clean of the river water that had already formed a large puddle on the soft red carpet. He was staring at Elsa as though properly seeing her for the first time. "That damn witchcraft actually worked," he mumbled and shook his head. "We don't have much time." He pointed impatiently at the bundles lying at their feet. "Hurry up and change!"

Lukas opened his bundle and pulled out a pair of slitted blue trousers and an equally blue robe that was far too large for him. He slipped into them and then pulled a laughing Venetian mask over his face. The others were changing into their own colorful clothes and masks; together, they looked like some kind of traveling circus. Jerome, in particular, had taken great pains in selecting his outfit, for which Paulus and Giovanni had already teased him repeatedly. In the end he'd opted for a red harlequin costume, along with a white mask and a tambourine, which he was now shaking theatrically.

"*Voilà*, how do I look?" he asked the others around him.

"Like a drunken clown," Paulus replied. "And if you keep shaking that thing, you'll look like a dead drunken clown."

"At least I don't have a gigantic warty nose," Jerome shot back.

"But you're about to have a bloody one . . ." Paulus began.

"Quiet, you two!" Zoltan barked at the quarreling pair. He himself was wearing a pitch-black costume and a golden devil mask with plaster horns. "Since we don't know where the scepter is, we'll split up into three groups," the commander continued, lowering his voice again. "If I know that pompous marquis, he won't have locked the scepter away—it'll be out on display, where anyone can see it if they know what they're looking for. So keep your eyes open! From what I've been told, there's a golden acorn at the tip of the scepter, with six oak leaves around it."

He glanced over at the shivering Elsa, who was now wearing a Medusa mask and a tight green dress. Her trembling hands were still clutching the *Grimorium*. "What about you, girl?" Zoltan asked sympa-thetically. "Are you strong enough to help look for the scepter, or should we leave you here with Lukas?"

Lukas opened his mouth to protest, but Matthias spoke up first. "I'll go with the two of them," he said. "If it becomes a problem, we'll return here to the exit and wait for all of you."

Zoltan nodded. "It's decided, then. Good luck, men!" He gave Bernhard and Jerome a sign to follow him. Paulus and Giovanni went with one-eyed Jurek, though Paulus was staring daggers into the back of Jurek's head as he walked behind him.

Matthias, Lukas, and Elsa were the only ones left. Matthias put on his own mask. His monk's cowl and hood covered his wet black hair and the pearls knotted into it. "Let's go, then," he said cheerfully. "The other two groups have gone to the upper floors, so we'll look around down here."

They walked down the hall, which soon branched off into other rooms and corridors. The walls were hung with elegant woven rugs and fine oil paintings, most of which showed hunting scenes or scowling men in gleaming armor. After a while, they spotted the first few guests coming toward them—two women and a man, all wearing masks.

Lukas held his breath, but the trio seemed not to suspect a thing. They went on laughing and chatting as they walked, passing Lukas so closely that he could smell the thick cloud of perfume surrounding one of the women.

Soon they saw larger groups of people, and it grew progressively louder around them. In one of the rooms, people were dancing bois-terously as a small ensemble on a velvet-covered stage played a cheer-ful melody. Here, too, all the guests were wearing masks and brightly colored costumes.

A masked woman approached Lukas, giggling as she held out a hand adorned with diamond rings. "Well, you're certainly short, even for a Venetian lover!" she said in German, pointing to Lukas's mask. "All the same, would the gentleman care to dance? It's ladies' choice."

Lukas coughed sheepishly, feeling the blood rush to his face. If he said anything, the woman would know he was only a boy! He was about to turn and walk away, but then the lady reached for his hands and began spinning him around wildly in time with the music.

"One would almost think you'd never danced a volta!" she laughed. "Where are you from, sir? Not from Venice, I suppose—wild Russia, more likely. Look here, it's quite easy. And one-two-three, one-two . . ."

Panicked, Lukas tore away and hurried over to Matthias and Elsa, who were watching the dance from near the wall, looking as though they'd been turned to stone. Together, the three of them hastened toward the exit. They were nearly at the door when the woman's shrill voice rang out behind them. "You there! Who treats a lady that way? How unbelievably impolite! May I at least inquire *who* it is that has just snubbed me so coldly? Go on, answer me!"

A hush fell over the room; even the music stopped playing. Lukas gripped Elsa's hand tightly and closed his eyes. Now they were done for! He should never have agreed to this adventure! But just as the woman was about to rip the mask from Lukas's face, Matthias stepped into her path.

"Signorina!" he hissed. "Mind what you say! The young man standing before you is, indeed, a Venetian. In fact, he is the son of the doge himself, the ruler of the sea republic! Only his exceptional manners keep him from speaking to you . . . or, for that matter, from having you thrown into the marquis's dungeon," he added darkly.

"Oh, p-pardon me, I had no idea," the masked woman stammered. "Ah, how can I . . ."

"Best just keep silent," Matthias whispered. "His Excellency is here without his father's permission. I am his godfather and confessor."

"Of course, I'll be as silent as the grave." The woman turned away and hurried back to her friends.

Matthias exhaled heavily. Small beads of sweat appeared on his forehead above the mask. "I expect we have until the chime of the next hour before the entire ball—and thus the marquis—hears of the supposed son of the doge," he told Lukas and Elsa quietly. "The marquis knows his own guest list, of course, so the ruse will be discovered. We can only hope that the others have better success, because *our* search, at any rate, is over."

They hastened back into the hallway and made their way toward the rear exit again. Abruptly, Matthias stopped in front of a door reinforced with thick iron bars. He hesitated. "We haven't checked here yet," he whispered.

Behind them in the hallway, Lukas heard several women giggling. He froze. He could handle almost anything, but not another dance. Besides, the lie about his identity was likely to be discovered at any moment. Perhaps they could just hide behind this door for a minute?

"Let's take a quick look before we turn around," Lukas suggested quietly. "At least until these masked hens behind us have gone." Cautiously, he turned the knob, and the door swung inward without a sound. Matthias and Elsa hurried in behind him before the women got too close. Lukas found himself gazing into a gloomy vault, a series of stone arches illuminated by individual torches. Lining the walls were swords, rapiers, battle-axes, halberds, pikes, and countless other weapons. More were on display in the many glass cases all around the room. Suits of armor stood against columns, shimmering dully in the flickering light.

"An armory!" Lukas blurted out in astonishment. "My God, I've never seen so many different weapons in one place!"

"Hm, I've heard that the marquis loves weapons," Matthias murmured. He walked toward a glass case containing a massive two-hander. "A few of these swords look quite old. Probably quite valuable as well."

"And look here!" Lukas hurried over to another display case, which held several basket-hilted swords, including one blade with a hand guard made up of winding roses. "A real schiavona! My father told me about these types of swords. The Venetian Guard carries them. If only Paulus could see this!"

"As much as I hate to interrupt you men," Elsa piped up, "I thought I'd just remind you that we're here to find Imperial Regalia, not to admire a weapons collection."

Lukas sighed, running his fingers along the schiavona case once more. "You're right, Elsa. Anyway, we're running out of time. We need to hurry up and—"

"Die," a voice interrupted from the entrance. "Is that what you were about to say, boy?"

Lukas whirled around in horror.

VII

The man in the doorway was around fifty and was wearing a tight red velvet skirt, a ruffled blouse, and a powdered wig. A silver rapier dangled at his side. Even in the dim light, Lukas could see that the man was made up like a woman—he was wearing rouge and lip stain. And he was grinning like an evil harlequin.

"Marquis Antoine de LaSalle," he said with a slight bow. "And you two lovelies must be the Lohenfels siblings I've heard so much about. Especially you, girl." He winked at Elsa, who retreated a step.

Matthias and Lukas stepped protectively in front of her.

"What do you want from us?" Elsa asked, hugging the *Grimorium* to her chest.

"Well, first of all, from the looks of it, *you* are the ones who want something from *me*, isn't that right?" LaSalle smiled. "You sneaked into my house uninvited and disrupted my festivities like dirty little thieves! And what does one do with dirty little thieves? One crushes them like lice." He snapped his fingers, and suddenly three tall soldiers appeared behind him, wearing crested helmets and cuirasses. Their hair was black and oily, and their eyes were so lifeless that Lukas initially thought they were wearing masks as well.

But then he understood.

"Frozen ones!" he gasped. "You command frozen ones!" Lukas's heart leapt into his throat. More than half a year had passed since his last encounter with the soulless creatures, yet they still terrified him just as much as they had the first time.

"Indeed, frozen ones," Marquis replied in a tone of respectful admiration. "My dear friend Waldemar von Schönborn gave them to me as a gift. Like machines, these former mercenaries obey my every command and cannot be killed." He giggled. "I believe the future belongs to machines anyway. Perhaps someday they will not even require magic." He smirked. "Get them!"

The last two words were directed at the three frozen ones, who now had their swords drawn and were hastening toward Lukas, Elsa, and Matthias with strangely stiff movements. There was a crashing, crunching sound nearby. Lukas turned and saw that Matthias had smashed one of the glass display cases. He tossed Lukas a short sword known as a Katzbalger and then picked up the two-hander, which was nearly two paces in length.

"So these monsters can't be killed?" Matthias asked with a grim smile. "Well, they'll have to prove it to me first." He moved toward two of the frozen ones, while the third lurched toward Lukas.

"Elsa, stay behind me!" Lukas commanded his sister, tossing his mask aside. Resolutely, he swung his Katzbalger and parried close to his body to block his adversary's first attack. The blow was so powerful that Lukas's sword nearly fell out of his hand. He preferred fighting with rapiers, which were both lighter and better suited to dexterous thrusts and jabs. With swords, on the other hand, it was mostly about swinging as hard as possible, so the stronger fighter often emerged victorious.

And when it came to sheer muscle power, the frozen one had an enormous advantage over Lukas.

The blows were raining down upon him as he retreated little by little. The bandaged wound on his upper arm was throbbing in pain.

Out of the corner of his eye, he saw Matthias swing the two-hander in a circle, actually managing to strike one of his two foes in the thigh. Blood spurted from the wound, yet the frozen one simply went on fighting as though nothing had happened.

Even without legs, he'd probably still crawl toward us, Lukas thought despairingly.

Elsa, meanwhile, was standing with her back against one of the columns, murmuring silently. Sweat was pearling on her brow, and Lukas suspected that the spell outside at the river had severely weakened her. He wondered if she would even be capable of casting another one. Lukas knew all too well how dangerous these monsters were. Once upon a time, they'd been people, Spanish mercenaries fighting for the Kaiser. But Waldemar von Schönborn had used his sorcery to make them into utterly invincible machines, designed for one purpose alone.

Killing.

Another blow hit Lukas's Katzbalger, and he stumbled against a glass display case. As he fell he knocked the case over, and it shattered with a deafening crash. Lukas found himself lying on his back among the shards. He reached for his sword, but the frozen one was already above him. He kicked Lukas's weapon away with the tip of his boot and then raised his sword for the final deadly blow.

In that instant, Elsa's loud, if slightly shaky, voice rang out.

"VADE . . . VADE SANTUATIS!"

The frozen one tumbled backward as though hit by some unseen force. Lukas got to his knees and searched desperately for a weapon— something, anything! Finally, he found a gilded mace amid the glass shards and clenched it tightly. Gasping for breath, he got to his feet and prepared for the next attack.

"Get the girl!" the marquis screamed, still standing in the doorway. To Lukas's horror, he saw that more guards had now stormed into the room. They were mortals, not frozen ones, but Lukas still knew that he and Matthias could never fight all of them at once—not successfully, anyway.

Unless Elsa can manage another spell, he thought. *Which doesn't appear likely.*

Elsa looked extremely weak, leaning heavily against the column, barely able to stay on her feet. Matthias, too, seemed to be nearing the end of his strength. His arcing swings with the two-hander were keeping the two frozen ones at bay, but now the newly arrived guards were pointing crossbows at him as well.

"Surrender!" the marquis barked. "The game is up! *Rien ne va plus!*"

Suddenly, the sound of rapidly approaching footfalls echoed out in the hallway, and more men burst into the vault. Lukas was a moment away from dropping his weapon, but then he saw who had just arrived.

Zoltan! It's Zoltan and the others!

Lukas had a glimmer of hope again. Zoltan and Bernhard went for the guards, while Giovanni, Jerome, and Paulus tore a few swords from the walls. Soon they were fighting like the Devil, with Giovanni and Jerome wielding two rapiers apiece and Paulus hacking at one of the frozen ones with the schiavona and a massive curved saber. Jerome kicked over one of the suits of armor, and it crashed to the stone floor, sending its individual pieces flying in every direction. He bobbed and wove with agility, fending off two of the guards at once.

"Out!" Zoltan called from the doorway, where he was fighting two more soldiers. "Hurry!"

Lukas looked over at Elsa, who was still slumped weakly against the column. As he hurried toward her, he saw one of the frozen ones closing in from the right. Lukas was still clutching the gilded mace in one hand, and now he wound up and smashed it against the frozen one's helmet with all his strength. The creature only grunted and continued walking. Lukas swung the mace again; this time he hit the frozen one in the face, hard enough that he actually stumbled back a little.

Giovanni hastened over to help. "Back to the exit!" he called, keeping the frozen one in check with his two rapiers. "We'll take Elsa in the middle!" Giovanni threw himself against one of the display cases, knocking it over along with a nearby suit of armor and sending both crashing down onto the frozen one. The mercenary twitched and flailed, but he was wedged beneath a long lance and couldn't get to his feet.

"Perhaps these frozen ones can't be killed, but at least they're dumber than rocks," Giovanni wheezed when he caught up to the two siblings. "Now let's get out of here, before these beasts get *really* vicious."

Lukas used the short breather to look more closely at the mace he'd grabbed in desperation. He weighed it in his hand thoughtfully. It was about the length of his arm, and it was well balanced, though not particularly heavy. After peering at it in the dim torchlight for a moment, he realized that, beneath the thin layer of gold plating, it was made of solid silver with many decorative elements—like the golden acorn at the tip, encircled by leaves.

Lukas blinked. *A golden acorn?*

Now Giovanni was gaping at the mace in Lukas's hands as well. Finally, he burst into loud laughter. "Do you know what you're holding there?" he chortled. "We've been turning over every stone, rummaging through every goddamned chest in the mansion, and meanwhile, this fellow here's been bashing helmets in with the imperial scepter!"

Lukas stared at the mace in disbelief.

Marquis de LaSalle seemed to notice what Lukas was holding at that very same moment. "The Imperial Regalia!" he shrieked. "Damn it, he's got the scepter! Don't let that boy get away!"

Crossbow bolts smashed into the wall all around Lukas and Elsa. Lukas took his sister's hand and ducked down as he ran toward the exit, where Zoltan and Jurek were already waiting for them. Giovanni followed right behind them.

"Quickly, to the back door!" Zoltan ordered. "If the Lord God is well disposed toward us, Bernhard will have secured us a boat by now. He ran on ahead."

They dashed down the hall toward the exit, with shouting guards in hot pursuit. At last, the door came into view, followed by the river shimmering black around the pier. Then, to Lukas's surprise, Bernhard really was there, waiting with a boat! He was in the river guards' rowboat, which was bobbing up and down on the Vltava. "In with you!" the giant called, laughing and waving an oar. "Every guard in the palace is after you. Lucky for us—means they don't need their boat any longer."

They jumped into the rowboat one by one, causing it to rock violently from side to side, nearly tipping it over. Bernhard rowed for all he was worth, his massive arm muscles bulging beneath his wet shirt. By the time the first guards reached the pier, the boat was already a good twenty paces away. A handful of bolts splashed into the water nearby, and then all was still.

"That was close," Zoltan said, breathing heavily. He shook his head in disappointment. "Too bad our mission was a failure."

"Oh, I wouldn't say that," Giovanni grinned, gesturing to Lukas. "See for yourselves. Our friend here brought us a little present from the armory. The marquis was so vain that he had the thing on display with his collection."

Lukas held up the golden scepter, which shimmered faintly in the moonlight. The oak leaves at its tip glittered like tiny tongues of flame.

"The scepter!" Zoltan blurted out, thunderstruck. "I'll be damned, this Lohenfels boy is a little devil."

They all cheered, and their celebratory whoops echoed in the night as the boat slowly glided beneath the stone bridge. The Vltava flowed sluggishly along; only a few lights were still aglow in the city.

Lukas was excited, too, but had a strange feeling he couldn't shake. He sensed they were being watched from somewhere in the darkness.

A short time later, they were all back at the Black Boar, which was illuminated by only a pair of candles. They sat around a table with the scepter in the center. Lukas could still scarcely believe that they'd actually succeeded. The battle with the frozen ones had left the imperial scepter slightly bent, but at least it hadn't broken. The friends had managed to carry off a few other weapons from the marquis's armory as well. Paulus had taken the Venetian schiavona, and Giovanni and Jerome had new rapiers that leaned gleaming and freshly polished against the counter beside Matthias's enormous crossbow and Bernhard's two-hander.

"And we can say with certainty that this is the imperial scepter?" Giovanni asked after a while, running his fingers along the gilded handle.

"Of course," Zoltan said, slapping his hand away. "There's no doubt of it." He rummaged around in his bag and then showed the boys three yellowing sketches of a diamond-studded crown, a golden sword, and a scepter with oak leaves at its tip. "Senno sent us these drawings last month. This is the imperial scepter, there's absolutely no doubt." Zoltan glanced around the table with a severe expression on his face. "And to make sure none of you boys get any stupid ideas, I'll be locking the scepter in my chest. If anyone tries to open it, I'll break their fingers. Several times. Just so that's clear."

"Which brings me to another question." Giovanni spoke up. "Who the hell sent us that anonymous tip about where to look?"

"Maybe it was someone who wants revenge on Schönborn and the marquis?" Matthias suggested. "Some confidant of theirs whose identity must be kept secret?"

"Maybe," Giovanni replied. "Still strange, though. And so is Senno's disappearance."

"That reminds me," Lukas interrupted anxiously. "Marquis de LaSalle knew about me and Elsa! In the armory, he mentioned 'the Lohenfels siblings.'"

"So? Of course he'd have heard of you." Jurek was cleaning his dirty fingernails with the point of his knife. "Schönborn and the marquis are friends." He glanced up at them with a sneering grin. "Besides, you introduced yourself in spectacular fashion in front of Wallenstein's palace."

"I know that was a mistake," Lukas snapped. "You don't have to remind me. But it occurs to me that I didn't see you anywhere during the fight with the frozen ones. Where were you? Drinking wine with the masked ladies?"

Jurek leapt up furiously, but Zoltan held him back. "Jurek was the rear guard," the commander assured Lukas. "We'd planned it that way. So stop bickering or—"

"Shh!" Elsa sharply interrupted. "Don't you all hear that?"

"Hear what?" Paulus asked from the corner where he'd been silently polishing his schiavona.

"Above us!" Elsa hissed, pointing toward the ceiling.

Now Lukas could hear it, too. It was a creaking sound, as though someone was tiptoeing across floorboards. Lukas remembered how he'd felt like they were being watched back in the boat. "Is there an attic up there?" he asked Jurek softly.

Jurek shrugged sullenly. "There's a ladder to it in the storeroom. It's no bigger than a chicken coop, you can barely stand up in there. It's probably just a cat."

"If so, it's a pretty damned big cat." Lukas signaled to Giovanni and Jerome, and the three of them crept past the counter to the storeroom. From there, a rotting ladder led up to a hatch. Lukas went up first, trying to make as little noise as possible, but the ladder still squeaked and groaned under his weight. Something rumbled overhead. He took two rungs at once the rest of the way, and finally popped his head through the opening.

The moonlit attic was full of old boxes and kegs. A nearby roof hatch stood open. For just a moment Lukas thought he spotted a leather-clad figure looking through it, then he heard rapid footfalls scurrying away across the roof.

"Damn it!" Lukas hissed and clambered the rest of the way into the attic as fast as he could. But he was too late—the stranger had already escaped.

Jerome and Giovanni finished climbing up the decaying ladder and joined him in the low-ceilinged room. Jerome shone a torch around the dusty attic, and soon they discovered a knothole in the floorboards large enough that they could peer down into the tavern.

"Damn," Giovanni muttered. "Whoever was here heard everything we said, and probably knows about the rest of the Imperial Regalia now, too."

"Who says he didn't know about them already?" Lukas added, looking thoughtful. "Remember that big secret informant of ours?"

"I don't think I would call him big, whoever he is." Jerome pointed down at the footprints in the dust. Sure enough, they were practically petite, like a child's. Jerome walked over to the roof hatch and gazed out at the clear night sky stretching above the rooftops. "Whoever it is, he must be an excellent thief, if he can climb so well and so quietly," Jerome added in an admiring tone. "I really hope we catch him next time around. I'd like to meet this fellow."

VIII

They spent the next few days waiting.

No new tips came in, and there was no sign of the mysterious eavesdropper, either. The imperial scepter remained in Zoltan's chest, which was kept in Zoltan's well-locked room. One look at his face was enough to tell the boys that even *thinking* of stealing it might cost them their heads.

Senno was still nowhere to be found. Lukas's hopes of him joining them were beginning to fade. Maybe the spell really had sent him to the other side of the world. At any rate, Lukas seemed to be the only one who was worried about Senno's absence. The others had never trusted the astrologer much anyway.

The young friends spent their time exploring the old imperial city of Prague, while Zoltan and his men did reconnaissance work. As far as Lukas was concerned, wandering through the Prague alleyways was one big adventure. The only city he'd ever known was Heidelberg, but Prague was far, far bigger. Everything here was louder, more colorful, more impressive. Unfortunately, it was also smellier, particularly in the summer heat.

Lukas often sensed ancient dark magic still lurking in Prague's nooks and crannies, in its out-of-the-way courtyards and churches, its rustic inns and patrician manors. He thought back to his mother's many stories of bridge spirits, house gremlins, and evil alchemists. There truly was something magical about this city.

The muddy roads were long and rambling, winding in every direction. Lukas often got lost in them, as though he were in a deep forest. Before the Great War, Prague had been the home of the German Kaiser, but then the Bohemian Protestants had taken up arms against Kaiser Matthias, throwing his governors out of a castle window. The Bohemians had wanted their own king, but in the end, they had been utterly decimated at the Battle of White Mountain. After that, the world had turned its back on Prague, and the old imperial city had been all but forgotten.

Around noon on the third day after their arrival, Lukas and Elsa strolled through the huge, lively marketplace, surrounded by shouting vendors, cartwheeling acrobats, and energetic musicians. A puppet theater in front of city hall was performing a play about a clever harlequin and a stupid king; the audience laughed and slapped their knees as they watched. Despite the heat, both Lukas and Elsa were wearing the simple farmers' hats Zoltan had given them that morning to help keep them discreet. There was always a chance that the marquis might have spies in the marketplace.

It was the first time that Lukas and his sister were out in the city alone. Elsa had hardly left the tavern; she'd spent most of her time poring over the *Grimorium*. Whenever Lukas tried speaking to her, she'd wave him away gruffly. Her face was pale, and there were dark circles beneath her eyes. Lukas had to remind her that she hadn't eaten anything since the night before. Only then did she finally agree to take her nose out of the magic book and leave the tavern with him. Even so, she still had it with her, like some kind of protective talisman.

"You're really spending too much time with that book," Lukas told her as he bought the two of them some boiled eggs and a small loaf of rye bread at one of the many market stands. "If you keep this up, you'll start eating the pages instead of breakfast."

He'd meant it as a joke, but Elsa scowled. "We need the book to beat Waldemar von Schönborn, don't you see that?" she snapped. "And I still don't understand even half of what's written in there! If we find ourselves face to face with Schönborn, what do you plan on doing? Are you going to defeat him with your ridiculous little rapiers and swords?"

"We did it once before," Lukas retorted.

"And nearly got yourselves killed in the process." Elsa shook her head. "Lukas, he's my father. Don't forget that. I know what he's capable of. I can feel it."

"And what are *you* capable of, Elsa?" Lukas asked softly. "I hardly know you anymore. You've changed. The book has changed you."

"You mean now I'm not the sweet little sister that can be bossed around," Elsa replied in a snippy tone. "You're just jealous that I can do magic and you can't, because the symbols in the book speak to me, not to you!"

Lukas stopped short and stared at her. Elsa had made that accusation once before, in Lohenfels Forest. "What are you talking about?" He sounded angrier than he'd intended. "I'm worried about you, that's all!"

"You and your friends ought to be worried about finding the other two pieces of Imperial Regalia instead." Elsa crossed her arms defiantly. "Leave the thinking and the sorcery to us women. All you men are good for is fighting."

Lukas was so furious that he crushed one of the boiled eggs in his fist and threw it against the side of a building. "Oh, do whatever you want!" he barked at her. "You'll see where that gets you!"

He turned away and stalked off amid the market stands, trembling with rage. Didn't his sister realize how much the book and the sorcery were changing her? Lukas knew they needed the *Grimorium* to help them find the Imperial Regalia and defeat Schönborn, but he also sensed that Elsa was increasingly losing herself in the book. Wasn't there any way out of this?

He was so deeply lost in thought that he didn't notice he'd left the marketplace and turned down a narrow alley. A handful of children hurried past him, and a beggar shuffled by, and then he was alone.

All at once, Lukas sensed that he was being watched yet again. It was the same feeling that he'd had back on the boat as they were escaping from the marquis. He jerked his head around and saw a shadowy figure duck into an alcove. Lukas hesitated. It might be a robber, some common thief on the hunt for another defenseless victim.

Or maybe it's the eavesdropper from the tavern, he thought. *Well, whoever it is, he's in for a nasty surprise.* Lukas drew his rapier and walked toward the shadowy alcove, ready to fight. The wound he'd gotten outside Wallenstein's palace was still throbbing. It had broken open again as he was fighting the frozen ones, and his arm had been slightly stiff ever since. But there was no time to worry about that now.

"Whoever you are, come out and fight like a man!" Lukas called. "Or are you too much of a coward?"

He was perhaps ten paces away when a leather-clad figure leapt out of the alcove, moving with lightning-fast reflexes. A cowl masked the short stranger's face. A leather quiver of arrows dangled from the figure's belt. A pair of almost delicate-looking hands were clutching an unusually small, sharply curved bow. Suddenly, an arrow came flying in Lukas's direction, grazing his upper arm, piercing his shirt, and nailing him neatly to a door.

"What the hell?" Lukas muttered, tearing free. But the next arrow followed immediately after. The stranger fired off half a dozen shots in quick succession, darting through the alley and changing direction again and again—ducking behind a barrel here, rolling across the ground there, even jumping over a pushcart parked in the alley. Each time, the arrows missed Lukas by a hair's breadth. The last arrow bored through his boot and nestled precisely between two of his toes. Lukas slipped off the boot, stumbling forward, and could only watch helplessly as the figure escaped. Soft, mocking laughter rang out as the stranger shouldered that odd little bow, leapt up onto a wall, and then sprang to a roof overhang, moving as nimbly and gracefully as a cat.

Lukas hurried toward the wall, but there was no sign of the mysterious archer. He shook his head, dumbfounded, as he stared at the holes in his shirt and his boot.

Who in the world was that?

Whoever it was, he was a champion marksman. Lukas bent down and picked up one of the arrows, squinting at it thoughtfully. Two unfamiliar symbols were etched into the shaft. The other arrows all bore the same two symbols.

They looked like ancient runes.

Knees still wobbling slightly, Lukas made his way back to the tavern, carrying one of the arrows as evidence. He kept stopping and glancing around suspiciously, wondering whether that spooky archer would reappear out of nowhere again. What had he wanted? Surely not just Lukas's coin purse. And what did these strange runes mean? They looked almost like some of the magical runes in the *Grimorium*.

All of a sudden, terror shot through Lukas's veins like ice.

Elsa!

Had the stranger been after her and the magic book? Had she been his intended victim?

Lukas ran faster. He never should have left his sister by herself, not in this huge, strange city. What had he been thinking?

He hoped desperately that it wasn't too late.

Heart pounding, Lukas dashed across the great stone bridge to the quarter below the castle. As he ran, he collided with a peddler carrying a large basket. The man shouted furiously after him, but Lukas didn't stop. He kept running and running until he reached the Black Boar tavern. Frantically he hammered out the secret knock on the door, and finally Zoltan opened it, looking astonished.

"Lukas!" The commander glanced up and down at the sweat-soaked youth, furrowing his brow. "Lord, look at you. Did something happen?"

"Is Elsa with you?" Lukas gasped, ignoring Zoltan's question.

Zoltan nodded. "She just arrived, but she went straight to her chambers," he said, pointing back into the tavern. "Something seems to have made her quite angry." He gave Lukas a stern look. "You, perhaps? Can't the two of you—"

Lukas exploded into giddy, relieved laughter, cutting Zoltan off midlecture. "Thank God! I thought that awful archer got her!"

"What archer?" Giovanni asked. He and the others were sitting at one of the old tables, sharing some bread, cheese, and wine. "What happened?"

Anxiously, Lukas told them about the masked assailant and his almost unearthly skill with a bow and arrow. "Best archer I've ever seen in my life," he said, laying the mysterious arrow on the table. "His technique is odd, though. He carries his quiver on his belt, not over his shoulder the way you'd expect. And he uses an odd bent bow and even stranger arrows that he fires off faster than anyone. I couldn't see his face."

"Sounds almost like those infamous assassins back in the days of the Crusades," Giovanni mused. "Though they usually fought with daggers rather than bow and arrow."

"And here's something else unusual." Lukas tapped the center of the arrow. "There are runes etched into this. Runes I've seen in the *Grimorium*! So I was thinking that Elsa—"

"Let me see." It was the voice of his sister. She'd just come down from the storeroom, apparently curious what all the commotion was about.

Lukas was so relieved to see her that he didn't even mention their earlier argument.

Elsa, for her part, still looked sullen and withdrawn as she reached for the arrow and peered intently at the symbols on it. "They're runes, yes," she said at last. "Not magic runes, though. I believe they're the type of runes the Welsh bards once used to write down their songs. The *Grimorium* does, indeed, contain a few of them as well."

Yet again, Lukas was astonished at how much Elsa knew about books. She'd lived with her father, Inquisitor Waldemar von Schönborn, for more than a year. During that time, he'd not only taught her sorcery, he'd also given her free rein in his enormous library and shared all manner of dark knowledge with her.

"So what do these runes mean, then?" Paulus asked. Like the others, he was standing around the table, eyeing the arrow with curious interest.

"That's an *F*, and this is an *E*," Elsa replied, pointing to each in turn. "Likely some sort of abbreviation."

"Frightening Essassins?" Jerome grinned. "Get it?"

Giovanni groaned. "Thank you for that exceptionally brilliant suggestion, Jerome. Anyway, it's more important to find out why the archer was after Lukas. It doesn't seem that killing him was the goal—from the way Lukas describes his skill, I expect he'd have had no trouble shooting our friend full of arrows."

Bernhard nodded, stroking his beard with one massive hand. "Our little scholar is right." He took the arrow and ran a finger over its sharp iron tip. "This is good workmanship, certainly no beginner's arrows. If this is the same fellow who was eavesdropping on us from the storeroom, we definitely need to have a talk with him."

"And how do you propose to arrange that?" Jurek looked at him skeptically with his one eye. "Our boy Lukas just let him slip through his clumsy little fingers for the second time."

Lukas's lips parted to make an angry retort, but Zoltan raised a hand to cut him off. "It's time for us to set a trap for him," the commander said. "Whoever it is, thanks to our inattention, he probably knows about the Imperial Regalia. We need to find out what he's planning." Zoltan smiled broadly. "And I've already got a plan. We'll lure him into a real mousetrap. This very night, in fact."

"And what's our cheese?" Giovanni asked.

Zoltan laughed grimly. "What do you think? The imperial scepter, of course. The most valuable piece of cheese the world has ever seen!"

IX

Zoltan's plan was as simple as it was brilliant.

The past few days had brought the commander no closer to learning the whereabouts of the two remaining Regalia items, but while out on one of his searches, he had spotted an abandoned Protestant church. Since the Catholics' victory at the Battle of White Mountain, the building had served as a stable and storehouse. It was in a run-down quarter full of poor folk and shady characters—and it was clearly visible from all directions.

"This fellow is as curious as a cat," Zoltan explained quietly to the others seated around the table. "And we're going to take advantage of that. Our bait will be the imperial scepter. We'll go out there with it tonight, and make sure that he notices us leaving. He'll follow us there. The church has only two entrances, and both will be easy to guard. Once he's in, he'll have no way out. The trap snaps shut!"

"What if he doesn't come?" Jurek asked.

"Trust me, he will," Zoltan replied in a low voice. "He knows our hideout here, and he wants to find out more about our plans. He doesn't dare return to the attic, but I suspect he's sneaking around outside somewhere. So we'll just dangle a carrot under his nose."

For the next several hours, as they waited for nightfall, they spent their time piquing their mysterious lurker's curiosity as much as possible. They took turns stepping outside and conversing in whispers, or setting off to purchase lanterns, torches, and ropes. They wanted to give the leather-clad stranger the impression that they were staging some great coup.

Elsa had retreated to her chambers with the *Grimorium* once more. Lukas had tried speaking to her several times, but she said she wanted to be alone. He figured she was still upset with him about the argument they'd had in the marketplace.

Lukas didn't join them at the market, either. The wound he had received fighting the guards simply refused to heal. Matthias had changed his dressing only the day before, but it was already beginning to soak through. Lukas removed his shirt, unwound the bandage, and regarded his shoulder. To his horror, he discovered that the wound had begun to fester. Matthias, who had remained at the tavern with Lukas and Elsa, came closer and inspected the injury with a worried look on his face.

"I don't like this," Matthias said as he dabbed the wound with a scrap of cloth, pressing the pus out. "Not at all. You should have rested your arm, rather than battling that damned frozen one and then running all over the city like a madman. That has to stop!" He shook his head with such force that the pearls in his braided hair jangled softly. "Perhaps it would be better if you stayed here with me and Elsa tonight."

"And give Jurek something else to whine about?" Lukas gritted his teeth and shook his head. "Never!"

Matthias sighed. "I suspected you might react that way. Well, then, let me at least change the dressing and put some herbs on there before the infection gets worse." He cleaned the wound and pushed a few sweet-smelling dried herbs beneath the fresh bandage as he wrapped it around Lukas's shoulder.

Lukas closed his eyes and tried to ignore the pain. He looked up again when he heard footsteps coming from the storeroom. It was Elsa. She approached and stroked his sweaty face sympathetically. The argument had apparently been forgotten.

"Matthias is right," she said with a caring expression on her face. "You *do* look quite ill. I'll prepare a brew of linden blossoms and willow leaves for you. It won't taste very good, but it will help."

Lukas tried to smile. "Has it already come to this? My little sister is mothering me?"

"You should be glad you have a little sister who mothers you instead of wishing the Devil would take you," Matthias said, pointing an admonishing finger at him. "My sister would never have done such a thing—though I suppose I was never particularly nice to her, either," he added with a grin.

"Neither is Lukas," Elsa shot back teasingly. "When he runs out of ideas, he throws boiled eggs at me. Or sings me lullabies! That's the worst of all."

They both laughed, and for one brief moment, things between them felt almost the way they'd been before.

Soon after, freshly bandaged and carrying a mug of linden-blossom tea, Lukas went upstairs to one of the sparsely furnished guest rooms. It held a pair of beds with straw-filled, bug-infested pillows. The rushes on the ground smelled moldy, and Lukas saw a mouse scurry into a hole in a corner of the room.

Wearily, Lukas dropped down onto one of the beds. How he wished he were a guest at Wallenstein's palace—presumably he would have a far more comfortable bed to sleep in there. But he knew they needed to attract as little attention as possible in their search, so this hovel would have to do.

Lukas shivered, and he realized that he had a fever. Matthias was probably right, he decided. Swimming in the cold Vltava, fighting the city guards and the frozen one, encountering that eerie archer, and then sprinting back to the tavern had all been too much for him.

All of a sudden, he felt so weak that he nearly retched with exhaustion. He laid his hand on the throbbing wound—it almost felt like it had a steady heartbeat. Why, *why* had he let himself get distracted for that one moment when he was fighting the guards? Because he'd been hoping Elsa would cast a spell. For a fraction of a second, he'd stopped relying on his own talent.

I could have been killed.

He thought about his father, who had taught him that one lightning-fast thrust or stab was often the difference between life and death. Many wounds were not immediately fatal. Far more painful, and far more dreaded, was what they called "wound fever," which carried a man off slowly. During the war, Lukas had known soldiers who were as strong as oxen, and he'd watched wound fever burn them from the inside out within just a few days. The only way they'd have even a shred of a chance was if the limb was amputated in time. The feldsher sliced off arms and legs using a bone saw, giving the unlucky soldiers only a bottle of schnapps to dull the pain and a piece of wood to bite down on.

Is that where I'm headed now, too?

Lukas wanted to call out to his sister, but he couldn't muster the strength. Instead, he thought of his dead mother. He'd heard her voice from time to time, as though from some distant world, but it had been a long while since it last happened. He still dreamed of her on occasion, but the figure in those dreams was less distinct each time—her contours were fading, as though she were slowly sinking into the fog of oblivion.

Lukas closed his eyes and took a deep breath, calming himself. He tried to picture his mother, to remember her laugh, her songs, her caresses. He drew new strength from his love for her.

And just like that, the familiar voice of his mother spoke within him. It was as clear as if she were standing beside him in the room.

The power is within you, Lukas. Feel it. Use it.

Lukas jolted upright and glanced around, but he was alone in the room. The moment had passed again. Perhaps it had only been a fever dream? But the voice had been so real. His mother had helped him conquer his fears before. Her voice had once come to him and told him how to defeat the inquisitor's phantom wolf. Would it help him now, too?

There! Her voice sounded once more, softly now, as though carried on the wind from some distant shore.

The power is within you, Lukas. Not only in your sister. The power is within you.

"What power, Mother?" he murmured. "What power?"

Lukas put his hand on the fresh bandage. His heart was filled with love for his mother—he missed her so much! Hearing her voice was like having her close again.

"Mother . . ." he whispered.

The power, Lukas . . . the power . . . the power . . .

The voice grew fainter.

Lukas took a deep breath and pictured his blood pulsing through his body, flushing the infection away, fighting off the malevolent forces inside him.

He breathed deeply again, turning all his concentration inward, and all at once, the pain in his shoulder seemed to lessen. His fever had broken as well! Astonished, he unwrapped the bandage, and he could barely believe his eyes.

Rosy skin now shimmered in the spot where the injury had been, and the exhaustion that was now spreading through him was like nothing he'd ever felt before.

The wound was gone.

The power is within me, too, he thought. *I have it, too.*

Then his eyes fell shut.

The last thing he heard was a soft ringing sound that seemed to come from another world.

X

Lukas awoke to chatter at the foot of his bed.

". . . has me worried. I looked at his wound before, and the infected blood may have already reached his heart. You all know what that means."

Blinking sleepily, he saw Matthias and Zoltan standing there, along with his friends, Giovanni, Paulus, and Jerome. All five of them looked extremely concerned. Night had already fallen, and several candles on the windowsill bathed the room in muted light. It took Lukas a while to get his bearings again, but then the memory came back to him.

My mother's voice! he thought. *The wound!*

Cautiously, he prodded the bandage, but the pain was gone. In fact, he felt refreshed—a little tired, though, as if he'd been working hard all day long.

"During the war, in a case like his, we would have amputated the arm just to be safe," Matthias went on in a whisper. Then he stopped, realizing that Lukas was watching him, and forced a smile. "Ah, Lukas!" he cried, attempting to sound cheerful. "I'm glad you're awake. Are you thirsty? I'll get you something to drink."

"Thanks," Lukas replied. "But I don't think that's necessary. I can get it myself." He moved to stand up, but Paulus held him back with his strong, massive hands.

"Lukas, you have a bad fever. Stay in bed. We'll take care of you."

"Damn it, I don't have a fever! Now stop treating me like I'm a small child. I'm fine!"

Astonished, Matthias came closer and felt Lukas's forehead. "It's true," he murmured. "His fever is gone, his cheeks are rosy. How is that possible? It's some sort of miracle."

Lukas pushed Matthias's hand away. "I told you, I feel much better. When are we leaving?"

Laughing, Zoltan clapped the dumbstruck Matthias on the shoulder. "Bernhard is right. You really are a damn quack, Matthias! And here I was thinking this little whelp was done for." He turned to the door. "Get ready, all of you. We'll leave in half an hour."

Matthias shot Lukas one last, baffled look before following his commander down to the tavern. Paulus, Jerome, and Giovanni breathed sighs of relief.

"Mon dieu!" Jerome exclaimed, grinning. "Matthias gave us quite a fright. We thought you were going to have to start wiping your ass with your right hand."

"Matthias must not be as good a field surgeon as he thinks," Lukas replied, rising to his feet. He felt bad about having to lie to Matthias, but he decided it would be better not to tell his companions about his miraculous recovery just yet. He didn't know what to make of it himself. His dead mother had spoken to him, and apparently, he had managed to heal himself through some sort of magic. Or had the whole thing simply been a feverish hallucination? Hastily, he picked up his doublet and rapier belt and put them on.

As he walked downstairs, Lukas sneaked another glance underneath the bandage. It was true—the wound had disappeared.

The others were already waiting for him down in the tavern. Elsa was standing with them, looking equally baffled to see her brother so healthy.

"I thought you were deathly ill!" she cried, embracing him tenderly.

"Must have been that bitter linden tea of yours." Lukas smiled, smoothing back her hair. "I suppose you should take care of me more often, little sister."

Elsa's expression turned suspicious.

Lukas thought back to what his dead mother had said. *The power is in you, Lukas. Not only in your sister.*

He decided not to say anything to Elsa yet, either. He shoved his rapier into its hanger and turned his attention to the others, who were already carrying their weapons, lanterns, and torches. "Shall we go?"

Zoltan looked at him uncertainly. "Are you sure you want to come with us? The injury may not be as serious as we feared, but if we end up in a battle . . ."

"I can fight as well as anyone here," Lukas broke in. "Maybe even better," he added defiantly.

"Now that's the angry little half-pint I know!" Zoltan grinned. "You certainly do remind me a lot of your late father sometimes." He reached for the imperial scepter, which he had just removed from the chest and wrapped carelessly in a few scraps of cloth, making sure that the gold and silver were visible underneath. "Well, then," Zoltan growled. "Let's draw this strange bowman out of his hiding spot. I can hardly wait to find out who it is we're dealing with."

They left the tavern and sneaked through the alleys. Their torches and lanterns were spots of warmth in the darkness of the narrow, unlit streets. The crew stopped again and again to make a show of whispering among themselves and glancing around. From time to time, Zoltan shifted the wrappings on the scepter, letting it peek out for a moment to keep their potential pursuer interested.

"I think I saw something," Jerome whispered after a while. "Up on one of the rooftops. Don't turn around!"

"Let's hope you're right," Bernhard replied. He had his two-hander on his back. Its cross-guard was almost the length of Bernhard's forearm, and its handle poked out above his head, making the giant look even more imposing than he already was. "I wouldn't mind exchanging a few words with him," he added with a somber look on his face. "Man to man."

"Only if I don't get to him first," Matthias replied, patting his large crossbow. He'd explained to Lukas that it was a "repeater" crossbow, a weapon invented in far-off China. Ten bolts fit into the strange wooden box above the groove, and Matthias could fire them all off quickly if necessary. The friendly man with the pearls in his hair had offered to stay at the tavern and watch out for Elsa, but Elsa had made it clear that she didn't need anyone's help, and then shut herself up in her room with the *Grimorium*. Lukas wished she would read something else instead.

They hurried onward, hunched down, until they finally reached the stone bridge flanked at each bank by a massive gate tower. The Vltava murmured softly beneath their feet.

"The rear gatehouse is guarded," Zoltan said quietly. "But I handed out a few coins this afternoon so that we would be allowed to cross." He winked. "Our pursuer, on the other hand, will have to swim across, so we should take our time."

They went over the bridge, and sure enough, the bored-looking watchmen merely nodded to Zoltan as they approached the rear tower. After passing the gatehouse, they descended into another labyrinth of dark, grimy streets, past tiny churches, gloomy squares, and dry wells. Before long, Lukas had lost his sense of direction completely.

After what seemed like an eternity, they reached a poor, run-down neighborhood, well away from the marketplace. Only a handful of the homes here were made of stone; the rest were mostly crooked huts and cottages that looked like they might collapse at any second. The foul-smelling morass tugged at Lukas's boots. Here and there, they heard hasty footsteps down an alley or spotted a pair of eyes staring out at them from a dark corner. In several alcoves and corners, men and women in tattered clothing stood around barrels with fire glowing inside. As Lukas and his friends passed them, their eyes flickered greedily, but none of the ragged figures dared stand in their way.

"All beggars and scoundrels here," Zoltan murmured to Lukas, wisely tucking the scraps of cloth more tightly around the imperial scepter. "Come here alone, and they'll eat you alive and spit out your bones. They won't come near eight armed men, though."

The troop did, indeed, look quite fearsome. Zoltan was out in front with Bernhard the giant and his two-hander, followed closely by Matthias. After them came Paulus, with his freshly sharpened schiavona prominently displayed on his belt. Lukas, Giovanni, and Jerome were marching along in the middle with their rapiers drawn. As usual, the one-eyed Jurek bore up the rear; a good half dozen knives dangled at his side, all of which he was equally capable of fighting with or throwing. Lukas still didn't trust the short, wiry man any farther than he could spit.

After a while, they came to a square bordered on two sides by wild, fallow fields. The small church across from them had seen better days. Its stained-glass windows were all broken; the collapsing bell tower loomed in the night sky like a rotten black tooth. The church portal hung crookedly from its hinges. Sounds of lowing cattle and bleating goats came from inside the building.

"A Bohemian herdsman uses the church as his stable," Zoltan said, shaking his head. "It's such a shame what the Catholic victors have done with the Protestants and their churches. As though they were not Christians! Well, so much the better for us." He turned to Jerome, who had the best eyes of any of them. "Did you spot our friend again?"

"I think he's still following us from the rooftops," Jerome replied. "I haven't noticed him in some time, though."

"I'm sure he's there. Well, let's lure him into our trap, shall we?" Zoltan leaned against the church portal, which opened with a creak. In the dim light of the torch, Lukas could make out several pillars, an altar bearing half a dozen empty birdcages, and all manner of junk. The church floor was covered with straw and manure, and the whole room stank terribly of animal waste. A pair of goats and a starved-looking cow stared at them from out of the rough-timbered alcoves in the aisles. There was no sign of the herdsmen themselves.

"They say this church is haunted," Zoltan remarked, turning toward the others. "After the Battle of White Mountain, the Evangelical priest was stabbed to death here on the altar, and his ghost has been lurking around here ever since, screaming for revenge. Supposedly, although I think the herdsmen merely invented the story so that they wouldn't have to guard the stalls," he added, winking. Then he pointed to his right, toward another small side door. "Bernhard, Jurek, Matthias, you hide near the side entrance," he ordered. "The rest of you, come with me. Remember, we don't attack until our friend has reached the altar."

Paulus, Jerome, and Giovanni hunkered down into the dark recesses on either side of the main church portal, while Zoltan and Lukas headed straight for the altar. Zoltan swept the cages and junk aside with a hasty motion, and then unwrapped the imperial scepter, displaying it atop the altar.

The scepter shimmered in the light of Lukas's torch, golden and seductive. The acorn and leaves at the tip twinkled like stars in the night sky.

"Well, let's see if our mouse can resist the cheese," Zoltan whispered and gestured to a staircase to one side of the altar, which apparently led to the crypt. "We want the fellow to think we're planning to do something with the scepter. Let's wait down there."

Zoltan and Lukas descended a few steps, and then came to a low arch with a row of stone sarcophagi. They waited there among the coffins in the darkness, listening.

Nothing happened.

Everything was still, and Lukas began to think they'd lost their unknown spy. He was just about to say as much to Zoltan, who was leaning against a sarcophagus with his eyes closed, as though asleep, when they heard the telltale sound of breaking glass. Zoltan was wide awake in an instant. He put his finger to his lips and signaled to Lukas.

The two of them crept up the stairs, crouching, until they could see the two portals and the interior of the church. Try as Lukas might, though, he couldn't see anything, apart from his companions' shadows in the alcoves. They appeared lifeless and frozen, like statues of holy men from some long-forgotten time. Had they been mistaken?

Another crashing sound.

Lukas scanned the room and spotted a figure standing high overhead, against what was left of a church window. The small, slender man was clad in brown leather and wore a black hood. Lukas recognized him immediately. It was the man who had ambushed him in the alley near the marketplace! As his eyes adjusted, he noticed the bow and the quiver on the man's belt.

The man seemed to hesitate, almost like he suspected a trap. But then he unrolled a rope, tied it to one of the window struts, and slid down without making a sound. When he reached the church floor, he lifted his head, as if trying to pick up a trail. Then he sneaked toward the altar.

Lukas was about to hurry up the stairs, but Zoltan held him back. "Wait until the altar . . ." he mouthed.

But just at that moment, Paulus and Jerome rushed toward the stranger, weapons drawn. The man spun around abruptly and sprinted back to the rope. Lukas dashed forward as well, hoping to block his path.

"God in heaven!" Zoltan shouted, drawing his sword. "Didn't I tell you to wait? Now go get him, or I'll feed you all to the goats!"

Still running, the man turned, lifted his bow, and sent a flurry of arrows at his pursuers. Lukas was amazed all over again at how quickly he could shoot—the arrows were raining down on them like hail. Matthias began firing off his crossbow as well. His bolts hissed through the air like angry hornets, but the stranger dodged every one, still firing back at them as he continued toward the rope.

Now Bernhard and Jurek were storming toward the dangling rope from the side entrance, but the diminutive man beat them there, Lukas close behind him.

The stranger clambered up the rope with the dexterity of an ape. Lukas was right at his heels. He'd always thought of himself as a particularly agile climber, but this hooded archer was even quicker. He reached the window and soon disappeared into the darkness. When Lukas finally came to the window as well, he saw that the fellow had a serious problem.

If he wanted to get down the church wall on the other side, he would need a rope. Specifically, the rope that Lukas had just finished climbing.

The hooded man was standing on a narrow ledge, apparently trying to decide what to do next. There was an alley between the church and the nearest roof, creating a gap likely five, six paces wide.

Lukas smiled triumphantly. There wasn't a chance that . . .

The man jumped.

Lukas gaped at the slender man, who landed on the opposite roof with catlike grace.

"What's going on up there, boy?" Zoltan barked from below. "Do you have him?"

Lukas recalled Zoltan's very recent threat to feed them all to the goats. He didn't actually believe the commander would make good on it, but fear of Zoltan's rage put the added spring in Lukas's step. After taking a few deep breaths, Lukas took off sprinting and leapt across the alley to the roof on the other side.

He landed hard on the slippery roof shingles, stumbled, and nearly fell off, before finding his footing again. The hooded stranger was already on another rooftop. As the silvery crescent moon rose over Prague, Lukas followed his adversary from roof to roof, always a few steps behind. He was determined to catch the man—if for no other reason than to prove to the others that he was capable of such a thing!

After a few more leaps, the stranger stopped abruptly in his tracks. Lukas looked around, trying to figure out why. He soon understood. The large stone house they were now standing on was surrounded by a rose garden and a tall iron fence with sharp spear points along the top. It was at least eight paces to the next roof.

That's too far, even for you, Lukas thought, relieved. *Now I have you.*

He reached for his rapier. The other man turned around and fired off three arrows in quick succession, but Lukas managed to duck behind a chimney for cover.

Then the arrows stopped.

His quiver is empty! Lukas realized.

"Give up!" he shouted. "Now!" He stormed out from behind the chimney, rushing straight toward the man.

But the stranger spread his arms out and did the impossible.

He jumped.

At first, Lukas thought the man might actually make it. He flew through the air like a great bird. But then gravity caught up to him after all. He flailed his arms like a drowning man as he tumbled down.

The man landed on the spear points of the iron fence, which bored through him like daggers.

"My God!" Lukas stammered. "That wasn't what I wanted to happen. I swear, that wasn't what I wanted!"

The delicate-looking man twitched like a fish on dry land as he tried desperately to escape his situation. He was obviously still alive, but his injuries had to be awful. Lukas glanced around, searching for another way down. He hurried to the other side of the building, the direction they'd come from, and discovered a fragile trellis covered in climbing roses. He carefully clambered down to the ground and then ran around to the fence on the other side. The archer was still hanging there, bent across one of the spear points. Lukas heard only soft moaning.

"I'm so sorry!" Lukas gasped. "If you'd only listened to me, this wouldn't have happened! Why did you have to try that impossible jump?"

Now he saw the man up close for the first time. Blood dripped from his body down the metal spikes, one of which had indeed pierced through the stranger's doublet. Lukas stroked the bloody leather cautiously.

"Hurts . . . ," the short, slight man whispered from beneath the hood. "Hurts . . . so . . . much . . ."

"Wait, I'll help you," Lukas said, once he had made sure that the man really no longer posed a threat. Gently he lifted the man up, and discovered he was far lighter than Lukas would have expected. As Lukas laid him between two rosebushes, the stranger's hood slipped off, revealing a mane of long red hair. A pale, freckled face shimmered in the moonlight.

Lukas was so startled that he nearly dropped her.

Her.

XI

Only at second glance did Lukas realize that the redheaded woman was still quite young—more of a girl, really. Probably fifteen or sixteen, he guessed.

The wavy red hair that had been hidden beneath her hood now surrounded her face like a halo. She was extremely pale; a thin rivulet of blood trickled from one corner of her mouth. Around her abdomen, where the fence point had gone through her, a dark, wet blotch was spreading steadily across her leather doublet.

Although Lukas knew the girl had to be in terrible pain, a delicate smile still played on her lips. "Congrat . . . ulations, little . . . hunter," she murmured. Lukas detected a trace of a foreign accent. "Shot . . . the deer . . . in the end . . . after all."

"Who are you?" Lukas asked, dabbing the blood from her lips, though he knew it wasn't doing her any good. The injury to her stomach was undoubtedly fatal.

"My friends . . . call me Gwendolyn," the girl coughed. "Though I doubt you're a friend." She smiled again.

"Well, friends don't spy on each other and follow each other around, either," Lukas replied dully. He regarded the redheaded girl. She was certainly pretty. He'd have liked to be her friend, but fate obviously had other plans for them. "Why did you follow us, anyway?"

Gwendolyn let out a rattling laugh. "Thieves like to work in the shadows," she replied wearily after a while. "You should know that, since you are thieves yourselves. I saw you coming out of the palace of the marquis, just as I was about to go in. I . . . eavesdropped on your . . . conversation. The Imperial Regalia . . . sounds like quite a treasure," she said between labored breaths.

"You think we're *thieves?*" Lukas furrowed his brow. So she wasn't following them on the orders of Schönborn or some other evil power? This girl was just a simple thief with her eye on their gold. In that case, her death would be even more senseless than he'd thought.

"What about your arrows?" he asked. "I saw the runes on them. Runes like the ones in the *Grimorium Nocturnum.*"

"The what?" The girl's voice was growing weaker. "They're letters. An *F* and an *E.* I carve them . . . in memory of my . . . father. Falcon Eye . . . He was a famous . . . Welsh . . . archer . . ." Before she could say anything more, she closed her eyes and her head lolled to one side.

"No!" Lukas cried. "You can't die! Oh, God, I'm so sorry, damn it, damn it . . ." Tears ran down his face. This girl was no tool of Schönborn's—she was just a harmless thief, and he'd driven her to her death. He'd never forgive himself for this.

Clumsily, he ran his hand through her hair, patted her cheeks, shook her gently, but Gwendolyn remained unconscious. Lukas wished desperately that Matthias would come by with his bandaging supplies, even though he suspected that there was nothing in the world that could heal the girl.

Nothing in the world . . .

Lukas gave a start when he realized what he had just thought. His mother's words came into his mind again: *The power is in you, Lukas. Not only in your sister.*

He closed his eyes, laid both hands on Gwendolyn's blood-soaked doublet, and murmured the phrase over and over again. "The power is in me. The power is in me."

But nothing happened.

Lukas cursed softly. It had all been in his imagination, a fever dream. His wound had healed naturally. Maybe it had been a miracle, maybe chance, but it was certainly no magic. All was in vain.

Heavy of heart, Lukas gazed down at the dying red-haired girl. She was so beautiful. Lukas felt strangely connected to her, even though he barely knew her. Her death seemed to reflect all the senselessness of this war, all the cold cruelty it represented.

"Don't die," Lukas whispered and shut his eyes again. He felt like he could see inside a body, as he had when his own wound healed, only it was Gwendolyn's this time rather than his own. He saw the torn tissue, the injured organs, the blood . . .

The power . . .

There was a soft ringing sound.

Lukas felt some sort of lightning bolt shoot from his fingertips. A slight tingling sensation swept through his body.

Gwendolyn twitched for a moment, and then her eyes opened. She looked at Lukas in astonishment.

"What did you do?" she began. Then she fell unconscious again.

Lukas stumbled backward and fell into the dewy grass of the garden. He felt unexpectedly weak, and his sweat-soaked shirt was clinging to him. He waited for a while before he got up and knelt beside Gwendolyn. Trembling in excitement, he cut a slit in her doublet with his knife and examined the skin underneath.

The puncture wound was gone; the skin was healed.

"Oh, Mother!" Lukas whispered. "You were right. The power is in me, too!" He still couldn't believe it. He could do magic, even if he wasn't sure how. He seemed to be able to heal people magically, without using any magic books or spells. Could Elsa do the same?

Gwendolyn's breathing was even now, and her cheeks were less waxy than they had been just a few moments before. Lukas was once again taken aback by how pretty she was, with her red hair, her freckles, her pale complexion.

A loud, gruff voice snapped him back to the present. "Hey, here he is! Here!" It was Bernhard, running over to him with his two-hander drawn. Apparently, the others had been searching for him.

"Hah, caught him!" Matthias shouted, following close at Bernhard's heels. He had his crossbow raised threateningly, and only lowered the weapon when he saw that the figure on the ground was no longer a danger. He stopped dead in his tracks when he saw Gwendolyn lying on the ground. "That's a girl!" he cried. "And what a pretty one, too."

"She fell from the roof," Lukas reported haltingly. "But she's alive. Don't worry—she's no henchman of Schönborn's, just an ordinary thief."

One by one, the others made their way to the abandoned garden. They stood around the unconscious girl, gawking in amazement.

"Just a thief, you say?" Zoltan growled. "Somehow I find it hard to believe." He clapped Lukas on the shoulder. "Good that you caught her. We'll take her with us to the Black Boar. When she comes to, I'll squeeze the truth out of this little tramp."

Lukas stared at Zoltan in outrage. *How dare he call Gwendolyn a tramp? He doesn't even know her.* He wanted to protest, but he was too weak. Bernhard tossed the girl over his shoulder as though she weighed nothing. Together they all started back toward the tavern.

Lukas wobbled along behind them as though in a trance, already suspecting that getting Gwendolyn to talk wouldn't be quite as easy as Zoltan thought.

XII

"Let me out, you stinking donkeys! You thrice-accursed swine!" They'd locked Gwendolyn in the cellar storeroom, where she'd been protesting loudly all morning. Zoltan had gone in to speak with her three times, but received only cursing and fist blows for his trouble—so far, Gwendolyn hadn't told the commander a thing.

Zoltan sighed once again at the sounds of screaming and hammering ringing out from the other side of the door. Despite his threats to the contrary, Zoltan didn't seem to intend to hurt her, but his severe expression deterred the others from asking too many questions on the subject. Even so, Lukas couldn't suppress a grin, and the others winked at each other on occasion as well.

"For a poor little bird who fell from the roof, that one sure has plenty of strength in her lungs." Bernhard plucked at his beard. "She'd have made a good Musketeer. Pity she's only a girl, albeit a rather pretty one. What do you think, Zoltan?"

"I think you should shut your mouth," the commander grunted. "I don't believe that little brat is an ordinary thief. Did you see the way she wielded that bow? I'm telling you all, that girl is a well-trained assassin, sent by Schönborn himself!"

"She said her father was a famous archer," Giovanni reminded him. "Someone called Falcon Eye. I asked around in the marketplace this morning, and word has it that there was, indeed, such a fellow in the Saxon army. A Welsh marksman, and a true legend! But they say he lost his life a year or two ago, here in Prague. He was in a tavern, protecting his daughter from a band of scoundrels, and someone stabbed him in the back."

"And the daughter?" Jerome asked.

"Redhead, supposedly quite pretty. Hasn't been seen since that day."

Jurek spat on the floor contemptuously. "Bah. Even if that is the daughter, it doesn't mean she isn't working with Schönborn. I wouldn't put anything past a redhead. They're in league with the Devil."

As if to confirm what Jurek had said, the caterwauling in the cellar grew even louder. Several of the men held their ears.

It was Elsa who resumed the conversation. "Red hair or not," she said, "I find it strange that the girl came away with no visible injuries. Matthias examined her while she was still unconscious." She glanced over at Matthias, who was sitting beside her at the table, looking contemplative. "Her doublet was soaked through with blood, but she had no wounds. Not even a scratch!"

"See?" Jurek hissed. "She's a witch. I told you."

"Right, and all one-eyed men have sacrificed an eye to the Devil," Lukas retorted sarcastically. He suddenly felt Elsa's eyes on him, but he avoided her gaze. Did she suspect something? He would tell her about the magic healing episodes soon enough, but not now, not in front of everyone. Especially not in front of Jurek, whom Lukas trusted less and less.

"That's enough," Zoltan exclaimed, slamming his fist down onto the table and standing up. "I'll talk to that beast whether she likes it or not! And this time, I'm not letting her wailing soften me up."

"Don't hurt her!" Lukas called after him.

"Oh, so now you're protecting her?" Elsa taunted him, crossing her arms defiantly. "Don't forget, even if she's not a witch, she's still a thief."

"I just don't want Zoltan to hurt her," Lukas insisted. "Is that a crime?"

Paulus laughed. "I'm starting to believe that the two of you had quite an enjoyable time together in that rose garden." He winked at Lukas. "But don't worry. If anything, Zoltan will just give your little darling a proper spanking."

The shrieks from the cellar fell silent, and Paulus nodded knowingly. "What did I tell you? Now she's getting soft."

"I wouldn't be so sure," Giovanni replied.

After a while, Zoltan returned to the tavern room. He wiped the sweat from his brow as though he had just come from a long battle of swords and shields. "The beast remains stubborn," the commander said curtly. "She says she'll only talk with Lukas."

"With Lukas? Oho!" Jerome ran his hand through his hair coquettishly, and the others laughed. "A little tryst in a beer cellar, *comme c'est gentil!* Perhaps we should play some music for you to dance to?"

"Oh, be quiet," Lukas replied wearily, but he felt the blood rising to his cheeks. He raised a questioning eyebrow at Zoltan, who nodded reluctantly.

"Go on down," he muttered. "But make it clear to her that this is her last chance. We can always let her starve down there. Everyone talks after a couple of days without food. And don't let the beast catch you off guard. She knows every trick in the book!"

Lukas went down the stairs to the tavern cellar and knocked on the door, but everything remained still on the other side.

"I'm coming in," he said at last, sliding the latch open. Cautiously, he stepped into the low cave, which stank of old beer. A ray of sunlight fell in through one tiny window, but most of the room was dark. Barrels as tall as Lukas himself lined the walls to either side.

"Gwendolyn?" Lukas asked in a tentative voice.

Suddenly, a shadow flew out from between two barrels and knocked him to the floor. Long red hair blocked his view.

"Gwendolyn!" he cried, shaking her off. "Don't! I thought you wanted to talk? There are a half dozen roughnecks upstairs who would be only too happy to torture every last scrap of information out of you."

Gwendolyn let go of him and stepped a few paces away as Lukas rose cautiously to his feet. He felt strangely insecure and awkward in her presence, and found himself struggling for words—even though she was the prisoner, not he.

"Yes, I wanted to talk," she said, green eyes glittering. "About what you did yesterday."

"What do you mean?"

"You know perfectly well what I mean," she replied in her unfamiliar accent. "I was near death, I could feel it. I remember you laid your hands on my stomach, and now there's not even a scratch on it! How is that possible? Are you a magician? Who *are* you people, anyway?"

"We're no magicians," Lukas replied. *At least, most of us aren't,* he added in his head. "But we're trying to stop an evil magician. He stole three pieces of Imperial Regalia, and we need to find them."

Gwendolyn hesitated for a moment, but then nodded. "The scepter, the crown, and the sword, right? I heard you talking about them." She grinned. "I bet those things are worth a lot of money."

"We're not interested in money, Gwendolyn."

"But I am. Money is the only thing that counts. Coins are hard, they don't melt away in your hand like love. They have substance. But what would a young pup like you know about that, anyway?"

"I'm nearly fifteen," Lukas retorted, blushing. "And you're not all that much older, so don't you talk to me about love."

Gwendolyn's expression hardened, and Lukas remembered that the girl had lost her father and presumably her mother as well, just as he had. He wondered whether she'd ever experienced love since.

"I have a proposition for you all," she said. "I'll help you find these imperial things if you'll pay me properly for it."

Lukas blinked. "You're our prisoner! Why should we cooperate with you at all, let alone pay you for it?"

"Because I know where the crown is." Gwendolyn winked.

Lukas stared at her in disbelief. "What?" They'd been waiting for days for another message from their mysterious helper, and now Gwendolyn knew what they needed? Absurd. "You're lying," he said. "How would you know where the crown was?"

"Oh, that doesn't matter. I just do. I give you my word." Gwendolyn raised her right hand solemnly. "Give me *your* word that you'll stand up for me to your smelly friends, and I'll help you find the crown. Swear it!"

Lukas hesitated. Gwendolyn was the finest archer he'd ever seen, and an excellent climber as well. If she really did know where the crown was hidden, they could only benefit from her help. And if she was lying, he didn't feel bound to his promise, either. Though he did feel that strange connection to her.

"All right," he said at last, raising two fingers in a V. "I swear."

Gwendolyn grabbed his fingers, spit forcefully onto them, and rubbed them against her own hand. "That's how we do it in Wales." She grinned. Then, out of nowhere, she stuck her hand down into her doublet.

Lukas froze. Was she *undressing*?

Gwendolyn smirked, and simply withdrew a folded note from her bodice. Lukas immediately recognized the handmade paper. It was the same type that the mysterious stranger had used for his last message. Lukas slowly realized just how Gwendolyn planned on helping.

She's skilled at more than archery and climbing, he thought. *She's a good thief as well.*

"Oh, were you all looking for this?" Gwendolyn cooed, fanning herself innocently with the paper. Then she shoved Lukas in the chest. "Go up there and tell your fat-assed saber-dancer friends that Gwendolyn is ready to negotiate."

◆ ◆ ◆

"Where in hell did you get that?"

Zoltan, like the others, was staring at the crumpled message in Gwendolyn's hands. They were all sitting together upstairs. Gwendolyn had taken the seat at the head of the table.

"Simple." She shrugged, smoothing the paper flat. "The morning after you nearly caught me in the attic, I came back and saw a fellow leave this note at your doorstep. I grabbed it and left."

"Our mysterious helper!" Lukas blurted out. "Did you recognize him? What did he look like?"

Gwendolyn pursed her lips. "Not sure. It wasn't quite light out. He was wearing a coat and a floppy hat. It could have been almost anyone."

"And you expect us to believe that?" Zoltan muttered.

"Believe what you want, but if you don't let me join you, you don't get the letter." Gwendolyn folded the note and stuck it under her bodice again. "So, what do you say? Are we in business or not?"

"And what if we simply take the note and slit your throat?" Jurek pulled out his long knife. "What will you do then, little bird?"

"You won't. Lukas promised. Isn't that right, Lukas?"

Every pair of eyes in the room turned toward Lukas, who flushed bright red. "Ah, that's true," he stammered. "I promised I would take her side."

"Oho, and what did she promise *you* in return, Lukas?" Paulus asked in a taunting voice. "Another trip to the rose garden?"

The others laughed and winked at one another. Elsa alone remained silent, eyeing her brother as though she suspected he was hiding something from her.

"Gwendolyn can help us," Lukas cried. "You saw for yourselves how well she can climb and shoot!"

"Why don't we go ahead and ask every unemployed mercenary we encounter in a dark alley to join us?" Jurek sneered. "We could invite half of Prague while we're at it. Or at least all the pretty girls. What do you say, Lukas?" He batted his eyes coquettishly, thrusting his hips.

Gwendolyn scowled at the others furiously. "Hellfire and damnation, I know what this letter says," she hissed. "And believe me, if you want to steal the imperial crown, you'll need all the help you can get. Every bit!"

"Well, spit it out already," Zoltan growled. "Where is the crown?"

Gwendolyn crossed her arms. "In the White Tower."

"The White Tower?" Bernhard shook his strawberry-blond head skeptically. "Where's that supposed to be?"

"It's up in the castle," Gwendolyn explained. "At the end of Golden Lane. The infamous Polonius Sendivogius works there. A dreadful alchemist who experiments on human beings." She shivered. "Polonius probably needs the crown for some sort of attempt to create gold. Golden Lane is crawling with charlatans and pseudomagicians."

"I've heard of that Polonius," Giovanni piped up. "A renowned alchemist who supposedly began searching for the Philosopher's Stone back in the days of Kaiser Rudolf. They say he is the only person who has ever successfully created gold, albeit in extremely small amounts. If that really is the same Polonius, though, he must be very, very old."

Paulus sighed. "I hate to say it, but right now, I wish we had our astro-babbler, Senno, here with us. He might know how to handle that alchemist quack."

"Polonius's laboratory is directly beside the castle torture chamber," Gwendolyn whispered. "The commander of the Red Archers occasionally turns prisoners over to him for his experiments."

"The Red Archers?" Jerome scratched his nose. "Who are *they*, now?"

"The Prague Castle's elite troop," Gwendolyn said quietly, as though afraid someone might be listening in. "They guard the castle, Golden Lane, and especially the White Tower, so that nobody can uncover the secret to making gold. The crown is hidden down in Polonius's lab. Trust me, if it were easy, I'd have already snatched it for myself." She pushed the letter over to Zoltan. "Here, read for yourself."

Zoltan skimmed the lines and then nodded. "The message appears authentic. At least, the handwriting is the same as the one that led us to the scepter." He pocketed the letter and turned to Gwendolyn again. "Now, how is it you think you can help us?"

"With this." Gwendolyn laid her small, crooked bow and quiver of arrows in front of her on the table. "The entrances to the White Tower are all heavily guarded, except for the windows at the top. Those windows are locked and secured with smooth copper shutters, and are nearly fifty paces overhead."

"Damn," Matthias murmured. "So we won't be able to tie a rope to an arrow and shoot it through the window to climb up. Arrows bounce off copper."

"None of you can do it, but I can." Gwendolyn removed an arrow from her quiver and ran her fingers over the runes carved into it. "I've considered breaking into Prague Castle before. While exploring the area, I noticed a single hook and eye underneath the battlements. They probably used it to hoist stone up when they built the castle, and then the masons forgot it was there. An arrow would fit through that eye." She stuck her chin out with pride. "By my honor and that of my father, Falcon Eye, when I hit that mark, we'll have a rope to climb up."

"Fifty paces? At night? Through an eye no bigger than your own?" Matthias shook his head. "As a trained bowman with years of experience, I can tell you that's impossible. Forget it!"

"I can do it!" Gwendolyn insisted defiantly. "My father taught me to shoot every squirrel down from a tree, even under a new moon. I could hit that eye blindfolded if I wanted to. You have my word!"

"Keep up this blustering and I'll pull your fur over your ears like a squirrel's," Zoltan warned her. He hesitated, clearly wrestling with himself. Finally, he sighed in resignation. "All right, I'll give you a chance. But only one!"

"You mean you actually want to bring her with you?" Elsa protested. "She's a thief! Have you forgotten already?"

"I know those Red Archers up at the castle," Zoltan replied. "They're not to be trifled with. Gwendolyn's plan is at least worth thinking about. And I haven't heard a better plan at this table yet."

Lukas exhaled in relief. "So, now there are ten of us?" he asked.

"Well, for the time being, anyway." Zoltan pushed a few beer tankards to one side and began sketching the layout of the castle onto the table with a piece of charcoal. When he finished, he turned and gave Gwendolyn a sharp look. "Now, tell us everything you know about Prague Castle. I repeat, everything! I have no interest in ending up as that alchemist Polonius's newest experiment."

XIII

They spent the next two days planning. After the conversation with Gwendolyn, even the most skeptical among them understood that they must use whatever support they could get. Unlike Lukas and Elsa's home, the Prague Castle was no small structure. It was a gigantic, heavily reinforced complex with trenches, a moat, ramparts, and walls that stretched up to the heavens. Saint Vitus Cathedral towered in the middle of it all. There were individual palaces, churches, chapels, and small servants' houses. Essentially, Prague Castle was less a castle than a city unto itself—and all of it was patrolled by the infamous Red Archers.

Lukas thought back to what Giovanni had said about the start of the Great War. The rebellious Bohemians had spontaneously thrown the Kaiser's delegates out of a castle window. Now, looking up at the high walls, Lukas could hardly believe the men had survived the fall. The Kaiser's subsequent revenge had been frightful. The imperial troops had completely annihilated their opponents in the battle at nearby White Mountain, and war had been raging throughout the German Reich ever since.

Elsa and Matthias stayed at the tavern while the rest of the group scouted the castle. It took them an entire day to stake out the massive enclosure from the outside. They disguised themselves as simple day laborers and farmers, laden with sacks, boxes, and handcarts. They cautiously approached the lower castle gate, where guards were thoroughly inspecting every single person trying to come inside—especially those planning to visit Golden Lane.

"Golden Lane gets its name from all the goldsmiths living there," Gwendolyn explained in a soft voice as they ducked behind the handcarts. "Which is why it's so heavily guarded. The White Tower is at the far end." She pointed to a beefy tower with narrow windows. "The torture chamber and Polonius's laboratory are both in there. No one has yet succeeded at breaking in."

There were at least half a dozen of those fearsome Red Archers standing at the entrance to Golden Lane. All of them wore blood-red tunics over their chain-mail shirts. They carried longbows and swords, and each one had an extremely alert, serious look about him. The guards eyed the companions suspiciously as they pushed their handcarts over the bumpy cobblestones. Several scantily clad women were lurking near the watchmen, occasionally making mocking remarks.

"What about the north side of the castle?" Zoltan asked. "It looks less guarded to me."

"It is." Gwendolyn nodded. "But only because the castle wall drops so far down on that side. But yes, fewer guards are posted along there, so if we do get anywhere near the White Tower, it will have to be from that direction. The hook and eye are on that side, too."

In the distance, Lukas saw countless watchmen in shining chain mail up at the top of the wall. He bit his lip. If even one watchman spotted them and alerted the other guards, all would be lost. They would meet their end in the Prague Castle torture chamber, like so many others before them.

"We need to know when the changing of the guard is." Even in plain farmer's clothing, Bernhard still cut an imposing figure. "If we can get up to the top of the wall at exactly that moment, we might have a chance. But we must figure that out quickly." He kicked a handcart so violently that it nearly fell apart.

"Oh, let me handle this." Jerome winked at them. "For a job like this, you don't need strength. You only need a little, shall we say . . . intuition." He peeled off his farmer shirt, revealing his fashionable red doublet. After combing out his blond hair with his fingers, he marched off, heading straight for the gate.

"God in heaven, what is he doing?" Zoltan hissed. "He'll land us all on the gallows!"

Paulus grinned. "I think I know his plan." Jerome was walking toward the women standing near the gate. When he got there, he chatted a little with the girls, and the group could hear them laugh. Finally, one of them kissed Jerome on the cheek, and he came back to the others, humming as he walked.

"No problem," he said. "I know when the changing of the guard happens."

Jurek gaped at him. "You what?"

Jerome shrugged. "Those girls stay there in hopes of spending a nice evening with one of the guards, so of course they know exactly which soldiers leave their posts, and when." He grinned. "I just made eyes at the girls, and they started talking. It's that simple."

Gwendolyn crossed her arms. "Just so you know, not all women are like that, you . . . you manicured swine!"

Jerome whistled through his teeth, and Lukas thought he saw Gwendolyn blush slightly. Could she have taken a liking to Jerome? He felt a slight pang in his chest. Why did the girls all fall for Jerome?

"Let's go back to Elsa," Lukas said curtly, turning away. "It doesn't seem there's anything else we need to do here."

◆ ◆ ◆

Zoltan wanted to find out as much as possible about the infamous alchemist Polonius, so Lukas, Elsa, and Matthias went out on a particularly tricky mission the following day.

Thus far, all they knew was that he was the Kaiser's favorite alchemist, and that he lived in his own palatial home near the White Tower. Otherwise, Polonius was like a phantom.

Near the castle grounds, there was an old cloister whose abbess was friendly toward Wallenstein and his officers. Zoltan had obtained the Mother Superior's permission for the three of them to enter the heavily guarded Prague Castle, so they headed there to see what information they could uncover about Polonius and his experiments.

"Saint George Cloister has an enormous library," Zoltan explained to them before they left the tavern. "If there's information to be found about that devilish alchemist, it will be there. The abbess knows you're coming and will allow you to poke around. Matthias will accompany you to protect you." He smirked. "Being the quack that he is, he can at least read the titles on the covers. Bernhard and Jurek can't do much with books beyond wiping their asses."

The castle grounds were a hive of bustling activity. Peddlers sold their wares, and soldiers patrolled the spotless streets. Only Golden Lane was blocked from their view—separated from the rest of the property by a second gate, where even more soldiers stood guard.

Lukas had been reluctant to go to the library at first. Elsa had always been the one interested in books, while he preferred tramping around the woods with his wooden sword and bow. But now that he was standing in the cloister library, the massive, towering bookshelves filled him with a deep reverence. So much knowledge had been collected here. Lukas glanced around the wood-paneled hall in amazement.

It must have taken them many years to catalogue all these books.

The gallery encircling the room at a height of around four paces held even more bookcases. Down on the main floor, the spaces between the countless bookshelves formed a labyrinth of winding, narrow aisles. The whole place smelled like dust, glue, and ancient parchment.

Matthias groaned when he saw the thousands upon thousands of books. "If we want to find anything in here, we'll probably have to split up, like it or not," he said, knitting his brow. "Otherwise we'll never finish. I'll work my way through there." He pointed to the right. "And the two of you look around upstairs." With that, Matthias disappeared down one of the many aisles, while Lukas and Elsa went up a narrow spiral staircase to the gallery.

The moment they reached the balcony, Elsa suddenly froze, as though rooted to the spot.

Lukas blinked. "What's wrong?"

Anxiously, Elsa pulled the *Grimorium* out from the leather bag beneath her dress where she often carried it. "The book!" she hissed. "It's heating up!" She clutched it in both hands and closed her eyes. "I think it wants to tell me something."

For a while she stood there motionless, moving her lips silently, while Matthias's steps echoed between the shelves somewhere down below.

"The *Grimorium* was here once before, many years ago," Elsa finally murmured, as if in a trance. "It . . . it was hidden here, I think. For a long time."

"Do you suppose our mother brought the magic book from this library?" Lukas asked, excited. "She was a young novice here in Prague, living in a cloister. Maybe it was this one?"

"Yes, she was here. But then . . ." Elsa shook herself, as though trying to escape a bad dream. "I see blood . . . lots of blood. A great battle . . ."

"The Battle of White Mountain?" Lukas put in. "It happened right near here!" He furrowed his brow. "But what was our mother doing there? What would a nun be doing on a battlefield?"

Elsa gripped the book tightly, eyes still shut. "Our mother . . . she is walking past many, many injured and dying people. She has the book with her. There are soldiers after her, wearing crested helmets, like the Spanish cavalry. They've caught up to her! They're throwing themselves at her . . ."

"The frozen ones!" Lukas whispered. Goose bumps stood up on his arms. "Those monsters have been after the book all this time? Go on, tell me more. What do you see?"

"I see . . ." Elsa hesitated. "Our father, it's our father!" she cried in astonishment. "He blocks the Spaniards' path, and he's fencing with them like the Devil . . . He's won! They're retreating! He just picked up Mother. He's carrying her on his back through rows of enemy soldiers. Now . . ." She fell silent.

"What is it?" Lukas asked. "Why aren't you saying anything?"

"The image . . . it's fading, it's disappearing." Elsa opened her eyes, breathing heavily. "Well," she said after a while, "now we know that our parents met in Prague. It must have been at that Battle of White Mountain. Father was fighting in the Kaiser's army. Maybe our mother was trying to protect the *Grimorium*?"

"From Schönborn's frozen ones." Lukas nodded. "Even that long ago, he was already trying to get his hands on the book. Maybe on our mother, too. Schönborn was always fascinated by what she was capable of as a white witch." He hesitated. He still hadn't told Elsa about his newly developed magical powers. This was probably the right time to do it, but for some reason, he was still hesitant.

"There's something you should know," he finally began. In a soft voice, Lukas told his sister about Gwendolyn's fatal wound, and how he'd healed it purely through the force of his own will. "Look at this," he said, undoing the top buttons of his shirt and gesturing to the rosy skin underneath. "I was wounded fighting in front of Wallenstein's palace, but it's completely healed, my fever is gone. Mother spoke to me. She told me I have the power in me as well."

"Our dead mother talked to you?" Elsa eyed him suspiciously.

Lukas nodded. "She's done that before. Back when I fought Schönborn's hell-wolf, do you remember?"

"Mother's never spoken to me." There was an unexpected icy note in her voice, and her expression darkened. "So you want to do magic now, too? Is that it? You want the *Grimorium* for *yourself*?"

Elsa's fingers instantly tightened around the book like spider legs, and Lukas gave a start. For one brief moment, it was not his sister standing before him but a much larger, darker apparition—a demon with gigantic, bat-like wings. But then the terrifying shadow vanished, and she was just a little eleven-year-old girl again.

An eleven-year-old girl with unbelievable powers, he thought.

"No, Elsa," Lukas replied gently. "I don't want the *Grimorium* for myself. After all, I didn't need it when I healed Gwendolyn."

"Gwendolyn, Gwendolyn!" Elsa mocked him. "All you ever talk about is *Gwendolyn*! That girl has knocked all the sense out of you, she's put a spell on you. *She's* the real witch!"

"What are you talking about?" Lukas replied indignantly. "I admit I think she's very nice, but I only stood up for her because I know she can help us." He tried to sound casual, but even he knew that it was only half-true. Elsa was right. Gwendolyn really did have him under a spell, just not the kind that involved magic.

"Let's not fight anymore," he suggested after a long moment of silence. "We're here to find out more about Polonius."

"Fine." Elsa nodded hesitantly. "But please, *please* stop talking about that stupid Gwendolyn all day." She turned away and began poking through the bookshelves. The books were organized by topic, but they couldn't find an "alchemy" section. After a thorough search of the balcony turned up nothing, they went back down the stairs. Finally, they stumbled upon several shelves of alchemy books in one corner of the hall. Elsa began flipping through one after another at random.

"Many people think alchemy is only about transforming worthless metals into silver or gold," she remarked. "But back when I spent all that time with Schönborn, he showed me other possibilities as well. Far more horrifying ones." Her lips tightened. "Alchemists have tried again and again to create hybrid creatures. Artificial human beings, or chimeras with eagles' talons and a lion's head, or basilisks—terrible snakelike monsters that can kill with their gaze alone."

"Sounds like this Polonius fellow is trying something similar," Lukas replied, shuddering. He went to a bookshelf farther to the left. "Look here! These books are all about famous alchemists, arranged alphabetically." He ran his finger along their cracked spines as he read. "There's someone named Avicenna, a Dr. Faust, an Edward Kelly, Paracelsus . . ." He stopped short. "Wait a minute! There's a gap here next to Paracelsus. One book is missing."

"The book on Polonius!" Elsa began frantically searching the nearby shelves, but the volume on Polonius was nowhere to be found. "Of all the books, *that's* the one missing," she complained.

"It's almost like someone's removed it from the shelf," Lukas murmured. "Someone who doesn't want us to find out any more about Polonius."

They heard footsteps approaching, and Matthias rounded the corner. "Well?" he asked. "Have you had better luck than me? All I found were boring treatises on plants and animals."

"Apparently, someone got here before us," Lukas said, pointing to the empty space on the shelf. "The book on Polonius has disappeared."

"Disappeared?" Matthias furrowed his brow. "Who would do something like that? Nobody knows we're here except the abbess, and Zoltan vouches for her. Maybe the book was simply misplaced?"

"Maybe." Lukas lapsed into a thoughtful silence. He recalled how Zoltan had told them all about the cloister library the night before, as they'd been sitting around the table. Had someone been eavesdropping on them?

Then he remembered that Jurek had hurried off shortly thereafter, supposedly to scout out the Prague Castle ramparts once more. He hadn't returned until late that night. What had he been doing all that time? Paying a visit to the cloister, perhaps?

Could they perhaps have a traitor in their own ranks, someone who was working with Schönborn?

Lukas decided to keep an even closer eye on Jurek.

XIV

The following night, heavy thunderclouds rolled in over Prague. Before long, torrential rain was hammering down upon the rooftops. The clouds enveloped the moon completely, leaving the city as dark as a dungeon, except for the occasional flash of lightning through the sky.

At the Black Boar, Zoltan peered out the window and then turned to face the others. "I was hoping to wait a little longer, so we could find out more about the alchemist," he muttered. "But opportunities like this don't come along very often. Nobody will see us outside in this weather, and the guards will be glad if they don't rust in place." He clapped his hands. "So gather your weapons and equipment. We're leaving in half an hour."

Lukas's heart began to race. It was time. Now they would see whether Gwendolyn's plan would succeed, and whether they could recover the second piece of Imperial Regalia, the crown.

If not, Lukas feared that the castle dungeon and death awaited them.

Or perhaps even worse, he thought, imagining the torture chamber in the White Tower.

Skeptically, he regarded Jurek, who was sorting his equipment. Was Lukas mistaken, or did the one-eyed man seem a shade more excited than the others? Had Jurek already tattled on them to Polonius? Lukas had considered going to Zoltan with his suspicions, but he had no real proof—only a vague feeling that there was a traitor among them.

They set off a short time later. It was still raining buckets, and within mere seconds, Lukas's coat was soaked through and water was running down his collar. It was pitch-dark. They'd brought along a small firepot to light the torches, but decided to wait as long as possible in order to remain undetected. At least the alleys were completely deserted. In this moonless darkness, even his sister walking directly in front of him was only a blurry shadow.

"Hurry!" Gwendolyn hissed from up front, where she was walking beside Zoltan. "Are you Black Musketeers or fat old men who fear the rain?"

Paulus shook himself like a wet bear. "That girl is already getting on my nerves," he snarled. "Acting like she's the leader! She's no older than I am."

"But a good deal prettier," Jerome teased him.

Paulus snorted. "Being pretty wouldn't keep me dry."

Hunched over, they marched up the castle hill, then headed off to the right and made their way through the bushes until they found themselves in front of a stone wall around three paces high.

"This is the lower castle wall," Gwendolyn explained as she started climbing up. "In this weather, we don't have much to fear, but we should still hurry before the guards spot us." With catlike agility, Gwendolyn slipped over the wall and soon disappeared.

The others followed, though Elsa had particular difficulty with the slippery stones, and it took her a while to make it over. At last, they were all standing on the other side. They found themselves in a wooded area with low trees and shrubs. It gave way to a small valley, which led to the moat and then finally the castle wall. Monstrous and black, it seemed to stretch straight up into the clouds. The lights jerking from side to side at the top told them that watchmen were patrolling the wall.

"Pretty damned high," Bernhard grunted. Fine rivulets of rainwater ran down from the end of his beard. "And pretty well secured. If you ask me, no army in the world could take the castle from this side."

"No army, but one girl," Gwendolyn replied, grinning. "Now come on already. Or do you boys need a break?"

They ducked down and ran through the woods toward the castle moat. The rest of the group trailed Gwendolyn, gasping for breath. Lukas noticed that Elsa was keeping a slight distance from the others. When he came closer, he saw to his astonishment that his sister's hair and dress were perfectly dry.

Elsa winked at her brother. "Gwendolyn may talk big," she said in a scornful tone, "but the only thing that can truly protect you here is my magic."

"Does that mean you're using the book right now?"

Elsa waved dismissively. "A simple spell I found in the *Grimorium* yesterday. I used it as you were climbing over the wall. No matter what the weather, it keeps you as dry as if you were standing under a roof. What do you think?"

"I think you shouldn't use that book any more than you have to," Lukas replied. "If you want to stay dry, just get under my coat. It's less dangerous." As he had so often lately, Lukas suspected that his sister was losing herself in the *Grimorium* more and more.

Elsa turned. "You're only jealous that you're wet and I'm dry," she said as she walked away. "That's magic, and I don't need my mother talking to me to do it."

Before Lukas could say anything in response, they had caught up to the others. The rain pattered down onto the black water in the moat before them, stirring up a foul stench that was probably from the many latrines along the wall-walk. Leaves and mildewed twigs floated in the dark sludge. Swimming in the Vltava, the way they had a few days before, suddenly seemed extremely pleasant and refreshing.

Gwendolyn led them over to a fallen tree trunk, and they ducked behind it. "I doubt anyone will see us in this wretched weather," she said, "but better safe than sorry." She unshouldered her bow and checked the string one last time. Then she withdrew a single arrow with a thin cord around it. The cord was rolled up into a spiral, and a thicker rope was knotted to the end.

She put her hand to her forehead and peered upward. Finally, she pointed the arrow toward the guard tower, which Lukas could vaguely make out through the rain.

"The White Tower," Gwendolyn said. "Can you all see the individual windows?"

Lukas squinted, but saw only a few distant, blurry rectangles. How did Gwendolyn expect to hit one of those windows in the dark, with the rain pouring down—let alone a single hook and eye?

Zoltan looked skeptical as well. "Maybe doing our climbing excursion in this weather wasn't such a good idea after all," he grunted. "No human alive can hit such a target in this rain."

"*I* can," Gwendolyn snapped. "Just give me a moment to concentrate." She closed her eyes and threw her head back, so that the rain flowed over her face. To Lukas, it looked like she was somewhere else entirely. "Weather like in Wales," she said. "Wonderful!"

"How can anyone think this weather is wonderful?" Jerome complained.

Zoltan made a harsh gesture to silence him.

Gwendolyn nocked the arrow, drew back the string in a fluid motion, and then stopped for a moment. She cried out a few words in a strange, lilting language Lukas had never heard before. Then the bowstring hummed, and the arrow flew toward its target.

An eternity seemed to pass. The length of thin cord unrolled, winding and curling, as it shot farther and farther overhead.

Finally, the cord remained suspended in the air, where it gently swayed back and forth.

"The cord got stuck on something," Jurek said in a scornful tone. "And we went out in this miserable weather just to watch her miss her shot."

Zoltan tilted his head. "They'll be changing the guard up there any moment," he warned. "If it doesn't work this time around, we'll come up with another plan. That's my last word."

Gwendolyn made no reply. Instead, she marched off into the darkness until she was no longer visible.

"Look," Giovanni said, pointing. In the air, the thicker rope rose like a snake and began a slow journey upward. "She's hoisting up the rope!" he exclaimed. "It looks like she's really done it." Giovanni laughed. "A hell of a girl, that one!"

"That remains to be proven," Zoltan muttered. But even he gave Gwendolyn an admiring nod when she returned, clutching the end of the rope in one hand. Her hair and robe were completely soaked—she had jumped into the moat to pull the cord that was threaded through the eye and raise the rope, not caring about the mud.

"I told you I could do it." She smiled triumphantly. "Now all we have to do is climb. First to reach the top gets the crown!" She used the rope to swing across the moat, and then tossed it back to the others before dashing off into the darkness again.

Paulus groaned aloud, as though only now realizing that their plan involved climbing a wall fifty paces high. "Damnation, let's get this over with, then." He tugged on the rope, testing it. "This thing may hold a lightweight like her, but a fellow like me? Oh, to hell with it." Still cursing, he gripped the rope with both hands, and soon he was dangling above the moat.

One after another, they climbed up. Bernhard carried Elsa on his massive back as she clung to his neck for dear life. Panting and gasping, the giant heaved them both to the top.

Lukas and Zoltan were the last of the group. The rope chafed Lukas's hands as he pulled himself up, bit by bit, not daring to look down. The wall was slimy and smooth as ice, so he could barely use his feet to support himself. Wind and rain roared around him. He could just make out Giovanni a short distance above him, but the rest of his friends were no longer in sight.

As he climbed, the rope grew slipperier beneath his hands. Sweat and rainwater ran into his eyes and nearly caused him to fall once or twice. Just as he was starting to think he would never reach the top, he saw a bright rectangle shimmering above him.

The others had managed to get the window open.

Lukas scrambled toward the opening, and strong hands pulled him up. Zoltan came wheezing in after him.

Without a word, Matthias pointed toward the right, where the others were already waiting on the wall-walk.

The cathedral bells tolled the twelfth hour. If Jerome's inquiries were accurate, they would now have precisely a quarter of an hour to get into the White Tower before the next guards came by.

Crouched and silent, they hurried along the narrow covered walkway, along which flickering pans of embers were placed at regular intervals. Their path ended abruptly at a heavy, copper-studded door.

Gwendolyn gestured to the entrance. "The White Tower," she said almost inaudibly.

Zoltan signaled to Jurek, who stepped forward with his ring of lockpicks and bent over the lock. Lukas remembered how Jurek had nearly failed to open the door to the marquis's palace last time around. *Was that deliberate?* He couldn't help but wonder.

It seemed to be taking an eternity this time around, too. As the minutes ticked by, Lukas listened for the watchmen's footsteps—and indeed, after a while he heard the sound of voices rapidly approaching.

"Damn it, Jurek," Zoltan whispered. "The guards are coming. Hurry up, or there will be a bloodbath here in a minute!"

"Almost got it!" Jurek hissed. "Just have to . . ."

"Let me do it," Elsa broke in, pushing Jurek aside. She laid the first two fingers of her right hand on the lock, murmuring a single word: "FORAMEN."

There was a click, and the door swung inward without a sound.

"Damn witchcraft," Zoltan muttered, wasting no time in stepping through the doorway.

The others followed him, slipping into the darkness one by one. Matthias closed the door behind them. Only moments later, Lukas heard footsteps out on the wall-walk. The sound of boots stopped for a moment . . .

. . . and then went past the door.

"What did your sister do just now?" Gwendolyn asked softly. She was standing so close to Lukas that her hair tickled his nose. "Was that more witch stuff? Are all of you magicians or something?"

"I'll explain later. Let's just look for that crown right now."

A dim glow appeared as Zoltan lit a single torch on the firepot they'd brought along. They were standing in a small vestibule with tapestries, shields, and spears adorning its walls.

A narrow spiral stairway led down. Zoltan placed his finger to his lips before descending. The others followed him.

They had only taken a few steps when a loud hissing sound echoed in front of them, followed by crashing and splintering noises as though something large had fallen to the ground. Bernhard and Matthias shouted. A black shadow rushed toward Lukas, seemingly out of nowhere.

And then chaos broke out.

The black, hissing shadows seemed to be flying all around them. Lukas held his hands up to protect his face, but something painfully scratched his skin. When he drew his fingers away, he saw a strange little creature fluttering just below the ceiling. At first he thought it was a bird, but then he realized to his horror that it was a black cat.

A black cat with bat wings.

Three of those cat creatures were assaulting them from above, try-ing to scratch out their eyes. The stairwell was far too narrow to fight in with longswords and rapiers, but Bernhard still tried to lunge at one of the cats with his two-hander. He stumbled and fell down the stairs with a loud crash.

Giovanni and Jerome drew their parrying daggers to fend off the attacks of the sinister hybrid beings. One of the cats fell to the ground, but then a second one flew screeching at Elsa. She froze in shock, gaping at the horror unfolding before her.

"Look out, Elsa!" Lukas shouted. He drew his weapon, but at the same moment, the creature let out a pitiful squeak and plummeted to the floor with a knife in its belly.

"Vile beasts," Jurek spat. "Thrice-accursed hellspawn!" He bent over the creature and pulled out his throwing knife, which he wiped on his trousers with disgust.

Lukas stopped, amazed that Jurek had protected Elsa. Maybe he wasn't a traitor after all?

Or is he only protecting Elsa because Schönborn wants her back alive? he thought.

Lukas could see a broken wooden cage on the steps.

"The cage was hanging from the ceiling here," Zoltan panted, pointing upward. "In the middle of the hall, as if someone wanted us to run into it like a trap. Our shouts probably alerted every guard in the castle. Hurry, barricade the door upstairs!"

Bernhard stormed up the stairs, tearing two lances from the wall as he went, and used them to jam the lock. There was no noise on the other side of the door yet. Lukas breathed a sigh of relief. Maybe they'd gotten lucky, and nobody had heard all the commotion. It was fairly improbable, though.

"What in God's name *is* that?" Paulus nudged one of the creatures with the toe of his shoe. "Looks like it flew straight up from hell."

"Probably one of Polonius's experiments," Gwendolyn replied. "They say he breeds chimeras." She shivered. "I always liked cats until now. The ones without wings, anyway."

"Wait a minute," Lukas said. "I thought there were three cats. Two are here on the ground, but where's the third?" He took a few more steps down until he came to a large arrowslit, through which wind and rain wafted. "Damn, got away," he murmured. "Wouldn't surprise me if the beasts are trained to warn their master."

"Then we really don't have much time." Zoltan raised his torch, which had nearly gone out. "Let's hurry."

Cautiously, they made their way down the stairs until they came to another door. This time, they were more careful. Zoltan turned the knob and then immediately took a step back as the door swung open with a soft squeak. When nothing else happened, they went in.

The room was perfectly round, and filled with all sorts of strange equipment and utensils. In the torchlight, Lukas could make out tables and shelves lined with flasks, ampullae, and mortars. The embers glimmering in the fireplace bathed everything in a faint reddish glow.

"*Mon dieu*, what is that? *C'est horrible!*" Jerome approached one of the tables and lifted a lifeless rat gingerly by the tail. Crippled bird wings, probably those of a pigeon, grew from the rat's torso.

"Another of the esteemed Polonius's experiments, albeit a failed one," Giovanni replied, clearly repulsed. "This must be his laboratory. Flying rats?" He rolled his eyes. "Rats on the ground are enough for me."

"Hands off that infernal thing!" Zoltan snapped at Jerome. "Go on, see if you can find anything that will point us to the whereabouts of the crown." The commander glanced over at another set of stairs, which seemed to lead to the cellar. "When we're finished in here, we'll look around down there."

They made a careful search of the room, repeatedly discovering the remains of horrible animal experiments. The tables, drawers, and cages contained half-dissected amphibians, mummified snakes and mice, a taxidermied rabbit, and even dried frogs threaded on a length of yarn.

As Lukas shut another drawer, thoroughly disgusted, Matthias suddenly let out a whistle of surprise.

"A chest," he called. "Seems pretty well locked to me." He reached under the table and pulled out a heavy oaken chest about the length of his arm, secured with five padlocks and reinforced with thick bands of steel.

"Whatever is in there, it must be pretty valuable," Paulus remarked.

"I can open it for you," Elsa offered, stepping toward the chest, but Zoltan held her back.

"For the last time, I don't want that magic nonsense," he barked. "Not unless it's absolutely necessary." He turned to Jurek. "Can you pick these locks?"

Jurek tilted his head from side to side uncertainly. "Possibly. But it will take me a while. By the time I finish, the guards will probably be here."

"I know how to get it done faster," Giovanni spoke up. He went back to one of the shelves and returned with a glass bottle marked *Aqua Regia*. "The name means 'king's water,'" he explained. "It's a mixture of nitric and hydrochloric acid, so it's the strongest acid in existence. It can even dissolve gold. Alchemists use it quite often."

Gwendolyn grinned. "I like you, know-it-all."

Once again, Lukas felt a slight pang in his chest.

They watched Giovanni drip the aqua regia onto the padlocks, which hissed and gave off acrid smoke. Cautiously, Giovanni tapped one of the locks, and it crumbled like a dry leaf.

"Impressive. You may be worth keeping around." Gwendolyn winked at Giovanni.

Lukas tried not to let his jealousy show. "Are we going to open this chest now, or what?" he groused. "We don't have all day."

"The boy is right." Zoltan bent over the chest and pried it open with a dagger. "Let's just see what's in th—"

A huge cloud of green smoke billowed out of the chest. Zoltan stumbled back. "Get away from that thing!" he exclaimed. "It's a trap!"

Hastily, they all took cover behind the tables as the green cloud slowly spread through the room. Lukas smelled something pleasantly sweet, like a meadow of flowers in late summer. At the same time, his legs grew heavy.

Poison! he thought, stumbling.

They coughed and clutched their throats, and one by one they fell to the floor. Jerome and Giovanni tried to flee, but the cloud had filled the entire room—green smoke swirled all around them.

Lukas held his breath as he crawled over to Elsa, who was leaning against a table. She had one hand in front of her nose and mouth, while the other reached under her dress for the *Grimorium*. Lukas could see that she was slowly beginning to fade.

This time, even the Grimorium *won't be able to help us,* he thought.

Jerome, Giovanni, and Matthias were already lying lifeless on the ground, while Zoltan, Paulus, and Bernhard continued to stagger through the room, knocking over ampullae and flasks with every step. Gwendolyn and Jurek were nowhere to be seen beneath the spreading bilious green fog.

Now even the giant Bernhard collapsed, knocking over a flask filled with liquid. A red puddle spread around him like blood.

Lukas was still holding his breath, but he could feel that he had only a few more seconds before he'd have to breathe again—before the poison defeated him as well.

Elsa's head slumped forward, and Lukas embraced her protectively. *Elsa! My little Elsa!* he thought. Tears ran down his face—he didn't know whether from his sorrow or the fog. In that moment, Elsa was once more the little sister he loved above all else. He wished so desperately he was able to take care of her now.

Once again, it was clear that they were powerless without Elsa's magic.

Or are we . . . ?

Still desperately holding his breath, although he was already nearly unconscious, Lukas recalled his mother's voice. His lungs were threatening to burst; his chest felt like it was being crushed by a boulder. Elsa lay in his arms like a tiny dead bird.

Elsa, you can't die! You're my little sister, I love you more than anything in the world. Mother, please, please help us!

Just as everything was beginning to go dark around him, he heard that warm, familiar voice—slightly distorted, as though from the other end of a tunnel.

You have the power, too, Lukas.

There was a soft ringing sound.

Lukas closed his eyes and embraced Elsa like he'd never embraced her before. As he did, he felt a warm wave wash over them, like water. His entire body screamed for air. He couldn't hold his breath even a moment longer. Lukas opened his mouth, expecting to breathe in the poisonous smoke . . .

. . . but nothing happened.

When he opened his eyes, he could barely make out a weak pulsing around him. The air surrounding him and Elsa seemed different from the rest of the room, more opaque somehow, with a faint pink tint. It was as though the siblings had been swallowed by a floating bubble.

Outside the bubble, Lukas saw his friends lying lifeless on the ground. He didn't know if they were dead or unconscious. He didn't have time to think about it. Footsteps echoed from the stairs leading to the cellar.

After a few moments, a terrifying creature appeared in the doorway.

At first glance, the being was a very tall, powerful-looking man wearing only a loincloth. His torso and upper arms were extremely muscular. But the creature wasn't really a man—it had the head of a bear on its shoulders, and long, sharp claws grew on its fingers and toes.

Then Lukas noticed that an iron collar was fastened around the creature's neck. A second man, who had been hidden in the dark stairwell until now, led the monster around on a chain like a puppy. The man was wearing a gray alchemist's frock that was far too large on his pale, spindly frame. His face was as wrinkled as an old, dried apple. Only his eyes had an oddly youthful gleam. He walked hunched over, and his back had a slight hump to it.

"Polonius!" Lukas whispered. Somehow he had the feeling that he'd seen the man before, but he couldn't remember when or where.

"Welcome to my laboratory," the old man replied in a gravelly voice. "My favorite little flier was right. Intruders!" He giggled. "Or should I say, new material for my experiments?" He glanced with pleasure around the room, where the others were still motionless on the floor. "Hm, fresh, strong human stock. Not like those starved creatures the captain normally brings me. This is good. Very good." He turned back to Lukas and Elsa. "Only you two were able to resist the scent of the lotus. The Devil knows why." He giggled again. "Well, then, Barnabas can play with you instead. He is my most successful hybrid to date. Barnabas, fetch!"

With that, Polonius released the chain, and the giant bear-man stormed toward Lukas and Elsa.

XV

At the last moment, Lukas managed to draw his rapier. Only then did he realize how exhausted he was. The spell had cost him a great deal of strength. On heavy legs, he moved into starting position and then lunged at the bear-man. His rapier bored deep into the fearsome creature's thigh.

The monster retreated, growling.

"Silly child!" Polonius chided him. "You hurt my little darling. Too bad that will only make him even more furious."

As if on cue, Barnabas let out a loud roar as he charged at Lukas again. Lukas dodged out of the way, but the bear-man caught him in the chest with one claw, leaving a bloody trail behind. Lukas gritted his teeth to keep himself from crying out.

All at once, he realized that the strange pink bubble around him and Elsa had disappeared. The sweet scent was gone, too. The poisonous cloud had dissipated. The others were still lying lifeless on the ground—dead or asleep, Lukas had no idea. Rapier in hand, he positioned himself in front of his younger sister, who stirred on the floor, moaning.

"Why don't you crawl back into the hole you came from?" Lukas snapped at the bear-man, trying to suppress the tremor in his voice. "I am a Black Musketeer, you don't frighten me!"

The bear-man took the chain between its massive paws and began swinging it in a large circle. The tough, heavy links flew just inches from Lukas's head. Lukas ducked underneath, risked a feint—and landed another hit on Barnabas, this time at chest height. But the monster only shrieked furiously and reached for a table, which he threw at Lukas.

"Elsa! Can you hear me?" Lukas looked over at his sister, who was still not quite conscious. As much as he hated it when she did magic, he could use her help right now. But Elsa's eyelids fluttered; her face was white as chalk.

The sinister creature was in such a battle frenzy that it seemed to feel no pain.

Lukas weighed his chances. Bringing the monster down would require a well-placed blow to the neck or chest. But was the creature standing before him truly a monster? He thought about what the alchemist Polonius had just said about Barnabas.

My most successful hybrid to date . . .

Lukas hated to think that the bear-man had perhaps once been an innocent prisoner, one of those unlucky souls the captain had given the alchemist for his experiments. What had Polonius done to him? Had he really once been named Barnabas? Could he have had a wife and children?

Another table splintered against the wall beside Lukas. Surely the guards had heard the noise by now. Fortunately, it seemed the poison had merely incapacitated the others, not killed them—Paulus and Jerome were beginning to stir again. There were signs of life from Giovanni and Zoltan, too, but his friends seemed a long way from being able to help Lukas fight the beast. He searched the room for Gwendolyn, and sighed with a little relief when he saw her twitch.

He would have to stake everything on one move.

When Barnabas stormed toward him again, Lukas feinted once more, so that Barnabas grasped at empty air. Then he aimed a high cut directly at his opponent's throat. The point of the rapier dug into the beast's rubbery skin, and for the first time, the bear-man appeared to feel pain. He stumbled back, pressing his clawed hand to his neck to stanch the gurgling blood. His eyes were wide, and something deeply human flickered to life within them.

In sympathy, Lukas lowered his rapier. He suddenly couldn't bring himself to deal the deathblow to the bear-man. Deep down, he knew that he was right—the monster had once been a man, and Polonius had abused him for his own purposes.

Lukas slowly approached the monster, who staggered away, whimpering. "You're a man, aren't you?" Lukas asked him in a soft, calming voice. "I'm sorry someone did this to you. Whoever they are, they should pay."

The words had a strange effect on the bear-man. "Barnabas . . . ," the creature croaked, drawing each syllable out. Tears sprang to his eyes. "I . . . am . . . Barnabas. A . . . man . . ."

"Whatever you were, you're my creation now!" Polonius screeched. "Obey your master, and kill this boy!"

Barnabas shook his head. "A . . . man," he rumbled. "No . . . creation." The look in his eyes hardened again, and he turned to Polonius. "No creation!" he repeated loudly. "And you . . . are . . . not my master!"

Claws raised, he started toward Polonius, who retreated in horror. "Stop that!" the alchemist ordered. "Didn't you hear me? I am your master! I command you to stop."

But Barnabas continued toward Polonius, one step at a time. Just as he was lifting his paw to attack, Elsa's voice rang out, loud and clear and strangely emotionless.

"PARNATIUS, EXCELSOR . . ."

To his horror, Lukas saw that Elsa was awake, pointing the first two fingers of her right hand at Barnabas. Her other hand was resting on the *Grimorium*, which she had taken out from beneath her dress.

"No, Elsa!" Lukas cried. "He can't help it!"

"FULGUR INFERNI!" Elsa continued. A satisfied smile played on her lips as a bolt of blue lightning shot from her fingers and hit the bear-man directly in the chest. His eyes flickered one last time, and for a brief moment, Lukas thought he saw the man that Barnabas once had been.

He collapsed, dead.

"What did you do, Elsa?" Lukas shrieked in despair. "He wanted to help us!"

"Is that the thanks I get for keeping that animal away from you?" Elsa grunted. Her eyes were cold and strangely unfamiliar. "You miserable traitor. I suppose you think I don't notice that you want to forbid me from doing magic so that you can become a wizard yourself? I see through you." Suddenly only the whites of her eyes were visible.

And once again, Lukas had the feeling that it was not Elsa speaking to him, but someone else.

"Elsa, what . . . what are you t-talking about?" he stammered. "I . . ."

Lukas stopped short when Elsa crumpled to the floor again, unconscious. The spell had apparently sapped her last ounce of strength. Trembling with rage, Lukas turned back to Polonius, who had followed the conversation with a secretive smile on his face. "You're the monster!" he shouted. "Not Barnabas!"

"And yet your sister is the one who killed him," Polonius replied with a giggle.

Lukas rushed at the alchemist, who barely defended himself. Lukas reached for his dagger and pressed it to Polonius's throat. The old man's skin smelled of cold ashes and sulfur.

"The crown!" Lukas demanded. "So Barnabas's death is not in vain, at least. Where is it?"

"Well, where do you think it is?" Polonius gasped through the headlock Lukas had him in. "In the chest, of course, you fool! I was planning a couple of fine experiments with it. My friend Waldemar von Schönborn was going to let me borrow it for a little while, so that I could uncover the secret of making gold." The alchemist let out an evil giggle. "The captain of the Red Archers promised me a pair of nice young prisoners to research on. But please, if the crown is that important to you, go right ahead and take it."

From the corner of his eye, Lukas saw Zoltan rise unsteadily to his feet, swaying. The others were slowly coming to as well. Above, in the stairwell, they heard furious pounding. The watchmen had heard them and were now attempting to force the door open.

"The crown, Commander!" Lukas called to the still visibly confused Zoltan. "It's in the chest!"

Zoltan staggered over to the chest, panting. He brought out a bundle wrapped in slightly singed velvet. He removed the cloth, revealing the shimmering octagonal golden crown. It was encrusted with colorful gemstones and pearls on every side, and a small cross gleamed at the front. "The imperial crown," Zoltan whispered in a weak voice, holding it reverently in both hands. He straightened up, seeming to recover a little more of his strength. "Let's get out of here!" he commanded at last.

Paulus rose from behind one of the fallen tables. "Ooohhh, my head," he complained, struggling to stay upright. "Worse than five liters of Bohemian dark beer. What kind of hellish poison was that?"

"Doesn't matter now." Giovanni was standing, knocking the dust from his trousers. He pointed to the upper stairwell where the noise was rising steadily. "From the sound of it, every Red Archer in Prague Castle is up there waiting for us."

Zoltan hastened over to Lukas and Polonius. The commander grabbed the alchemist and shook him like a sack of flour. "Is there another way out of here?" he shouted. "Start talking, now! Otherwise I might come up with a few experiments to perform on you."

"All right, all right, keep calm," Polonius whined. "I'm an old man! If you continue to treat me this way, my heart will stop, and then I won't be able to say anything more."

"The way out!" Zoltan repeated as the guards above them began breaking the door down.

"Yes, there's a way," Polonius gasped. "Down in the tower cellar." He giggled. "It may not be the most pleasant escape route, but it does lead out of the castle."

"Show us," Zoltan ordered, gripping Polonius by the scruff of his neck and dragging him down the stairs like a doll. The others had regained consciousness now, though Gwendolyn still looked particularly weak and needed Paulus to prop her up. Matthias was carrying Elsa, who had yet to reawaken. Bernhard and Jurek were holding each other upright, though the small one-eyed man was nearly collapsing under the bearded giant's weight.

Lukas was about to join the rest of the group, but he let his gaze sweep around the room one last time—and stopped. There, under one of the tipped tables, was the *Grimorium*! It must have fallen from Elsa's hands after her last spell. No one else seemed to have noticed that it was gone, Elsa included. Beside it lay the waxed cloth and the small leather bag Elsa kept the book in.

He shivered a little as he recalled the words she'd spoken earlier, the coldness in her voice. She'd called him a traitor, claimed he wanted the *Grimorium* all to himself. Well, she was probably somewhat out of her senses. That had to be it—the spell had weakened her.

But another thought had crept into Lukas's head, and he couldn't seem to drive it out.

The Grimorium *is changing Elsa. It's making her evil.*

Gingerly, Lukas picked up the book and slid it into the bag with his fingertips. Then he followed the others down to the tower cellar.

Here, too, there was another perfectly round room. A small, dirty cell was connected to it—presumably the place where the bear-man Barnabas had been locked away. On the other side of the room, there was a tiny bay with a dirty cloth hung in front of it. The others were gathered around it.

"It's the latrine!" Jerome shook his head in disgust. "*Merde!* This lousy alchemist wants to send us through the filthy latrine! Doesn't anyone *ever* think of my clothing?"

"I'm afraid you have no other choice," Polonius said and gestured toward the stairs, where the footfalls of the approaching watchmen were growing progressively louder. "I occasionally use this shaft to dispose of the remains of my experiments, so I know it leads directly to the castle moat."

"You'd better be telling us the truth, or I'll make you regret it," Zoltan growled.

"We really want to let this bastard live?" Bernhard asked, drawing his two-hander and coming threateningly close to Polonius. "Are you serious about that, Commander?"

"He's the Kaiser's alchemist," Zoltan responded. "As much as I would love to hack him into tiny pieces, we don't want to end up with any more trouble on our hands than we already have."

"A wise decision, gentlemen." Polonius smiled cruelly. "Now hurry up, or you'll end up full of Red arrows. And that would be *such* a pity, wouldn't it?"

Zoltan drew the curtain aside, revealing a bench with a hole in the middle. When he pulled the bench away, a foul-smelling shaft came into view.

"My doublet is practically new!" Jerome complained.

"Your doublet or your life," Zoltan replied. "And now, in with you." He lifted Jerome into the rank, excrement-clotted shaft and dropped him like a stone.

The guards came thundering down the second flight of stairs.

"Hurry!" Zoltan called to the others. "I'll hold them off!"

He drew his broadsword as the others slid down the shaft one by one. Lukas hesitated when he saw that Elsa was still out, but Matthias nodded to him. "I'll take care of her, don't worry." He smiled reassuringly. "Go on, jump. And wipe that shaft nice and clean for me with the seat of your pants."

Before climbing into the shaft, Lukas secretly wrapped the *Grimorium* in the waxed cloth, slipped it back into the bag, and then stuffed the bag beneath his shirt.

A second later, he was falling.

The shaft was nearly vertical. It was smeared and slick, and Lukas didn't want to think about what kinds of things Polonius had sent down it. Above him, he heard shouts and clashing weapons, and then he reached the end of the shaft and fell silently into the night, down the castle wall. Almost immediately, he landed in the putrid water of the moat.

Lukas held his breath, struggled, got caught on some sort of slimy algae, and then finally reached the surface. He glanced around and saw to his relief that Matthias and Elsa had survived the fall unharmed as well.

Like the others, Lukas crawl-stroked to the shore of the moat, where he lay, breathing hard. They all struggled out of the water, exhausted. Lukas shivered in the rain, which was still pouring down from the sky. At least the moat water had washed away the worst of the shaft residue.

A gasp cut through the air behind him, and Lukas saw that Zoltan had reached the shore, fresh blood dripping from a cut on his cheek.

"Respect," the commander wheezed. "Those accursed Reds are skilled not only with their bows, but with their swords as well." He heaved himself out of the moat. "But at least now they know what it means to tangle with a Black Musketeer." He wiped some mud and a few dead leaves from his hair, and then he held the crown up, grinning. "Through the shite and back into the light," he said.

Zoltan limped a little as he led the way back into the city. Relieved, Lukas fell in step with the others.

With the filthy crown in hand, the commander really did look like a severe, indomitable king.

XVI

When they finally returned to the tavern, long after midnight, Lukas couldn't fall asleep. Too much had happened up there at the castle, and the scratch he'd gotten from Barnabas the bear-man was hurting. But the wound wasn't all that deep. This time, he wouldn't need magic powers—a simple bandage and a little herb salve would suffice.

Lukas tossed and turned in bed, while Paulus, Giovanni, and Jerome all snored loudly nearby. Elsa, lying beside him, twitched in her sleep. She had only awoken for the briefest of moments when Matthias had laid her into bed. Occasionally she mumbled something indistinct, as though talking to someone. Apparently, she was having nightmares.

Lukas regarded his sister, who had changed so much over the past two years. She looked young and vulnerable, but earlier at the White Tower she had seemed much older.

Old and evil.

Like an evil old witch, Lukas thought, shivering.

Elsa's sleeve had slipped upward a little, revealing the thumbnail-sized mole near her right elbow. Her father, the inquisitor Waldemar von Schönborn, had the same mole. Elsa had always denied their similarities, but Lukas was beginning to suspect that they were more alike than either of the siblings had suspected.

Far more alike . . .

Lukas thought back to what Elsa had said just after she had brought down the bear-man with that bolt of blue lightning. She'd called him a traitor, but it had been as though some stranger was speaking through her—she'd seemed completely different. Lukas knew what had caused that change.

It's the book.

Immediately after they'd returned to the tavern, Lukas had hidden the *Grimorium* underneath their bed. He still wasn't sure what to do with it. Now, as he stealthily reached for it, Elsa began tossing and turning violently in her sleep. Lukas froze when he realized his sister was staring at him with open eyes. Once again, only the whites were visible.

"The power . . ." she murmured. "Don't risk it . . ."

But then she closed her eyes again and rolled over onto her side.

Moving as silently as he could, Lukas got up and sneaked to the door, *Grimorium* in his hand. His friends remained blissfully asleep as he hastened downstairs. He needed to be alone for a while so he could think. Zoltan had scratched the worst of the muck from the crown and then returned it to the chest beneath his bed, where he kept the scepter. Gwendolyn was sleeping in a small chamber next to his.

Gwendolyn was the only person Lukas would have enjoyed seeing at that moment. He thought she might be able to advise him on what to do with the *Grimorium*.

He certainly didn't know.

Lukas went into the kitchen, where a few embers were still glowing in the oven. After laying on some fresh pieces of wood, he sat down near the reddish glow of the fire and began cautiously flipping through the book. It was the first time he'd looked at the *Grimorium* closely—Elsa had always kept it from him.

He was astonished all over again at how inconspicuous the *Grimorium* was, this infamous *Book of the Night*. It was bound in plain black leather like a prayer book. As he turned the pages, Lukas came across strange, disturbing images of people in cages with bonfires burning underneath them; other illustrations showed mythical creatures with wings, long misshapen noses, or ears the size of doors. A man with goat horns and the legs of a buck was playing some type of flute, while men, women, and children followed him, dancing.

In between the pictures, there were sentences in a spidery, rust-red script that reminded Lukas of dried blood. He had no idea what language they were in—they looked sort of like Latin, and yet not. Here and there, he even found words that looked similar to German. Others were more like the ones Gwendolyn occasionally spoke.

Fulmen ad solictris donnerblitz per justatem . . . nos cysgod . . .

Lukas knew that the *Grimorium Nocturnum* was ancient. The bard Taliesin had written it down many, many centuries ago, back in the age of the Druids. It came from up in the North, in a faraway land by the name of Wales—the place Gwendolyn was from. Maybe she could tell him more about some of the words in the book.

Suddenly Lukas heard whispering in the air. It took him a while to realize that the whispering was coming from out of the book. The *Grimorium* was speaking to him. Or was it some other dark being?

The power, Lukas . . . the power . . . It is yours as well . . .

Lukas straightened up, and his gaze grew hard. The past few days had proved to him that he could do magic, too. Maybe the *Grimorium* would help him find the last piece of Imperial Regalia, the sword of Charlemagne. And not only that! He could stop wars, change the Reich! He could become Lukas the Great. A young king on the German throne. He could . . .

The power, Lukas. The power, the power . . .

Lukas snapped the book shut, and the whispering fell silent. What was wrong with him? What was the *Grimorium* doing to him? This was probably why his mother had hidden the book instead of continuing to use it.

The *Grimorium* changed the people who used it, drew them to the dark side. It made them evil.

Lukas was filled with an overwhelming desire to throw the book straight into the oven, but he was too afraid of what he might unleash—a furious, invincible power that could destroy him and all his friends. By now he was certain the book was slowly devouring his sister from the inside. He couldn't let her keep it any longer. But what could he possibly do?

He glanced around the kitchen, searching. Finally, he stood up and went to one corner, where he saw a stone floor tile protruding slightly. He lifted it up and scratched away the clay underneath until he had a small hollow that was the perfect size for the *Grimorium*. Carefully, he laid the book inside and pushed the tile over it. He would figure out what to do with it tomorrow. He was too tired tonight, too exhausted.

Just as he was about to go over into the tavern, the door opened and Zoltan entered. The cut on his right cheek had scabbed over and would probably soon become a scar. "Heard some noise and thought there were thieves afoot," Zoltan grunted, eyeing the boy suspiciously. "What are you doing in the kitchen so late at night? You look sick and worried. Everything all right?"

"Yes, I . . . ah, I was hungry," Lukas said, grasping for an excuse. "I ate a little of yesterday's bread. That's all."

Zoltan didn't seem entirely convinced, but eventually he waved the thought away—something else seemed to be on his mind anyway. "That Gwendolyn," he began. "Perhaps I was mistaken about her after all. She's brave and has helped us a lot. The same goes for your sister, by the way." Zoltan tried to smile. "Looks like we men need the girls a little more than we thought."

"Do you mean you need Elsa, or you need the *Grimorium*?" Lukas asked in a gloomy voice.

Zoltan shrugged. "You know I don't like that magic any more than you do. Once upon a time on the battlefield, we fought with swords, not with this . . . this dark power. I don't even want to imagine what our world will be like if wizards like Schönborn come to run it." He grasped for words. "But I have to admit, without Elsa's abilities, we probably wouldn't be in possession of two pieces of Imperial Regalia."

"The book is changing her," Lukas said.

Zoltan sighed. "Are you sure? She's a damned clever girl, Lukas. Perhaps she's simply growing up. Have you ever considered that?"

"Elsa told me more or less the same thing," Lukas responded gruffly.

The commander laughed. "There, you see?" He clapped Lukas on the shoulder. "It's past time we were in bed. Maybe our mysterious helper will bring us another message soon."

Plagued by dark thoughts, Lukas crept upstairs and got back into bed. He was so worn out that he was asleep in seconds.

XVII

Lukas startled awake to the sounds of loud voices coming from the tavern. He looked around and realized that he was alone in the chamber. The morning sun shone in through the gap between the closed window shutters.

He dressed hurriedly and went downstairs, where the others were sitting around a table in animated discussion. They all seemed very anxious. When Zoltan noticed Lukas on the stairs, he waved him over with an imperious motion. "You didn't look well at all last night," he said, "so I let you sleep. But it's good that you're awake now. It's one catastrophe after another here."

"What happened?" Lukas murmured, still completely worn out.

"What *happened?*" Elsa echoed, leaping up from her seat at the head of the table. She was shaking all over, and her eyes glittered feverishly as she ran her hands through her hair. "The *Grimorium* is gone! *That's* what happened, damn it!"

Instantly, Lukas was wide awake. For a moment, he'd forgotten that he'd hidden the *Grimorium* the night before. Now it came rushing back to him, along with all his fears and worries about Elsa. He'd been afraid his sister would be very, very angry when she realized the book was no longer there. But this was beyond even his wildest expectations. Elsa was completely beside herself.

"It's gone!" she kept repeating, over and over again. *"Gone, gone, gone!"*

"Maybe you lost it up in the White Tower," Lukas broke in. "You were unconscious . . ."

"Oh, please," Elsa hissed. "Gwendolyn has it!"

"Gwendolyn?" Lukas turned to the others at the table, baffled. Only then did he realize that Gwendolyn was not among them.

"Seems it's true," Bernhard replied. "Gwendolyn is gone, and so is the book. Put two and two together." He sighed. "She's just a dirty little thief after all."

Zoltan shook his head sadly. "And I'd nearly begun to trust her. What a fool I was!"

"It can't be," Lukas cried, taking the last few stairs in one great leap. "I'm sure Gwendolyn doesn't have the *Grimorium!*"

"Lovesick idiot!" Jurek let out a derisive laugh. "How would you know, hm?"

"Because." Lukas struggled for words, desperately racking his brain. He could clear up their suspicions by just admitting that he'd hidden the *Grimorium* himself, but what would the others think of him then? Even worse, Elsa would get the book back. He wanted to prevent that at all costs, at least until he knew what exactly the *Grimorium* was doing to his sister.

"What would Gwendolyn do with the book?" he said instead. "She can't do magic. She probably can't even read."

"She can sell it, though." Giovanni shrugged. "Lukas, I don't want to believe it, either, but the evidence is overwhelming. Why would she disappear without a word? And why would the *Grimorium* suddenly disappear at the same time?"

Lukas didn't have an answer to that. He was disappointed and hurt that Gwendolyn had left without so much as a good-bye. "So, what do you plan to do now?" he asked in a flat voice.

"What do you think?" Matthias asked. "We're going to look for her. If she wants to sell the book, she'll have to go to a dealer, an alchemist, or a scholar of some sort. At any rate, she won't remain invisible." He reached for his crossbow and began setting his oiled bolts in the box above the groove. "And when I lay eyes on her, even that little bow of hers won't help her."

Zoltan nodded grimly. "We'll hunt her down, and by God, we'll find her. Her and the *Grimorium*!"

"But . . ." Lukas began, but then realized there was no use. The others were already discussing how they would divide up their search for Gwendolyn.

Elsa, meanwhile, kept slamming her fist down on the table, as though trying to conjure up Gwendolyn's speedy return. "I'll kill her!" she snarled. "When I get my hands on that harlot, I'll kill her!"

Lukas shuddered. He hated to think what his sister would do to Gwendolyn if she did get the magic book back.

He was mostly silent during the discussion and planning that followed. Eventually, he and Giovanni were assigned to ask around the marketplace for Gwendolyn. Elsa would join Paulus and Jerome, who would look for her near Prague Castle. Lukas was glad that he and his sister were going to be separated. He hardly knew Elsa anymore, plus he was afraid she might see through him.

After they had finished checking the marketplace without success, Lukas and Giovanni strolled across the stone bridge toward Wallenstein's palace, knowing that plenty of wealthy merchants lived in the area. But none of them had ever heard of Gwendolyn, either. Finally, around midafternoon, they started back for the tavern.

"You like Gwendolyn a lot, don't you?" Giovanni asked after a while.

Lukas furrowed his brow, blushing. "What makes you think that?"

"I'm not a fool, Lukas. The way you act when she's around, the way you talk, the way you look at her . . ." Giovanni laughed. "You're in love, admit it. In love with a thief!"

"What if I were?" Lukas snapped. "What business would it be of yours?"

Giovanni halted in his tracks and gripped Lukas's arm. "I'm your friend, remember? I just don't want you to end up on the road to disaster. Pretty girls have been the ruin of many men."

"Oh, leave me alone with your clever sayings," Lukas retorted, jerking his arm free. "We should be worrying about Elsa, not Gwendolyn. Did you see how she was acting at the table earlier? That book has completely taken over her mind! Now that it's gone, she's losing control of herself."

Giovanni nodded solemnly. "You're right. Elsa's changing—it's unnerving. That book is truly a curse." He sighed. "Maybe it's for the best that Gwendolyn has run off with it. At least now the *Grimorium* can't do any more harm."

"God in heaven, how many times do I have to tell you? Gwendolyn hasn't run off with the book! She . . ." Lukas broke off midsentence when he saw Paulus and Jerome approaching, waving them over excitedly. They were now less than a stone's throw from the Black Boar.

"Zoltan's caught Gwendolyn!" Jerome called to them. "He tracked her down in the new part of town, at a peddler's! She fought him tooth and nail, and now she's back down in the beer cellar, ranting and raving."

"And the book?" Giovanni asked.

Paulus wiped the sweat from his brow. "She didn't have it," he wheezed, still out of breath from running. "Stubborn little beast isn't talking, but the commander says he'll beat it out of her." He knitted his brow. "This time old Zoltan genuinely means it, I'm afraid."

Lukas froze in horror. If Zoltan was convinced that Gwendolyn knew where the book was, there was no doubt that he'd hurt her terribly.

The commander of the Black Musketeers was a good man deep down, but he was also a soldier. He'd made it fairly clear that they needed the *Grimorium* to continue their search. Zoltan might well send one-eyed Jurek and his knives down to torture her.

Lukas wrestled with himself. What should he do? If he admitted the theft, Elsa would never forgive him, plus the *Grimorium* would continue to change her. On the other hand, he would save Gwendolyn. Beautiful, red-haired Gwendolyn—who hadn't actually stolen the book.

Elsa or Gwendolyn . . .

"I have to tell you all something," he said after a while.

"What, that you're in love with Gwendolyn?" Jerome giggled. "We've all known that for a while."

"No, that's not it." Lukas shook his head. "It's about the book. Gwendolyn doesn't have it."

"How would you know?" Paulus asked.

"Because *I* have it. So let's go put an end to this circus, once and for all." Lukas left his dumbfounded friends standing there and walked toward the Black Boar with a grim expression on his face.

"Why would you do such a thing, Lukas? Why?" Zoltan was staring at the boy, shaking his head repeatedly. They were all sitting around the table in the tavern again, except this time Lukas was standing before them like a defendant in court. Elsa was huddled like a spider at the farthest end of the table, clutching the *Grimorium* tightly. Lukas had retrieved the book from its hiding place in the kitchen and returned it to Elsa. Since then, his sister had neither spoken to nor looked at him.

"Again, *why* did you do it?" Zoltan repeated. "You know we need the *Grimorium*!"

"Because I wanted to protect Elsa," Lukas replied quietly. "The book is turning her evil. I know it." He turned to Zoltan. "You said yourself that you don't like witchcraft. Just look at what it's turned her into."

"Liar!" Elsa hissed, still avoiding his gaze. "You wanted the book for yourself! Now you've realized that you have magic powers, too, so you want to take it away from me!"

"Is that true, Lukas?" Zoltan asked. "Did you want the book for yourself?"

Lukas shook his head but remained silent. He had the feeling that he was saying all the wrong things.

Finally, Zoltan leaned back and crossed his arms. "If you say so, boy." He was silent for a while before continuing. "You're right, I don't like this witchcraft nonsense. But from the looks of it, it's our only hope of preventing something even worse. And you, Lukas, you betrayed everything the Black Musketeers stand for: honesty and loyalty! God in heaven, I need to be able to trust my people!" He sighed deeply. "I suppose we all need a break from one another. Especially you and your little sister. And because Elsa and the *Grimorium* are essential to our mission, you'll stay behind on our next foray. That will be best for everyone."

"Isn't that a bit harsh?" Matthias put in. "The boy didn't mean any harm by it. If he promises that—"

"Quiet, now!" Zoltan barked, cutting him off. "That's my final word. We've wasted enough time as it is. Now, let's go retrieve that blasted imperial sword, so we can return to our regiment already."

"We'd have to know where it was first," Bernhard said.

Zoltan whipped a letter out from beneath his doublet. It was written on the same fine handmade paper as the first two. "I just found another message outside, in front of the door," the commander explained. "Our wonderful stranger has finally told us where to find the third piece of Regalia."

Excited murmuring broke out around the table.

"So, where is the sword?" Matthias asked. "Tell us, Commander!"

"I'll tell you as soon as we've brought this young man down to join his beloved in the cellar."

"You're really going to leave me here?" Lukas was thunderstruck. "But . . ."

"You stole that book, Lukas," Zoltan replied. "Behavior unworthy of a Black Musketeer, even if your intentions were supposedly noble. It's better if you stay here and calm down."

"But what about Gwendolyn?" Lukas asked. "She had nothing to do with the theft, so there's no reason to keep her here!"

"She still hasn't explained why she ran off so suddenly. Stubborn little beast won't say a word." Zoltan shook his head. "I can't trust her, so she's staying here, same as you."

"If Lukas has to stay behind, then so will we," Giovanni said in a firm voice. He turned to look at Paulus and Jerome, who nodded resolutely as well. "We're his friends. All for one, one for all. We swore an oath to one another."

"Don't be ridiculous," Zoltan grunted. "That doesn't help anybody. I need every single one of you. Especially now, when we search for the imperial sword."

"One for all and all for one, *c'est vrai*," Jerome repeated solemnly.

"It's all right, Jerome." Lukas squeezed his hand. "Go ahead and go."

"But—" Paulus began.

"Zoltan is right," Lukas interrupted, straightening up and glancing around at his friends. "It doesn't help anyone if you stay here with me. If we ever want to be done with this madness, we need the third piece of Imperial Regalia." Dropping his voice to a whisper, he added, "Do it for Elsa. She needs your protection."

Giovanni hesitated, but then nodded. "Well, if that's what you think, all right. But only because you asked us to, you bullheaded fool."

Zoltan signaled to Bernhard and the one-eyed Jurek. "Bring the boy down to the cellar," he ordered. "I don't want him to get any foolish ideas."

"I promise you that we'll look after Elsa," Matthias whispered to Lukas, before the other two led him down into the cellar.

This time, Gwendolyn didn't pounce on Lukas like a feral cat. She was leaning against one of the barrels in the back, facing away from him. Her red tresses shone in the faint evening light that fell in through the small window. The door slammed shut behind Lukas, and Bernhard's and Jurek's footfalls echoed in the stairwell. Then all was silent.

After standing there for some time with no reaction from Gwendolyn, Lukas cleared his throat. "Looks like we'll have to tolerate each other's company for a while," he said in a quiet voice. "I told them that you didn't take the book."

Gwendolyn made a dismissive gesture. "Should I be grateful to you or something? You're no better than that rabble upstairs! They think I'm a witch because I have red hair, and they don't trust me a bit. It's always been this way. Even when Father was still alive," she added in a darker tone. "We never belonged. 'Filthy Welsh scum,' they called us. All three of us."

"Three?" Lukas asked. He was happy that Gwendolyn was speaking to him. "You mean you, your father, and your mother?"

"No, my mother died a long time ago. I mean my father, Jussi, and me."

"Jussi?" Lukas blinked.

"My younger brother. He's a hunchback, and he's not quite right in the head. The other boys always attack him, especially now that Father's dead and I have to leave him alone so often." She paused, biting her lip. "He cries a lot. He's probably terrified right now because I'm not with him."

"You were with your brother this morning, weren't you?" Lukas asked cautiously. "Why didn't you say so?"

Gwendolyn shook her head. "No one can know about him. The guards will throw him in a madhouse, or beat him to death like a rabid cur. I promised Father I would look after Jussi!"

"But you can trust us," Lukas said.

"Trust you?" Gwendolyn laughed. "The way you all trust me? Forget it! You won't tell me what's going on with all this witchcraft around here, either."

She turned away again, and for a time, the only sound was the buzzing of some flies that had wandered into the cellar. "So why are *you* down here?" Gwendolyn asked after a while, breaking the silence. "Did you get in a fight with your friends?"

"You could say that," Lukas sighed. "I'm down here because I'm the book thief." He summarized what had happened and explained why he had stolen the *Grimorium*.

Gwendolyn listened attentively. "A real magic book, then," she said when he finished, nodding in admiration. "I've heard the stories about Taliesin the bard, the one who wrote it. He's from Wales, where my family is from. It's a mountainous, inhospitable region with its own language. No one has ever conquered us. In Wales, we still believe in magicians, elves, pixies, and spirits. Speaking of magicians, though . . . you can do magic, too, can't you?" She winked at Lukas. "You used it to heal me. Why don't you just cast a spell to get us out of here?"

"I don't know if I can," Lukas replied. "Doing magic has only worked for me three times. I don't think I'm as good at it as my sister yet."

"But you don't need a book to do it. Plus, you're a good fighter. I like good fighters. Magical fighters, mages, like the legendary Manawydan from our beautiful Wales." Gwendolyn stood up and came over to him, smiling. "Lukas the Mage. Doesn't sound half bad."

She ran a hand over his head. Lukas blushed, and desperately hoped that she wouldn't notice in the dim light.

"I say we wait until things quiet down up there," Gwendolyn suggested softly. "Then you try to conjure us out of here. All right?"

Lukas nodded silently, tongue-tied. He didn't dare dash her hopes, for fear of disappointing her.

The sun had set, and night had fallen. Loud voices rang out upstairs for a moment, followed by footsteps. Finally, the tavern door slammed shut and everything was still again.

"Your supposed friends are off looking for the imperial sword now, getting their noses bloodied in the process," Gwendolyn said with a smirk. "Go on, work your magic," she said, gesturing to the cellar door.

"I'll . . . try." Hesitantly, Lukas went up to the oaken door, which was locked from the other side with a heavy latch. What was he supposed to do? Put his hand on the knob? Mumble something? He didn't have the first idea how to go about it. The other times, the power had simply flowed out of him. Maybe that would work this time, too.

He pressed his hands against the door, closed his eyes, and concentrated.

Open! he thought.

Nothing happened.

"What's wrong?" Gwendolyn asked. "Don't you have to say some magic words or something? That's how the marketplace magicians always do it. You have to mumble something like 'abracadabra' or 'simsalabim.' Something Latin."

"I've never been that good at Latin," Lukas stammered, frantically searching his mind for the words for "open" and "door." It had been years since his last Latin lessons with Castle Lohenfels's then chaplain, and he'd always hated the subject.

Finally, he remembered the words.

"PORTA PATEFIAS!" he cried, trying to give his voice a dark, threatening tone. When nothing happened, he repeated the phrase, waving his hands around in the air. "PORTA PATEFIAS! PORTA PATEFIAS, damn it!"

Gwendolyn eyed him skeptically. "You don't have any idea how to open it, do you?"

Lukas shook his head in defeat. "The other times, the magic just came out of me somehow. I heard the voice of my dead mother, and then it happened. I don't know what I'm doing wrong."

"Well, Mister Would-Be Magician, then we'll just stay imprisoned here until your friends come let us out. If they ever come back, that is," she added gloomily. "They might also get torn to pieces by spirits and ogres, and then we'll be left sitting in here until we rot." She withdrew to a dark corner of the cellar, where she curled up and sulked.

Too ashamed and embarrassed to reply, Lukas went to a different corner and sat down. A while passed without either of them saying a word.

Lukas bit his lip. He'd wanted to impress Gwendolyn so badly, and now he'd ruined everything. He brooded silently, wondering what he'd done wrong. Once again, he shut his eyes and tried to call his mother's voice to mind, but he couldn't do it. And there was nobody he could ask for advice! Not even Senno, who had once told him so much about magic.

Lukas still couldn't understand what had happened to the astrologer on that magical journey from Castle Lohenfels to Prague. Maybe he really was stranded somewhere across the sea, trying desperately to reach them. Or was he dead? At the bottom of the ocean, perhaps, or twenty feet underground?

The mysterious messenger . . .

Lukas blinked. A realization hit him. What if Senno was right here in Prague? What if all of this was just some sort of great test, serving some higher purpose? Could Senno be the stranger sending them the letters? It certainly sounded like the sly sort of thing he would do, even if Lukas couldn't imagine why.

A soft melody jerked him out of his thoughts. It was Gwendolyn, singing a song in a foreign language—probably Welsh, Lukas thought. The song sounded both cheerful and sad, and it gave Lukas renewed courage.

"Paham mae dicter, o Myfanwy . . . "

When the song ended, Lukas turned to Gwendolyn. "That was lovely," he said. "What was that you were singing?"

"A song my father once taught me. It's about the beautiful queen Myfanwy, who shuns all of her suitors. I sing it to Jussi a lot when he can't sleep." She sighed. "I hope he's all right. I promised the old peddler half a guilder if he'd take good care of him. If I could only get out of here!" Furiously, she pounded the barrel she was leaning against. Then she stood up, went over to the door, and kicked it. "This is so unfair. I haven't done anything wrong, and I still have to waste away down here with a puny little charlatan."

"Don't call me puny." Now anger was bubbling up within Lukas as well. "Charlatan, fine, but not puny!"

"Puny, puny, puny!" Gwendolyn kicked the door with every word. "Hah, I can do better magic than you! Listen. *Abracadabra, farting bear, open up, door, see if I care!* It's Gwendolyn, the redheaded Welsh witch!"

Smirking, Gwendolyn turned to look at Lukas—but her expression changed instantly when she saw that Lukas was staring at her with his mouth hanging open. "Th-the door," he stammered.

The latch slid aside, and the cellar door creaked open.

Giovanni, Paulus, and Jerome were standing on the other side. Their robes were torn and dirty, their faces blood-streaked. The right sleeve of Giovanni's shirt was soaked with blood as well. Lukas didn't think he'd ever seen so much terror on his friends' faces.

"What happened?" he asked apprehensively.

"All is lost!" Giovanni gasped. "You were right, Lukas. Your sister, she . . . she really is a monster."

XVIII

In the light of the single torch in Jerome's hand, the three friends' faces appeared chalk white, ghostly. Now Lukas noticed the blood on the blades of their weapons as well.

"What happened?" he asked again. "What about Elsa? Tell me!"

"We were on our way to the third hiding place," Paulus replied, breathless. "But the whole thing was a trap! Someone had tattled on us to the city guards. They were waiting for us just beyond the Vltava Bridge. Must have been at least two dozen!"

"I have my suspicions about who the traitor was," Lukas remarked grimly. "But go on, what happened?"

"It was a unit of Red Archers," Jerome went on. "Old, battle-hardened warhorses who knew every trick in the book. Giovanni took an arrow and . . . and . . ."

"And then what?" Lukas prompted him, sensing that his friends hadn't gotten to the worst part yet.

"Elsa cast a spell," Paulus replied darkly. "She brought that damned book out and mumbled a few words, and then the nightmare began. All of a sudden, the guards were being attacked by some invisible *thing that only they could see.* It must have been terrifying. They were crying and screaming and . . ." He broke off, shaking his head.

"And then something just tore the guards to pieces," Giovanni finished. "Shredded them like paper. I'll never forget the sound as long as I live. Only a few of them managed to flee. We ran from it, too, as fast as our legs could carry us." His face was deathly pale. "We lost sight of Zoltan and the others. We had no idea where they were, or if they made it out alive, so we came back here."

"I warned you all about my sister," Lukas murmured tonelessly. "Now, I fear it may be too late." Deep down, he sensed that Elsa had gotten away from him. The *Grimorium* had taken control of her.

"You have to stop your sister, Lukas," Giovanni ordered. "Who knows what she'll do next? She seems to be capable of anything! No doubt the guards who managed to escape have alerted every available unit in Prague. If you don't stop Elsa, the entire city will be a bloodbath!"

"She won't listen to me," Lukas replied in a glum voice. "I'm the one who stole the *Grimorium* from her, remember? To her, I'm a traitor and a thief."

"But you're still her brother. Doesn't that count for anything?" Gwendolyn was standing behind him. She'd crept up like a cat. "Believe me, I know how strong the bond between siblings is," she said. "We have to try, at least."

"We?" Lukas turned to stare at her in amazement. "You're free, Gwendolyn. There's no reason for you to help us. You can go your own way."

"That would suit you all just fine, wouldn't it?" She folded her arms defiantly. "You're forgetting that I want my share. I brought you to the imperial crown, and your commander owes me a pile of gold for it. I wonder how tall the pile will be if I return your sister to him?" She paused, furrowing her brow. "Assuming Zoltan is still alive, of course. But that's a risk I'll have to take."

"And perhaps they're together out there," Giovanni replied. "All I know is that we need to leave here as quickly as possible—if someone told the Red Archers where we were going tonight, they probably know where we're staying as well."

"Damn it, you're right," Lukas cried, starting for the stairs. "Let's get out of here! Hopefully it's not too late to . . ."

All at once, the sounds of loud voices and thundering footfalls came from the other side of the tavern door.

"*Merde,* they're here already," Jerome said in a low voice. "Hurry, we'll take the back exit."

They ran to the kitchen, where another door led out into a rear courtyard. Lukas glanced back and realized that Gwendolyn hadn't followed. She was still standing in the kitchen, looking around as though searching for something. "What are you doing?" he whispered. "We need to go!"

"I'm not going anywhere without my bow," she replied curtly. She began rummaging through different boxes and chests, even as the guards outside began kicking the front door down with their boots. Now it would be only a matter of seconds before they were inside the tavern.

"Ah, listen, we'll get you another bow." Lukas tugged at her sleeve. "We really don't have time for this—"

"I'm Welsh," Gwendolyn broke in. "Our bows are like children to us. Here! Here it is!" She drew her oddly curved bow out of the chest in the very back corner, along with her quiver. "*Now* we can go," she said.

When Lukas and Gwendolyn went out to join the others in the courtyard, they saw that it was already too late. Several of the guards had rounded the tavern and were blocking their escape route. More soldiers in Red Archer uniforms were emerging from the tavern and approaching from that direction. The courtyard was too narrow for them to use their longbows, so they drew their swords resolutely.

"In the name of the Kaiser!" called one of the guards, likely the captain. "You are under arrest for theft, heresy, and—"

That was as far as the man got before Paulus rammed the grip of his schiavona into his stomach. Jerome and Giovanni moved toward the other soldiers with their rapiers drawn. There were at least three Red Archers for each of them. Lukas threw himself into the middle of the fray, thrusting and jabbing his rapier in every direction as he searched desperately for a way out. The back courtyard had only one narrow exit, and the guards were blocking it. Even if they managed to defeat the ones they were fighting now, they'd never make it through the cramped passage. And they didn't have time to climb up onto the roof.

We'll have to try, at least, he thought. *Otherwise Elsa's lost, and maybe the entire city with her!*

Just then, Lukas heard a buzzing sound, followed by horrified shrieks coming from the guards. It was Gwendolyn, hailing down arrows on the men. Lukas thought back to how she'd shot at him in the marketplace alley just a few days before, and marveled once again at her ability to use the bow with such unbelievable speed, even in these tight spaces.

Bows were normally only used for distance fighting, but Gwendolyn loosed her arrows equally well in close combat—and it took her only seconds between one shot and the next, though she was continuously changing position. Now Lukas realized that she wasn't even readying one arrow at a time, but often held several arrows in her hand at once. She whirled through the courtyard, aimed, fired, scooped up arrows in a single, fluid motion, causing chaos among the guards, who began throwing themselves on the ground or hiding behind barrels, thinking they were facing an entire army of archers.

"Damn it, they've gotten reinforcements!" the captain shouted, looking around for the invisible enemy fighters. "Take cover, men!"

"Now!" Gwendolyn whispered to the boys. "Let's go!"

They ran out of the courtyard and into the alley before the watchmen could figure out what had actually happened. They didn't stop until they were several streets away and the Red Archers' shouts had faded into the distance.

"That was amazing!" Lukas panted, gesturing to Gwendolyn's bow. "Where did you learn to shoot like that?"

She shrugged. "My father taught me. We Welsh often ambushed the infernal Normans up in the mountains." She grinned. "By the time they'd drawn their longbows, they had at least five holes in their chests."

"Unfortunately," Giovanni said, "Gwendolyn's archery skills won't help us find Elsa." He gritted his teeth and gripped his upper arm. The arrow wound he'd gotten when the Red Archers attacked the group in the city earlier seemed to be causing him tremendous pain.

"If Zoltan and the others are still with her, I'm sure they're looking for the imperial sword," Lukas pointed out. "You all know where that is, right? So all we have to do . . . is . . ." Lukas trailed off, realizing that all three of his friends were looking down at the ground abashedly. "Wait, you *don't know?*" he cried in horror.

"Ah, *non.*" Jerome toyed with his rapier in embarrassment. "Zoltan only told us that we were headed someplace inside Prague's Jewish quarter. He said this time we were going into the lion's den, and that he'd tell us the rest when we needed to know." He shrugged. "I suppose he was suspicious that there was a traitor in our midst."

"Jurek!" Lukas hissed. "Jurek is the traitor. Think about it! He was the reason we nearly didn't make it into the marquis's palace, and I'm sure he was the one who stole the book about Polonius from the cloister library."

"We can worry about Jurek later," Giovanni said. "Right now, the most important thing is to find Elsa, so let's go to the Jewish quarter. Maybe someone there has seen your sister and the others."

"Provided that the entire quarter hasn't already gone up in flames," Paulus added, scowling. "When Elsa has that book in her hands, I wouldn't put anything past her."

With only patchy moonlight illuminating their path, the friends crept silently through the alleys of Prague until they reached the Vltava Bridge again. Innumerable torches flickered on the other side of the river around the gatehouse. Shouts occasionally rang out.

"Damn, might have guessed that," Paulus growled. "All hell's still loose over there. We'll never get across the bridge."

"Let's find another way over, then," Giovanni replied, already running down to the river, where several fishing boats were bobbing in the protective safety of a stone jetty. At this time of night, the quay was deserted. "The chaos gives us one advantage, at least," he said quietly to Lukas.

They jumped into one of the boats and untied the mooring. Soon they were drifting along the Vltava. Paulus took the oars and rowed with powerful strokes to the other bank, where the river lapped at a slippery quay wall.

Now they were only a good stone's throw from the bridge. Occasionally the calls of the watchmen reached their ears, but otherwise all was still. They docked quietly at a rotting, rickety pier and sneaked toward the houses nearest the riverbank.

"The Jewish quarter starts up there," Gwendolyn whispered, pointing to a couple of small, squat houses with darkened windows. "Follow me!"

Before long, they reached a wall at least three paces high, interrupted at regular intervals by individual buildings. There was no door—even the windows were small, like arrowslits. To Lukas, the whole quarter seemed like a separate town inside Prague.

"They've locked the Jews in here?" Paulus asked in disbelief.

Gwendolyn laughed softly, shaking her head. "More the other way around. The Jews are locking everyone else out. They are tired of being accused of terrible things." She shrugged. "But it's all just about money."

Giovanni nodded. "The Christians find they can avoid having to repay their debts by driving their creditors out of the city, or simply killing them. It keeps happening in cities all over Germany."

"I'm not surprised that Mister Bookworm here knows all about it," Paulus broke in, turning to give Gwendolyn a distrustful look. "But what about you? What business do you have with them?"

She grinned. "Let's just say that Jewish people and Welsh people have something in common. Nobody likes us because we're different. Now, stop running your mouths already and follow me."

"Well, I can see why nobody would like that big-mouth," Paulus grunted as he trudged along behind Gwendolyn. "What man would enjoy having a girl order him around?"

They tiptoed through the streets bordering the walled-off Jewish quarter. After a while, they came to a large, locked gate between two buildings.

"Maybe we can climb over this," Giovanni whispered, cautiously glancing around in all directions. "Or we can try climbing the wall itself."

Gwendolyn marched up and hammered on the gate with her fist.

"Have you gone mad?" Giovanni hissed. "They're going to hear us!"

"That's the idea," Gwendolyn replied.

And indeed, after a few moments, a small hatch opened in the door. A face appeared on the other side. "Who's there?" a harsh voice asked. "Jew or goy?"

"Neither," Gwendolyn replied curtly. "It's me, your red witch."

"Gwendolyn!" The voice suddenly turned friendly. "Well, why didn't you say so? What a nice surprise!"

The door opened, revealing a man in a guard's uniform, except with a strange yellow ruff at the neck, and only a club instead of a sword. He smiled broadly and wrapped his arms around Gwendolyn. "Haven't seen you in a long time. How's your brother?"

"Apparently, our new leader knows these Jews pretty well," Jerome murmured to Giovanni. "I have to admit, they do seem strange—with their weird customs and words."

"They could say the same about us Christians," Giovanni retorted. "We transform wine into the blood of Christ and chew dry Communion bread that we say is the body of our Savior. Even back when I was a novice monk, I didn't quite understand that." He grimaced in pain and clutched the makeshift bandage on his arm. "All that matters now is finding Elsa."

Gwendolyn exchanged a few quiet words with the guard and then turned to address the others. "He says the guards in the Jewish quarter haven't heard anything about a little girl or a group of men intruding here," she told them. "But they may have sneaked in somehow. At any rate, we seem to be on the right track. Here in the quarter, there have been rumors about unusual strangers going in and out in secret for several days."

They suddenly heard footsteps marching in the alley outside the quarter.

"Soldiers!" Gwendolyn hissed. "Hurry, get in here! We'll be safe in the Jewish quarter for a while, at least."

The friends hurried through the gate, which shut behind them with a thud.

"Now what?" Lukas asked.

"Now we go to Rabbi Bushevi," Gwendolyn responded. "If anyone can help us, it's the rabbi. Come on, you *schmucks*! That's Yiddish for 'slowpoke idiots'!" She waved the boys over.

As they hurried down the road leading into the Jewish quarter, the sound of marching boots on the other side of the wall slowly faded away.

XIX

As they traveled deeper into the Prague Jewish quarter, Lukas noticed how close together the houses were here. The streets were narrower than in the rest of the city—many of the back alleys were only an arm's length across. To Lukas, it almost seemed like the old, multistoried buildings were leaning forward to peer more closely at the tiny visitors. In the darkness, he could make out a bakery, a smith, and a tavern with strange curlicued lettering on the iron sign above the door.

"This is like a little village," he said, astonished.

Gwendolyn nodded. "The Jews formed ghettos like this across Germany after they were driven out of their homeland."

"What was that funny yellow neck ruff that the guard had on?" Lukas asked her.

"That marks him as Jewish," Gwendolyn explained. "The rabbi can explain all of that far better than I can—he could be a great help to us." She sighed. "We probably should have come to him for advice much sooner."

Lukas wanted to ask Gwendolyn how she knew the rabbi and the Jewish quarter guards so well, but she had already hurried on ahead.

He had this aching feeling that she no longer took him seriously after his failed attempt at magically opening the door.

At least I didn't make quite as much of a fool of myself fighting the Red Archers, he thought.

They came to a fairly large square, containing only a single building with a high, sharply slanted roof. The guard stopped and gestured to the entrance. "The honorable rabbi is in the synagogue, praying," he whispered. "He's worried about our community. Strange, unsettling things have been happening around here." He hesitated. "But it's probably best if he tells you about them himself."

Lukas knitted his brow.

Unsettling things . . .

He suspected that these things had something to do with their mission.

Respectfully, the friends stepped inside the synagogue. It was built entirely of stone, with wooden chairs along the walls. Numerous bronze candelabras bathed the room in ceremonious light. Hanging on the back wall was a thick, gold-embroidered velvet curtain with a six-pointed star on it.

For the most part, the synagogue reminded Lukas of the churches he'd seen, except instead of an altar, it had a raised podium in the center. An old bearded man in a black rabbinical frock was standing at the podium, hunched over a large book. His torso rocked back and forth slightly as he murmured a prayer under his breath. Twisted locks of gray hair hung down from beneath the small cap on his head.

Gwendolyn made a throat-clearing sound, and the old man paused, looking up. He seemed annoyed at first, but then a smile spread across his face. "Gwendolyn!" he exclaimed in delight. His voice was soft and musical, with an unusual accent. "What a *mazel*! So glad to see you." Still smiling, he turned to the others. "Aha, I see you've brought a few nice goyim with you."

"Venerable rabbi," Lukas said with a bow. "We're looking for my younger sister, and we think she may have gone into hiding in your quarter. She's in great danger. And so is your quarter . . . the whole city, in fact!" He hesitated, unsure how much to tell the rabbi. Gwendolyn gave him an encouraging nod, so in the end, he recounted everything—the search for the Imperial Regalia, and especially the story of Elsa and the *Grimorium Nocturnum*. "That book is making my sister evil," Lukas concluded. "It's awakening dark powers within her. We need to stop her."

Rabbi Bushevi, who had been listening attentively, tilted his head back and forth, causing the twisted locks on either side of his head to sway. "Some books are sent by God; others carry the seed of evil within them," he said gently. "When we humans are too weak, the evil seed sprouts within us." He closed the enormous tome on the lectern and walked toward Lukas with measured steps. "And you believe your sister is here because the imperial sword is hidden somewhere in this quarter?"

Lukas nodded. "Zoltan, our commander, said it was. We don't know more than that, unfortunately. The last two Imperial Regalia objects were protected by magic and magical beings. I'm afraid the sword probably will be as well."

"Magic and magical beings, hm . . ." The rabbi's expression turned contemplative, and after a few moments, he hit his forehead. "Almighty God, is it possible?"

"What do you mean?" Gwendolyn asked, but Rabbi Bushevi had already hurried on ahead.

"Follow me," he ordered brusquely with an impatient beckoning motion. "We mustn't waste any time."

They hurried into a nearby room, from which a narrow staircase spiraled to the upper floor. The steps creaked and groaned under the elderly man's weight as he led them up, holding a single candle to light the way. "I never would have thought that it would be goyim I brought up here," he murmured. "But in such dark times, the old rules don't apply, I suppose. May the community forgive me."

They came to the synagogue attic, which was packed with boxes, parchment rolls, and tattered books. The rabbi used his candle to light a seven-armed candelabra. Spiderwebs the size of pillows hung from the rafters, and several mice squeaked in some far-off corner, likely frightened by their sudden arrival. The disorder was unimaginable—it was clear that nobody had tidied up in there for ages.

"Ah, why are we up here, Rabbi?" Giovanni asked. "You do know that we're running out of time?" He gripped his injured arm and coughed at the cloud of dust that he had kicked up with his boots.

Rabbi Bushevi made his way over to a larger chest and opened it. "This is why."

Curious, Lukas peered inside. The chest was empty apart from a few crumbs of dirt and scraps of paper. "I don't understand."

The rabbi set the candelabra on the floor and gestured for the friends to sit down on the smaller boxes nearby. "I'd like to tell you all an old story," he said quietly. "Then you'll understand." He cleared his throat. "Half a century ago, a famous rabbi lived here in the quarter. He was the most learned man of his day, and was even granted frequent audience with the Kaiser. His name was Judah Löw. He had mastered the art of kabbalah—mystical incantations and prayers that you goyim like to mistake for magic."

The friends scooted closer, as the candlelight cast huge, dancing shadows across the roof overhead.

"In those days, the Christians accused us of terrible things and attacked our quarter. Rabbi Löw decided to create a golem—a magical guard made of clay—to protect us."

"I've heard of those," Giovanni breathed. "Golems are monsters made of earth that obey their master alone."

"Clever boy, you'd make a good rabbi someday," Rabbi Bushevi said with a tired smile, but then his expression immediately turned serious again. "The golem helped us protect our quarter, but after a few years, we no longer needed it. The Kaiser himself had forbidden anyone to bring false accusations against us, under penalty of death, so Rabbi Löw brought the golem up here, to the roof of the synagogue. He reversed the spell, and the creature collapsed into a pile of clay." Bushevi gestured to the chest. "Rabbi Löw put the clay in here and covered it with old prayer shawls and parchment rolls, so that no one else could awaken it for evil purposes."

"But there's nothing in here," Jerome said, confused.

Giovanni gulped. "There's no clay in the chest because someone else has reawakened the monster."

Rabbi Bushevi nodded somberly. "I'm afraid that wherever the imperial sword is hidden, it is guarded by the golem."

A gust of wind whistled through the windows and blew several of the candles out, leaving them in near-total darkness.

Lukas shivered. If Elsa really was somewhere in the Jewish quarter, looking for the sword with Zoltan and the other Black Musketeers, they would find themselves facing a powerful opponent. He needed to get to his sister as quickly as possible.

"So how long has this pile of dirt been walking around out there, then?" Paulus asked.

Rabbi Bushevi shook his head. "The guards in the quarter reported seeing a man running away from the synagogue a few days ago. Since that day, people have occasionally heard stamping, and there's talk of large shadows on the street at night. But nobody has actually seen the golem yet."

"Because he's guarding the sword," Lukas said thoughtfully. "But where?" He raked a hand through his hair. "We have to act quickly. If Elsa fights this golem, the ghetto will end up leveled. I'm sure of it, especially after hearing what she did to the guards on the bridge."

"At least then we'll know where she is," Paulus replied grimly.

Gwendolyn sighed. "There are hundreds of houses here, thousands of potential hiding places. It's quite a shame that Zoltan didn't tell you more than that the sword is hidden somewhere in the Jewish quarter."

"Well, that's not totally true," Jerome piped up. "Zoltan said we were going directly into the lion's den."

Giovanni rolled his eyes at Jerome. "That's just an expression you use when you're going somewhere dangerous . . ." He broke off, and a grin spread across his face. "Wait a moment. Maybe you're not all that stupid."

"That's what I keep telling you!" Jerome exclaimed. "But seriously, why do you say that?"

"What was the name of the creator of the golem again?" Giovanni asked, turning to Rabbi Bushevi.

"Rabbi Judah . . ." Bushevi began, but Lukas cut him off.

"Löw!" he exclaimed, suddenly catching on as well. "*Löwe,* German for 'lion.' Judah Löw, Judah the Lion. *He's* the lion!"

"But wouldn't that rabbi have died by now?" Paulus asked.

Bushevi nodded. "Buried at the Jewish cemetery. Judah Löw has a grave of honor there, a sort of stone burial tent, as rabbis are entitled to." Now he stopped as well. "Do you think that's . . ."

"The lion's den." Lukas nodded. "The imperial sword is at the Jewish cemetery, in the rabbi's grave."

Anxious excitement overcame them all; the friends talked wildly over each other as the wind rattled the attic windows outside.

"And you little goyim plan to stop the golem?" Rabbi Bushevi asked.

"Of course," Lukas replied. "But daggers and rapiers probably won't be enough to defeat it."

"No, they won't." The rabbi smiled. "It will have to be destroyed the same way it was created."

"Which is how?" Gwendolyn asked.

"Bringing the golem to life requires a great many mystical incantations," Rabbi Bushevi explained. "But the most important thing is a note that the golem's master places inside its mouth. The note has a powerful word on it. Only when that note has been removed will the golem turn to clay again."

"Let me make sure I understand this correctly." Paulus looked skeptical. "You want us to reach into its mouth and fish out a scrap of paper? Is that it?"

"In essence, yes."

Jerome grinned. "I don't suppose we can just ask it nicely to open its mouth?"

Rabbi Bushevi shrugged. "I can't say I know. The only person I know of who has ever created a golem and destroyed it again was Rabbi Löw, and he's been dead for many years."

"I suppose we'll just have to try, then," Giovanni said. He was about to stand up, but then quickly doubled over, cringing in pain.

"What's wrong with him?" The rabbi regarded Giovanni with a worried expression. "Is he sick?"

"He took a bad arrow hit on the arm," Lukas replied. "He needs to see a doctor, but I'm afraid we don't have time for that." He'd already considered trying to heal Giovanni magically, but ever since his failed attempt to cast a door-opening spell back at the tavern, Lukas was convinced again that he couldn't do magic after all. He hoped desperately that they wouldn't need magic to fight the golem. He preferred good, honest fencing a hundred times more.

"Let me see, child." Rabbi Bushevi beckoned to Giovanni, who winced as he got up and walked over. The old rabbi rolled up his shirtsleeves and eyed the boy's injury, which was wrapped in a tattered strip of cloth as a makeshift bandage. Although not especially deep, the wound had a strange dark rim around it, as though the flesh had been singed. Giovanni was pale, and gritted his teeth as the rabbi took his arm.

"That looks bad," he said, dabbing at the coagulated blood. "Very bad. Quite possible that the arrow was poisoned."

"It'll . . . be . . . all right . . . ," Giovanni managed to get out from between his clenched teeth.

Bushevi furrowed his brow as though wrestling with a decision. "You're right, he really should go to a doctor," he said at last. "But time is short." He went over to a chest and withdrew a large cloth of some sort, which he tore into long strips. "A holy tallit," he said reverently. "Hopefully God will forgive me for using it as a bandage. But if what you've told me is true, this is far more important." Bushevi plucked a few tiny bits from an old papyrus roll, leaving only a single letter on each scrap. Then he gathered the scraps up in his hand, blew on them, and murmured a long prayer in Hebrew.

"What is he doing there?" Paulus asked quietly. "Has he lost his mind?"

Rabbi Bushevi raised his head and winked at the boys. "Don't worry, I'm not crazy. In the Jewish kabbalah, we believe that every letter and every number has divine power. I'm giving your friend a strong word to take with him. The word is *gevurah*." He sprinkled the bits of paper onto Giovanni's arm and wrapped them up carefully with the strips of cloth.

"*Gevurah* stands for strength, power, and victory," the rabbi explained as he worked. "It will help the wound heal faster, and it will give you strength and courage in your fight against the golem." His expression darkened. "You will need that protection, especially on this ominous night. Mars is completely in Leo, so hatred and warfare are in the air. And the *dybbukim*, the evil ghosts of the dead, wander the cemetery."

"Well, *those* are certainly spectacular prospects," Jerome said with a sigh.

When the rabbi was finished wrapping the bandage, Giovanni moved his arm cautiously back and forth, and then blinked in disbelief.

"Amazing! It doesn't hurt as much anymore!" he exclaimed. "What kind of magic is that?"

"It's not magic." Rabbi Bushevi smiled. "It's only faith." Then the rabbi spread out his arms and looked around at the friends. "And now, go with God!" he said in a firm voice. "May *gevurah*, fifth of the *sephirot*, the strength of the Eternal and Almighty, be with you all, and—"

"Yes, yes, fine, enough pompous words." Paulus's schiavona clattered in its holder as he rose abruptly to his feet and cracked his knuckles loudly. "Let's go see if this lump of dirt is really plodding around the graveyard watching the imperial sword."

XX

Thick fog descended around the synagogue and drifted in pale wisps through the alleys. The single oil lamp in Giovanni's hand gave off a hazy glow.

Rabbi Bushevi had given them directions to the cemetery, along with the lamp and several pine-pitch torches. Lukas had been briefly tempted to ask the old man to join them, but the rabbi had to be over seventy, and nobody knew what else awaited them in the cemetery besides the golem. After their last encounter with the alchemist Polonius and the bear-man, Lukas was expecting the worst. And then there was Elsa . . .

Lukas walked up front beside Gwendolyn. Since they'd left the synagogue, she'd hardly spoken to him. He cleared his throat a little awkwardly. "Ah, listen," he began. "Maybe it's not such a good idea for us to fight this golem without Zoltan and the others. The rabbi said it could only be defeated through magic."

"So what's the problem?" Gwendolyn replied, smiling. "You can do magic, can't you?"

"Are you making fun of me now?" he asked, pained. "You know I can't, you saw it yourself!"

Gwendolyn's face turned serious again. "You saved my life when I was lying in the rose garden dying," she said. "And I know you used magic to protect your sister in the alchemist's laboratory. I saw that strange little cloud just before I passed out. So you *do* have magical powers, Lukas." She poked him in the chest with her finger. "You just have to remember how to unlock them and believe in yourself. Preferably as soon as possible."

"I hope I can," he mumbled. Wanting to turn his thoughts in a different direction, he asked, "So, what exactly did you do here in the quarter to make the rabbi and the guards like you so much? I doubt you just came over and showed them a few archery tricks."

Gwendolyn grinned. "Amazingly enough, that's exactly what I did. About a year ago, a mob of so-called Christians decided it was a good time to storm the Jewish quarter again. Just as they were about to break down the gate, I sent a shower of arrows flying at them." She giggled. "Those idiots thought that the Jews had hired an entire army of English bowmen, and fled with their tails between their legs. Since then, everyone in the quarter has been nice to me and my brother, Jussi." Her expression grew solemn again. "Which is more than I can say for a lot of Christians."

"Christians were the ones who burned my mother to death, too," Lukas replied in a dark tone. "Sometimes I wonder if God actually exists. Why does he let things like that happen? This whole eternal war is being waged in his name."

Gwendolyn shrugged. "Maybe God doesn't care about us."

"I don't believe that. My mother always said God loves us. Love is the strongest power that—"

"Well, well, turtledoves, what's all this chatter about love?" Jerome broke in, trotting up from behind them. "We'd be happy to give you two some time alone, but I'm afraid we have a golem to kill first."

"Very funny, Jerome." Lukas turned away, walking faster. How had he ended up talking about love like that with Gwendolyn anyway?

A chest-high wall faded into view through the fog, and dozens of gravestones were just visible in the darkness behind it. A few paces to the left, there was a small gate standing wide open.

"Look, up there," Giovanni said, gesturing with the lamp. "I think we've reached the cemetery." He knelt down with the lamp and squinted at the ground. There were numerous footprints in the mud around the gutter. "They're still fresh," he said quietly. "Men's footprints, and one set from a small girl. We're on the right track."

Lukas's heart began to race. Elsa was somewhere in this cemetery, and she wasn't alone—it seemed that Zoltan and the others were with her. He listened carefully, but all he heard was a distant bell chiming the twelfth hour.

"The witching hour," Paulus grunted. "Perfect time to visit a grave-yard. What did the rabbi call the spirits of the dead? *Dybbukim?* Well, let's go say hello." He stalked through the gate, and the others followed him.

Only once they were inside the cemetery did Lukas notice just how many headstones there were. Innumerable markers of all sizes poked out of the ground, many crooked or crumbling. Tendrils of fog floated overhead; an owl hooted somewhere nearby. Oil lamps were burning beside a few of the graves, but otherwise it was completely dark.

"The Jews only have this one cemetery," Gwendolyn said in a soft voice. "People are buried on top of each other, because there's simply not enough space. I'm afraid that before long, there will be so many gravestones in here, you won't be able to put one foot in front of the other."

"You don't happen to know where that Rabbi Löw's grave is, do you?" Jerome asked.

Gwendolyn shook her head. "We'll have to look for it. Rabbi Bushevi said we'd recognize it by the lion."

Together they wandered around in the darkness, trying to navigate the labyrinth of headstones. Although it was summer, the cemetery's few trees were all completely bare of leaves; their twigs and branches stretched out over the graves like spindly fingers. Peering more closely at the stones in the lamplight, Lukas saw that many had symbols carved into them: a book, a harp, a loaf of bread. After a while, he found a few with animals on them as well. But none showed a lion.

"Let's go a little farther in," Giovanni suggested. "There are more graves over that way."

Furiously, Jerome kicked a loose clump of earth. "*Mon dieu,* doesn't this cemetery ever end? It's like the entire world is buried here." A soft moaning sound interrupted Jerome's complaining. "A *dybbuk!*" he whispered. "I shouldn't have disturbed its rest. Now it's rising from the grave!"

"I'm not so sure," Paulus muttered. "That sounds more like the eternal song of the battlefield. If you ask me, someone is badly injured."

"Maybe it's an injured *dybbuk?*" Jerome speculated.

"It's coming from over there." Lukas pointed toward the back wall of the cemetery. "Let's go take a look. Stay cautious, we still don't know where that golem is."

Quietly, they tiptoed from grave to grave until they came to a single marker standing by itself near the wall. It was about hip height, and its two angled stone slabs made it look like the roof of a small house. Lukas took the lamp and hurried over to it.

He saw stone pinecones, bunches of grapes . . .

And the figure of a lion underneath.

"I've found it!" he called softly to his friends. "The grave of Rabbi Löw."

Suddenly the eerie moaning started again, but much louder this time. Whoever it was, they were right nearby. Lukas turned around and saw a large figure lurching toward him from out of the fog. Its arms were outstretched, and it was stumbling more than walking.

Like a dead man dragged from the grave, Lukas thought. *A dybbuk or . . . ?*

Or a creature made of earth and clay.

The golem! Lukas realized. *Guarding the grave of its old master!*

And then it reached him.

XXI

Only when the sinister-looking figure was standing right in front of him did Lukas see its clothing, which was all too familiar: black leather, bucket-top boots, a hat with a red feather in it. This was no *dybbuk* and no golem.

"Zoltan!" he cried. "It's Zoltan!" To his horror, Lukas saw that Zoltan's doublet was streaked with blood, and his left arm hung lifelessly at his side. He was dragging his right leg behind him, leaning on his sword for support. He looked half-dead.

"Betrayal," Zoltan rasped. His face was pale as ashes. "Flee, boys . . . you . . . must flee . . . from here . . ." He collapsed right in front of Lukas with a groan.

"What happened?" Giovanni asked, breathless, as he and the others ran over to join Lukas and Zoltan.

"He said something about betrayal," Lukas replied. "Apparently Zoltan and the others have been lured into a trap yet again. I bet it's that damned Jurek!" He knelt down to Zoltan, who was gasping for breath. The commander of the Black Musketeers had his eyes shut tight and looked like he was in terrible pain. In the glow of the lamp, Lukas saw blood pouring from a wound on Zoltan's stomach that had been hidden under his leather doublet.

What happened? Lukas asked himself. *Who did this to Zoltan?*

"Where are the others?" Gwendolyn asked. "Elsa, Matthias, Bernhard?"

"Well, we know what happened to Bernhard, at least," Paulus spoke up in a dark voice, stepping from behind a nearby gravestone— and dragging a heavy, lifeless body into view. Lukas flinched. It was Bernhard, and there was a crossbow bolt in his neck.

"My God," Lukas breathed.

Paulus knelt down and examined Bernhard's wound. "There's nothing more we can do for him." He shut Bernhard's eyes, which had been staring vacantly up into the night sky. "God rest his soul. He was a good fighter." He balled his hand into a fist. "To hell with the cowardly assassin who did this!"

Jerome glanced around. "It had to have been several. Zoltan and the other Black Musketeers would have had no trouble with one. We'd better take cover—those cockroaches may still be nearby!"

Though Bernhard's death filled Lukas with grief and outrage, he immediately sprang into action like a soldier in battle.

Just as Zoltan would have advised me to, he thought.

He crouched down beside his commander, so that the rabbi's grave protected him from at least one side. The others sought cover among the gravestones as well.

Gwendolyn slipped behind one of the stunted trees. She nocked an arrow and gazed out into the darkness. "Damned fog," she grumbled. "This is worse than in Wales. Can't see more than three paces ahead!"

Lukas bent down over Zoltan and shook him gently. He was still alive, but judging by the large red stain on his doublet, the commander had already lost a great deal of blood.

"What happened?" Lukas asked him again. "Where is Elsa? Is she injured? Dead?"

Zoltan shook his head slowly. "Not dead," he panted. "He . . . has her."

"Who?" Lukas asked. "The golem? Schönborn? Jurek, the traitor?"

Zoltan clenched his teeth and moaned, apparently overwhelmed with pain again. "Jurek . . ." he began.

"I knew it!" Lukas hissed. "I never trusted that fellow, not once!"

Zoltan tried to say something else, but all he got out was a groan.

"Ah, *mon dieu!*" Jerome's voice echoed out from behind another gravestone farther on. "Here's another body."

Please, let it not be Elsa! Lukas thought. *Please, God, not Elsa!*

"Who is it?" he asked, desperate. "Is it Matthias?"

"Non," Jerome replied. "It's . . ."

Just then, a crossbow bolt slammed into the gravestone Paulus and Jerome were crouched behind. There was a crunching sound as the bolt bounced off the stone and fell to the ground. Another shot whistled across the cemetery and landed in the dirt not far from the badly injured Zoltan. Instinctively, Lukas ducked down and reached for the bolt to study it more closely. It was very long, and it seemed strangely familiar to him, shot from a large crossbow.

From a very large crossbow.

"Give up!" a voice rang out from some distance away. "You don't have a chance!"

Lukas flinched. He knew that voice, but he never would have thought he'd hear it like *that*, so evil, hissing like a snake, without its usual friendly note—the friendly note that had fooled him for so long.

Matthias was the traitor.

"Matthias!" he whispered. He shook his head, still hardly able to believe his own ears. "Oh, God, why? Why?" Lukas cautiously raised his head, and sure enough, he recognized Matthias standing there in the moonlight. The fog had lifted for a moment, revealing his broad shoulders and the pearls in his black hair. Lukas had trusted him! He had always been kind to Lukas and Elsa. How was he the traitor and not Jurek?

"Matthias!" Jerome exclaimed in disbelief. "*Ce n'est pas vrai!* Please tell us that you don't have Zoltan and the others on your conscience!"

"Nothing personal, boys," Matthias replied in an almost friendly tone. "I actually like you all. But we Black Musketeers are mercenaries. Killing people for money is what we do. Everything else is just empty words." He spat audibly on the ground. "With the money I'll receive for this, I'll be able to buy my own tavern, get married, and enjoy the sunset for the rest of my life. I was just tired of doing other people's dirty work and getting only a few silver coins for it."

"Talk all you like, you're still a filthy, dishonorable traitor!" Paulus screamed from his hiding place beside Jerome. "You've dragged the name of the Black Musketeers through the mud. Shame on you!"

Matthias shrugged. "Better dishonorable and rich than honorable and dead." As he spoke, he set another bolt into the magazine of the crossbow. Lukas knew it held up to ten shots, and he assumed that they were the same bolts that had killed Bernhard—and Jurek, he now realized. He looked at the severely injured Zoltan. The wound was that of a crossbow as well. They'd probably been so shocked that they hadn't even defended themselves.

"Come on out, boys!" Matthias called again. "There's no point in hiding any longer. You can still avoid a bloodbath."

"Oh, and what will you do when we all rush out together?" Paulus growled. "It doesn't matter how many bolts you have, you can't fire them all off at once."

Matthias sighed. "*Surely* you don't think I'd come here alone." He stuck two fingers into his mouth and whistled. The shadows of three large soldiers appeared from behind the nearby headstones. From their helmets, Lukas could see that they were Spanish mercenaries. In their massive hands, the swords and sabers they held looked like cute little toys.

Frozen ones! Lukas realized. *The Devil's mercenaries! Doesn't this nightmare ever end?*

Then he spotted the Marquis de LaSalle, standing a little farther back in his ruffled shirt and powdered wig, holding a rapier. Apparently, all of their enemies had joined forces against them!

"Your friend is right," the marquis called, swishing his rapier through the air. "Surrender! There are five of us, including three invincible frozen ones. You three boys may be good fighters, but you see what we did to your commander and those other two Black Musketeers." He giggled. "Bernhard and . . . Jurek, was it? It's amazing how easily a couple of crossbow bolts can take down legendary mercenaries."

"You won't have it so easy with us, coward," Jerome replied. "We will avenge our friends' deaths. *Je te le jure!*"

Lukas's heart beat a little faster when he realized what the marquis had just said. He'd counted three boys, not four. LaSalle and Matthias didn't know about him and Gwendolyn. Matthias probably assumed they were still locked in the tavern cellar.

Gwendolyn wasted no time taking it to their advantage. She left her hiding spot behind the tree and was now sneaking from gravestone to gravestone with her bow in hand, preparing to ambush their adversaries from behind. Lukas glanced over at Jerome and Paulus, who were already reaching for their weapons with determination. Giovanni was nowhere to be seen. Lukas could only hope that nothing had happened to his friend.

"Try and stall them," Lukas hissed at Paulus, who was only a pace or two away. "Until Gwendolyn can attack from behind. Then we'll strike."

Paulus nodded. "So, Matthias," he called loudly, making a noise of contempt. "What does it feel like to be a miserable traitor? Did the marquis promise you so much gold that it will be worth burning in the deepest pits of hell for?"

The Marquis de LaSalle let out a taunting laugh. "You fools. Matthias has been betraying you from the very beginning. He was the one leaving you those messages outside your door, and none of you had the faintest idea."

Lukas froze. Could that be true? The messages leading them to the three hiding spots had come from him? That didn't make any sense. Even if Matthias had been working for the marquis, why would he do something like that? Why would he tell them where the Imperial Regalia was hidden? Lukas didn't understand anything anymore. Paulus and Jerome looked confused as well. Lukas wished Giovanni was nearby just then, but he was still nowhere to be seen.

"Matthias, is that true?" Jerome called. "Did you lead us to the places where the pieces of Regalia were hidden?"

"How else do you think you ended up in the marquis's armory?" Matthias asked, still refilling the magazine of his crossbow. "Without me, you would never have found the imperial scepter. And you only discovered the poisoned chest in Polonius's laboratory with my help." He laughed softly. "You all stumbled past it like blind men."

Lukas thought hard, and one by one, he recalled all the little moments that they should have noticed, all the clues they'd missed. Matthias had probably also been the one who hid the book about the alchemist Polonius from him and Elsa in the cloister library.

"None of it matters now," Matthias went on, raising his crossbow again. He glanced up at the sky as though checking something. "The fog will lift soon, and then nothing will be standing in the master's way," he said, looking pleased. "Now all that's left is the cleanup. I'll get my gold, and I can finally leave this rotten city. So come out already, before the marquis sets the frozen ones on you."

"What are you talking about, Matthias?" Paulus asked from behind the grave. "What nonsense is that? Who is this master, and what has he gotten?"

Lukas clenched his fists as a terrible suspicion crept over him. The hairs on his neck stood on end.

Where is Elsa? he thought. *What have they done with her?*

Just then, Gwendolyn appeared like a ghost from behind another gravestone farther away. Now she was directly at their enemies' backs. With a determined expression on her face, she drew her bowstring and nodded to Lukas.

"Now!" Lukas shouted.

There was a buzzing sound, and then a cry of surprise.

Gwendolyn fired arrows off like bolts of lightning. One hit Matthias in the shoulder, and he groaned in pain, dropping his crossbow. More arrows rained down on him, the marquis, and the three frozen ones.

Amid the general confusion, the three boys leapt out from behind the headstones, rapiers drawn. Lukas glanced around once more for Giovanni, but it was like the ground had opened up and swallowed him. Lukas hesitated for only a moment—they couldn't wait any longer.

It was time to attack.

"Together against death and the Devil!" Paulus shouted.

"To hell and beyond!" Lukas and Jerome responded.

For Zoltan, Bernhard, and Jurek! Lukas thought.

Then they launched themselves at their enemies.

XXII

Only seconds later, Lukas was standing before a frozen one who was swinging his saber like a berserker. Lukas ducked underneath the saber before going into a riposte and landing a low cut that went deep into his adversary's side. The Spaniard swayed for a moment, only to resume his attack with even more determination. His eyes were as white and empty as glass marbles.

Having fought them before, Lukas knew how dangerous the frozen ones were. They kept right on fighting, regardless of how many times they were injured. It was actually impossible to kill them. Fire kept them at bay for a while, but a single torch or lantern likely wouldn't be enough.

Lukas dodged the soulless Spaniard's next blow. This time, the blade whizzed past just inches from his face. Lukas began focusing entirely on his opponent's neck. If he could hit the frozen one's throat, maybe blood loss would stop him, however briefly.

Lukas risked a feint and then swung a high cut at the Spaniard, sending his rapier thundering down from overhead. But at the last moment, the frozen one brought his saber into position, and their blades collided with such force that Lukas nearly dropped his weapon.

Paralyzing pain shot up his arm. The frozen one grinned malevolently and wound up for another strike.

I'll never win this fight, Lukas thought. *And it seems I can't do magic, either. It's hopeless!*

Desperately, he looked around for his friends. Paulus and Jerome were fighting the two other frozen ones; Gwendolyn was on the ground, struggling with the marquis. Her bow was lying nearby, useless—the marquis must have ambushed her hiding spot. She needed help. Where was Giovanni? Lukas still didn't see him anywhere. Had he fallen into some kind of trap?

At any rate, Matthias posed no further danger. The traitor had collapsed beside his giant crossbow, riddled with Gwendolyn's arrows. At this distance, it was impossible to tell whether he was still alive.

Lukas nearly didn't see his adversary's next attack before it was too late. He dodged it at the last possible moment, but stumbled over a burial mound and fell to the ground. His rapier skittered out of his hand.

Now the frozen one towered over him like a giant, and lunged at him with the saber. Lukas rolled to one side, and the blade bored into the wet ground. The next attack came only seconds later. Lying on his back, Lukas scooted away until he reached the rabbi's grave. He tried to stand up, but slipped against the wet stone.

For a moment, Lukas hoped that his magic might help him. But he wasn't sure what to do. Wave his hands and yell out some sort of spell? Something in Latin, perhaps? In his panic, all Lukas could come up with was the Latin word for "go away."

"Vade!" he cried, over and over again. *"Vade, vade!"* He stretched out his right arm, the way he'd seen Elsa do. *"Vade!"*

But the frozen one only laughed as he raised his saber for the fatal blow. *"Vas a morir,"* he said in a rattling voice that sounded like it came from deep within a grave. *"Pequeño bastardo . . ."*

This is the end! Lukas thought. *At a cemetery, how fitting.*

Just then, a large shadow rose up behind the Spaniard like an angel of vengeance. A blade whistled through the air and sank deep into his back. The frozen one let out a grunt of surprise and took a step forward. Only then could Lukas see who had dealt the blow to his assailant.

It was Zoltan.

The commander was swaying, but he was standing upright. Sweat pearled on his brow as he lifted the huge broadsword he was gripping tightly with both hands. He began swinging it at the Spaniard, who retreated little by little. Zoltan's first blow would have been fatal to any other opponent, but the frozen one had only stopped for a moment— and now he went on the attack.

Leaning against the rabbi's grave, Lukas watched the duel between two equally matched opponents—though one was severely injured, and the other was an invincible undead creature. Saber and broadsword crashed into each other with such force that sparks flew.

Zoltan was pale as a ghost; he had lost a great deal of blood, was limping slightly, and just lifting the sword was obviously a struggle for him. Even so, he showed once more why he was the leader of the legendary Black Musketeers. Crooked cut, high cut, parry, winding cut, wrath cut . . . The commander shifted from one guard and position to the next so quickly that the Spaniard was always a fraction of a second behind. Soon, his armor was full of scratches and tears, many of which were dripping blood. Still he kept on swinging his saber as though nothing had happened.

Zoltan fought with determination, but Lukas could see that his movements were getting progressively slower and more erratic. His utterly inexhaustible force of will seemed to be fading. The wound on his stomach, where he'd been hit with a crossbow bolt, was no doubt unbelievably painful; it was a miracle that Zoltan was still able to fight at all.

The Spaniard seemed to have noticed that his opponent was at the end of his strength. He redoubled his efforts, went straight into the riposte with greater frequency. Suddenly, he left himself exposed, completely out of nowhere; Zoltan's sword shot forward, piercing the frozen one's cuirass . . .

. . . where it stuck fast.

"No!" Lukas cried. "Commander, watch out! It's a trick!"

But it was already too late. As Zoltan was still tugging at the hilt of his sword, the frozen one swung his saber and felled the old warhorse like a tree. Zoltan glanced briefly up at the sky, as though a star was shining up there just for him. Then he tipped to the side and collapsed in a heap, where he remained, lifeless.

Blood seeped into the cemetery ground. Zoltan's eyes stared blankly into the darkness.

The great commander of the Black Musketeers was dead.

"You monster!" Lukas shrieked, over and over again. He snatched up his rapier, leapt to his feet, and lunged at the soulless Spaniard. The frozen one, panting slightly, turned to face his new assailant as though preparing to chop another log into firewood.

Lukas knew he didn't have a chance, but he still swung at his enemy like a madman. The frozen one had killed Zoltan, a man Lukas had loved almost as much as he'd loved his own father. Rage bubbled up within Lukas—he saw red. He was going to hack this monster to pieces, even if it cost him his life.

His blows were fast and precise, but Lukas still knew that he would eventually make a mistake, that his strength would fail him just as Zoltan's had.

And that would be the end of him.

A grin flickered on the frozen one's face, almost as though he could tell what Lukas was thinking. Soulless though his creations were, Inquisitor Waldemar von Schönborn seemed to have imbued them with his own cruelty.

"*Vas a morir,*" the Spaniard growled again as he swung.

Suddenly there was a crashing sound like broken glass, followed by a hissing sound. The frozen one's expression changed. Lukas thought he saw pure horror glittering in the creature's eyes. A moment later, he realized why.

The Spaniard was burning.

His entire back had burst into flames. Roaring, the frozen one tossed his saber aside and began swatting helplessly at the fire. He spun around in a circle like a dervish, which only fanned the flames. The other two frozen ones began screaming as well. Lukas raised his head and saw that they were stumbling through the cemetery, also burning—massive torches stomping around among the gravestones like will-o'-the-wisps, rolling on the ground, and then finally crawling off into the shadows of the night.

Soon the horrific scene was at an end, and all that was left of the undead terrors was a faint scent of burning flesh and cloth.

Gasping, Lukas straightened up. Had that been magic? Had he managed to cast a spell after all? He stared at his own hands in astonishment.

But then he spied Giovanni waving an oil lamp back and forth with a grave look on his face. He was wearing neither a shirt nor a doublet. The lamp had gone out, but Lukas noticed a few scraps of cloth stuffed inside it—Giovanni's clothing.

"May I present my latest invention?" Giovanni held up the lamp, grinning. "Prague Fire. Never fails against undead and other unnatural riffraff." He held the lamp to a burning candle standing near one of the gravestones. "I remembered how we fought these beasts off during our last adventure," Giovanni explained. "With fire." He pointed behind himself. "As the rest of you were having your little chat, I collected these oil-filled lamps, and then sealed them with strips of cloth from my shirt and doublet. The stuff burns just like tinder." He shivered and rubbed his bare arms.

"I hate to say it, but your little carnival show probably saved our lives. That, and Gwendolyn's arrows." Paulus walked over to Matthias, who was slumped lifelessly against a headstone, with his large repeater crossbow on the ground beside him. Paulus gave him a contemptuous kick. "This one here's probably already burning in hell."

Matthias's body tipped to one side, and Lukas stared into the traitor's dead eyes. Three arrows protruded from his chest—Gwendolyn had done a thorough job.

Where *was* Gwendolyn? She'd been fighting the marquis earlier.

Lukas swallowed hard as he regarded the dead man one last time. He'd always liked Matthias. It hurt to realize that all his friendliness had only been for show.

Now he'd gotten what he deserved.

"Forget the bastard," Jerome said quietly. "Come on over here and pay your last respects to our commander. He deserves a proper good-bye."

They followed Jerome, who knelt down beside Zoltan, eyes downcast. Lukas had a hard time fighting back his tears. Zoltan had known Lukas's father—the two of them had been good friends. With the commander's death, it felt like his father was even further away than before. Lukas's memories of him were gradually fading, like lettering on old paper.

Maybe I could have helped Zoltan, Lukas thought. *Maybe my magic would have worked on him.*

Lukas would have liked to try. But now it was too late.

Paulus removed his hat and wiped his eyes. Lukas had never seen his large, surly friend cry before. He cleared his throat. "A man like Zoltan had to die in battle," Paulus said, his voice cracking. He balled his hands into fists. "But not like this, killed by a cowardly traitor with a crossbow. By God, I swear I'll avenge him! Matthias is lucky that he's already in hell. Otherwise, I'd carry him there myself."

"Zoltan was the best mentor anyone could have," Giovanni said quietly. "I've never seen a more experienced fighter."

"Though he could certainly light a fire under a person's behind sometimes." Jerome nodded thoughtfully. "Do you remember how he—"

"All right, you mourning doves, is anyone here still interested in the living?"

Lukas jumped when he heard Gwendolyn's voice and saw her pop up from behind a grave like a cheerful ghost. They'd actually forgotten about the girl for a moment. Lukas knew he'd need to put his grief aside. Gwendolyn was right, they had to dry their tears and keep going. They had to worry about the survivors right now.

Especially about Elsa, who was still nowhere to be found.

XXIII

Gwendolyn approached the four friends with a serious expression, wiping her hunting knife on her leather trousers as she walked. Lukas was relieved to see her apparently unharmed.

"That painted hobgoblin probably thought fighting a girl would be easy," she said, nodding toward the marquis, who was lying on the ground near the cemetery wall. A pair of crows perched on a nearby headstone, eyeing LaSalle as though getting ready to land on him.

"Tried to skewer me like a rabbit with his rapier," Gwendolyn went on with a wry smirk. "But besides archery, my father also taught me a couple of dirty tricks to use on overly pushy men."

"Is he dead?" Jerome asked.

"Not quite, but soon." Gwendolyn turned around, dagger raised, but Lukas grabbed her arm to stop her.

"Don't!" he exclaimed. "We have nothing more to fear from him, and he might be able to tell us where Elsa is. We're running out of time!"

The Marquis de LaSalle let out a hoarse, gurgling sound. It took Lukas a while to realize that he was laughing.

"You fools!" he wheezed. "You ran out of time long ago! You think you've won, but you're all just marionettes in his game."

"What are you talking about?" Lukas went over to the injured man, who struggled into a sitting position, propped against the wall. "What game?" He saw that the marquis's leg was bleeding severely. The wound didn't strike him as life threatening, though he probably would never run again. "Stop talking nonsense, just tell us where Elsa is!" Lukas insisted.

The Marquis de LaSalle's lips twisted into a spiteful grin. Together with his powdered wig and makeup, it made him look like an evil old woman. "Your sister is gone! The golem took her. It's bringing the little brat to him right now. Everything is going according to plan, and there's nothing you can do about it now."

"My God, the golem," Lukas breathed. "So it *was* here at the cemetery." He bent down and shook the marquis wildly. "Where did the golem take Elsa? Tell us! Where is Elsa?"

"Calm down, little one," LaSalle taunted him, giggling. He glanced up at the sky for a moment, where stars were steadily coming into view. "It's too late anyway, so I might as well tell you. I'm sure the golem has already delivered your sweet little sister to Polonius by now."

"That hunchbacked alchemist?" Paulus asked as he strode up to join the others. "I should have drowned him in his own latrine when I had the chance."

"Polonius is probably a henchman of Schönborn's, just as the marquis is," Giovanni mused aloud. "The alchemist commanded the golem to kidnap Elsa, and now he's long gone with her." He furrowed his brow. "Somehow I have the feeling that everything was about Elsa this whole time. But I can't make sense of how this fits with the Imperial Regalia yet."

"The imperial sword!" Jerome cried, hitting his forehead. "Maybe that sword will help us figure out where Elsa is." He glanced around. "Where is it, then?"

"If what Giovanni says is true, and Polonius hasn't taken the sword with him, then it must be hidden in this grave." Lukas walked over to the tomb of Rabbi Löw, not far from the cemetery wall. "Remember what Zoltan said: the sword is in the lion's den. Hm, but where is that? We're running out of time!"

Lukas regarded the grave thoughtfully. The two angled stone slabs made it look almost like a tiny church, just the size of a man. Tentatively, he ran his hand over one massive slab and then the other. Vertical stone tablets were positioned at either end, adorned with columns and archways. Above that, there was a carving of a lion with paws raised. Strange lettering covered the entire tomb. A stone pinecone was at the very top.

"Let me." Paulus stepped up to the grave and took hold of one of the slabs. "I'll just lift this up for a moment so we can look—"

But Lukas held him back. "I'm not so sure. These slabs look like they haven't been touched in a long time. Look at the moss and lichen in the cracks."

"Maybe Mister Powdered Wig knows where the sword is," Gwendolyn piped up. She turned and strode toward the marquis, making a threatening gesture with the hunting knife. "Come on, spit it out, flea-wig. Tell us before I carve a pattern into your other leg."

"You'll have to do some of the thinking for yourselves," LaSalle retorted. "You're clever little children, aren't you?" He giggled, looking as though he'd just had a wonderful idea. "It's certainly a hard nut to crack! I wonder which of you will manage it?"

"I bet your skull isn't a hard nut to crack," Paulus said, raising his fist.

"Stop," Giovanni broke in. "We can figure this out without him." He rounded the grave, tracing the carved columns, gates, and lettering. The others watched in silence.

"Giovanni's managed to figure everything out thus far," Jerome remarked in a soft voice. "But I still think we should tickle the answer out of this *saligaud*, this bastard. Even if he is a countryman of mine."

"Maybe Lukas can conjure the sword out," Gwendolyn put in. "It has to be somewhere nearby."

"Lukas can do magic?" Paulus looked confused. "Lukas, is that true? You didn't tell us that you—"

"Gwendolyn, what are you talking about?" Lukas snapped. "How many times do I have to tell you? I *can't do magic!*"

"Oh, that's right, I nearly forgot," Gwendolyn shot back, sulking. "All you can do is wave your arms around and yell 'abracadabra.' Because you don't have faith in yourself! You're a coward, and it's driving me mad, you know that?"

"Shut up already," Giovanni grouched, clearly deep in thought. "How is a person supposed to . . ." He stopped. "Nuts!" he cried abruptly. "That's it, isn't it?" He turned to look at the marquis. "That's why you said we had a hard nut to crack. 'Nut' is the solution!"

Lukas glanced over at the Marquis de LaSalle, whose lips had narrowed into a thin white line. The taunting look was gone from his face. Apparently, Giovanni had hit the mark.

"This is a pinecone from a cembra pine," Giovanni explained, cheerfully pointing to the stone decoration. "It's often used on tombs as a symbol of resurrection, and it's also known as a cembra nut! So, let's see . . ." He felt around on the pinecone, and then rotated it cautiously. It made a grinding sound.

"It twists off!" Gwendolyn exclaimed in surprise.

And indeed, there was a screw at the bottom of the pinecone, allowing it to be rotated out. Gingerly, Giovanni reached beneath it. "There's a hollow underneath," he murmured. "And there's something inside, I can feel it." He fumbled around a little more before pulling out a golden handle wrapped in silvery threads. "Help me, this thing is damned long!"

Paulus, who was nearly two heads taller than Giovanni, took the handle and pulled on it. An ornate golden sheath came into view, with a long sword inside it.

"The imperial sword!" Lukas exclaimed. "We actually found it!"

It wasn't long before the holy weapon lay before them in all its glory. The golden sheath was adorned with likenesses of past leaders; blue enamel glinted here and there between them. The friends stared in awe at the most valuable of all the Imperial Regalia.

"When I think about how many German emperors have been crowned with this sword," Paulus murmured, "it almost makes me feel like one myself." He leaned over to pick it up, but Gwendolyn beat him to it, snatching up the sword and drawing it from the sheath to hold it up in the moonlight.

"Kneel before Gwendolyn, the redheaded queen of Wales!" she cried. "Well? How do I look?"

"We don't have time for these games," Lukas grumbled. "My sister is out there somewhere with a golem!"

"You're right," Paulus admitted. "I'm sorry. I can't help it. I'm the son of a weaponsmith, so I've always had a weakness for swords. Hey!" he shouted, because Gwendolyn had nearly thrown the weapon down onto his feet. "Are you crazy?" he barked at her. "Do you have any idea what this sword is worth?"

"I know exactly how much it's worth," Gwendolyn replied in a tone that was completely serious—and furious. "Nothing! A traveling peddler might give you a few guilders for it, that's all!"

"It's not worth anything?" Giovanni stared at her, baffled. "What makes you think that?"

"It's obvious, you idiots. This sword is nothing more than a cheap fake!"

They all fell silent for a moment, and then Lukas bent down and picked up the sword. Two of the blue enamel plates had fallen off and broken. "Gwendolyn is right," he said, amazed. "This is just iron and colored glass." Lukas scratched the sheath with his fingernail, and flakes of gold paint peeled away. "The whole sword is nothing but a cheap bauble. Now we know why Polonius didn't take it with him." He turned to look at Gwendolyn. "How did you know?"

Her eyes glinted with fury. "I'm a thief, have you forgotten? I've seen many such fakes in my life. We thieves have to be able to distinguish real jewelry from those fake glass-and-iron circlets that ladies drape themselves with. This fake isn't even very well made." She stamped her foot. "Damn it! The only reason I went along on this adventure was because I thought I would end up earning enough for Jussi and me. My brother needs a good home, where people will take care of him. Am I supposed to pay for that with this . . . this toy?" Tears shone in her eyes.

A derisive laugh suddenly rang out. Lukas turned around and saw that it had come from the marquis. "Well, you clever little scamps," LaSalle smirked. "Didn't I say you were in for a surprise?" He began laughing like a maniac. "It's a game! An evil game, and you've all lost!"

"Do you know what this means?" Giovanni whispered to Lukas. "If this sword is a counterfeit, then the scepter and crown probably are as well. It was a trick this whole time."

"To be honest, the scepter did feel surprisingly light to me when I had it in my hand," Lukas mused. "And none of us looked closely at the crown except for Zoltan, who was a fine soldier, but no goldsmith."

"Actually, I looked at the crown for a very brief moment yesterday when Zoltan was away," Jerome confessed. "He left the chest open for a minute or two when the third message came in. I swear, I only put it on for a few seconds. Some of the gold flaked off. I thought I'd broken it, so I put it back as fast as I could."

Paulus stared at him in outrage. "And you're only telling us this now, you French charlatan?"

"If you'd let me look at it just once, I would have noticed that it wasn't real," Gwendolyn chided them. "But no, I'm just an honorless thief that nobody trusts."

"Stop fighting already!" Lukas ordered. "That doesn't help anything. Think about what all of this can possibly mean." He shook his head. The longer this went on, the less he understood what was happening. First, it turned out that Matthias was the mysterious messenger who had led them to the Imperial Regalia. Now they had discovered none of the three pieces of Regalia were even real. What was the purpose of the whole charade?

"Why go to all the trouble with hiding places and counterfeit Regalia?" Lukas wondered out loud. "None of this makes any sense."

"Hm, the messages, the treasure hunt, the battles . . . if you ask me, someone was trying to distract us," Paulus mused. "Someone who wanted to make sure we didn't get in the way of his real plan. And I think I know who that someone was."

"Schönborn!" Lukas balled his fists, feeling the color drain from his face. "You think the inquisitor is behind all this?"

Giovanni nodded. "Schönborn probably orchestrated it all just to lure Elsa to Prague." He scowled. "And he succeeded. Because of this supposed Imperial Regalia, we followed him out here blindly, like mice following a cat."

"But what exactly is his plan?" Lukas asked.

"Whatever it is, Polonius probably used the golem to bring your sister to him." Giovanni muttered a curse in Italian. "I knew there was something fishy about those messages. How could we be so stupid? Schönborn led us all around on a merry chase, even Zoltan and Senno!"

Lukas ran over and grabbed the marquis, who was still laughing. "Where did Polonius bring my sister? Where is Schönborn? Tell us, or I'll make you pay!"

LaSalle's laughter died away. He seemed very tired. He had obviously lost a great deal of blood. "I don't know, I swear," he insisted. "He never told us. That was his big secret. But I have a guess."

"Which is what?" Giovanni asked.

"I'll make you all a deal. You let me live, and I'll tell you. Do I have your word?"

They were silent for a while, but finally they all nodded in agreement.

"Enough blood has been spilled already," Lukas said with a shrug. "Your death won't bring back Zoltan and the other Musketeers." He raised his hand. "All right, I swear. If you talk, I'll bind your wounds, and we won't harm another hair on your head."

"As much fun as it would be with that wig of yours," Paulus grumbled.

The marquis scowled at him, but then he straightened up and began to speak in a low voice. "The master frequently mentioned White Mountain to me. I saw him travel up there on occasion. Not many people seek out that sinister place!"

"White Mountain?" Jerome asked. "I've heard that name somewhere."

Lukas nodded. "Yes, you have," he said quietly, shivering—and not only from the cold wind howling around the gravestones.

The circle is closing, he thought.

"White Mountain isn't far from Prague," Lukas went on in a shaky voice. "The first major battle of this eternal war was fought there nearly fifteen years ago." He hesitated and then added, "That's where my parents met."

After they had finished bandaging the marquis and tying him up, Lukas explained how he and Elsa had stumbled upon a dark secret at the cloister library—and that his sister had seen visions of the Battle of White Mountain.

"The *Grimorium* must have been hidden there for a long time," he said. "It conjured horrible images into Elsa's head, battle scenes with many dead men. Our mother was in the vision, fleeing from the frozen ones. My father stood in their way and saved my mother. After that, the book came into my family's possession, and Schönborn has been looking for it ever since."

"And now the book is returning to that sinister place." Jerome shuddered. "*Mon dieu!* Cemeteries aren't especially nice destinations, but old battlefields? I hate to think of all the things that might still be lying around there."

"There must be a reason why Waldemar von Schönborn has chosen that particular place," Giovanni said thoughtfully. "The inquisitor lured us here to Prague so that he could get his hands on Elsa—that much is clear. He wants her and the book, because she and the *Grimorium* are a unit. But what is he doing up on White Mountain?"

"The wigged hobgoblin mentioned Schönborn going up to the mountain regularly," Paulus noted. "He's obviously making preparations of some kind there."

Lukas pondered, gazing up at the sky. The fog had completely cleared by then, and the stars overhead glittered like diamonds. He wondered if Elsa was looking up at them as well. Or was she unconscious . . . or perhaps even dead? As children, they'd often sat at the top of the Lohenfels keep and stared up at the firmament. When their father was off at war, they'd imagined he was seeing the same stars at that very moment. Then the distance between them hadn't seemed quite as drastic.

The stars . . .

Lukas gave a start. He thought back to Rabbi Bushevi's words. And then to what Matthias had said.

The fog will lift soon . . . then nothing will be standing in the master's way . . .

"The stars!" Lukas cried. "It must have something to do with the stars! The rabbi said something about an ominous night, remember?" He knitted his brow. "What did he say again? Mars is in Leo, or something?"

"Astrologers and fortune tellers always associate Mars with war and destruction," Giovanni replied with a dark look on his face. "Not a good sign."

"Wait a minute," Jerome broke in. "You mean that now the fog has lifted, Schönborn is doing some kind of horrible ritual underneath these stars?"

Giovanni nodded. "And Elsa must play an important role in that ritual."

"A sacrifice!" Lukas gasped. "My God!" He grabbed his rapier. "Time's wasting. Hurry, we need to go!"

He looked over at Gwendolyn, who was standing uncertainly beside the fake, dented iron sword. He assumed this was good-bye, and Lukas was annoyed at himself for having such a hard time with it. He still felt almost magically drawn to the red-haired girl. "I suppose you're staying here," he said haltingly. "There aren't any more treasures to retrieve, and I can't promise you a reward. The only prize I'm after now is my sister's life. So . . ."

"Why, don't you want me around?" Gwendolyn interrupted him gruffly.

"No, that's not it, it's just . . ."

"Then stop talking such nonsense." She picked up her bow and checked the string. "A girl's been kidnapped. You think I plan on sitting around in the cemetery, twiddling my thumbs? We women have to stick together." She grinned. "Besides, none of you have any idea where White Mountain is, so I will have to help you out of a bind yet again."

Paulus rolled his eyes. "If she were a boy, I'd have strangled her by now," he whispered.

"And if you were a real man, I'd have peppered your boastful ass with arrows by now," Gwendolyn said, smiling. "But I don't shoot at children." Her expression turned serious. "Now, let's get going before it's too late."

XXIV

They had no time to give Zoltan and the other Black Musketeers a proper burial, so they simply carried their bodies over to the cemetery wall and laid them beneath an old willow tree, whose branches hung down like a protective tent. One last time, the friends bowed to the legendary commander of the Black Musketeers before starting off to look for Elsa.

As they hurried past the rows of gravestones toward the cemetery gate, Lukas's thoughts turned back to the friendly giant, Bernhard—and especially to Jurek. Lukas felt terrible for having falsely suspected Jurek for so long. Yes, the one-eyed knife thrower had been rude, often vicious, toward him. Perhaps he'd even hated Lukas. But he'd been no traitor.

The moon had traveled farther in the clear sky, and Lukas guessed it was already after midnight. Elsa had been kidnapped hours ago. Time was running out.

They ran as fast as they could through the deserted-seeming Jewish quarter, and soon arrived at one of the gates in the wall. Gwendolyn exchanged a few words with the watchmen, who then let them pass without delay.

"I told them to go check the cemetery," she said quietly. "The guards will tell Rabbi Bushevi as well." Grinning wickedly, she added, "And the wigged fellow we've left tied up there will have to explain what he's doing among all those dead men."

They smiled at her and continued on.

"Say," Giovanni asked as he strode alongside Lukas through the dark, empty Prague alleys, "was it true, what Gwendolyn said earlier? Can you really do magic? You never told us that."

Lukas sighed quietly. He'd been afraid this conversation was coming. "To be honest, I don't know myself," he replied. "I've only managed it three times so far, and never until we came to Prague. I healed my own wounds, then Gwendolyn's fatal injuries, and I managed to protect myself and Elsa from that poisonous cloud in Polonius's lab. I don't know why it worked or how I did it. I tried it again a little while ago, and nothing happened."

"And you didn't use any spells or books or magical hand gestures, like Elsa does?" Giovanni asked.

Lukas shook his head. "Elsa once said that all these words and gestures and talismans are just helpful tools, they're not strictly necessary. Remember how she brought us to Prague? There were those cute little wooden figures of the castle, the cathedral, and the bridge, but Elsa said she didn't actually need them—the power came from inside her. The objects just helped her awaken it."

"Well, then, you just need to awaken the power inside you, too," Giovanni replied.

Lukas let out a mirthless chuckle. "If only it were that easy. My insides are pretty mixed up at the moment."

"All right, then, we'll have to rely entirely on our weapons," Giovanni said decisively. "It wouldn't be the first time. I just hope they're enough against dark sorcery."

Lukas recalled the blessing the rabbi had given them not long ago— the word *"gevurah,"* which stood for strength and victory. Both of those seemed hopelessly optimistic to him at the moment. But no matter how dire the situation seemed, he couldn't leave his sister in the lurch. Not even now, when the book was clearly drawing her to the dark side, turning her into an evil sorceress.

Lukas had lost Elsa to Schönborn once already. That time, it had taken him over a year to find her again and rescue her from Schönborn's clutches. The inquisitor was probably stronger than ever now, and he wasn't alone. He had Polonius at his side, that alchemist who could create hybrid creatures, and he had a real, live golem.

Plus, I still don't know if I can really do magic, Lukas thought. *And if so, how?*

Staying away from the main roads, Gwendolyn led the friends along the Vltava toward the south. They came to a decrepit suburb full of shady-looking drinking holes and shabby inns; the mud in the alleys was an inch thick. From time to time, sinister-seeming figures approached them, but then quickly retreated at the sight of the boys' rapiers and Gwendolyn's bow.

They found a fishing boat bobbing beside a putrid pier, and used it to cross to the other side of the Vltava. Now they had left the city behind; meadows, farms, and barley fields stretched out before them. Out here, the moon and the countless stars shone so brightly that they could see their way fairly well.

A cool breeze wafted across the river. Shivering, Lukas glanced around. On the other side of a forested valley, a bare hill rose up from the horizon, dark and threatening. A chill ran down Lukas's spine, for reasons he couldn't quite explain.

"White Mountain," Gwendolyn announced. "All around us here," she said with an expansive gesture at the shadowy meadows, "people fought and died during that first great battle of the war. People have avoided this area ever since, claiming that it's haunted. Especially up on the hill."

"Haunted?" Halfway out of the boat, Jerome hesitated. "You all know I'm not afraid of any fight, not even with those frozen ones. But ghosts?"

"Oh, don't be like that," Paulus muttered. "This certainly isn't the first battlefield we've ever seen. And that fight was years and years ago."

"The people of Prague say that the ground on White Mountain was completely soaked with blood," Gwendolyn continued. "Thousands of their countrymen lost their lives." She gestured up at the hill. "The Bohemian rebels barricaded themselves up there. The hill was considered impossible to take, but then a monk showed the Kaiser's army a portrait of the Virgin Mary, claiming the Bohemians had defiled and destroyed it. After that, there was no stopping them. The imperial troops stormed the hill, shouting 'Santa Maria' all the way. It was a terrible slaughter."

"One that continues even today," Lukas murmured. "And it all started here. Schönborn truly couldn't have chosen a better location for his ritual."

"Well, then, let's stop him before it's too late," Giovanni said, buckling his rapier on and jumping from the boat to the shore. "We managed to outwit Schönborn once before. Why shouldn't we succeed a second time?"

The others followed him in silence.

The meadow they were crossing now was swampy; Lukas's feet kept sinking deep into the bog. As they stepped, the wet ground made gurgling noises as if laughing at them. It wasn't long before Lukas's boots were soaked through and he was struggling to walk. The others were having trouble as well. It felt like something was grabbing at their feet. And there was an eerie howling sound—distant at first, but growing closer.

"What is that?" Paulus asked. "Wolves?"

"This close to the city?" Giovanni shrugged. "I don't think so."

"Hey, look!" Jerome exclaimed. "There's a light! Something's moving through the meadow."

Sure enough, a handful of tiny, fiery balls were flitting across the field. Sometimes they moved lightning-fast, sometimes more slowly. They came closer, but then suddenly shot away again, like curious little animals.

"What are those things?" Paulus grunted. "They're far too big to be glowworms." He stomped toward one of the balls to get a closer look.

"Don't!" Lukas screeched.

But it was already too late. Paulus sank down into the meadow, which had given way to brown, peaty-smelling marsh. Within seconds, he was up to his hips in it. "Damn it!" Paulus shouted. "There's something pulling and tugging on my feet." He thrashed wildly about, and then finally pulled a rusty sword out of the muck. Paulus threw the sword as far away from himself as he could, his face white as chalk. "By my soul!" he whispered. "I could swear there was a skeleton hand on my leg just now. Is that possible?"

Lukas raked his hands through his hair. What was this place, and what horrible spirits were haunting them?

"Here, take this!" Gwendolyn called. She tossed Paulus a rope while the boys stood frozen in shock.

"What in the Devil's name? There *are* hands grabbing at me!" Paulus gasped, clinging to the rope. "I can feel them. Well, come on, you lazy fools, pull!"

They all grasped the rope and tried to drag the heavy Paulus out of the moor. It felt like they were battling some invisible force living deep within the bog that refused to release its prey.

"Harder!" Jerome shrieked. "He's already sunk to his chest!"

They pulled and yanked the rope for all they were worth, and finally Paulus slid out of the bog with a wet, smacking sound. He crawled as quickly as he could to a halfway-dry patch of grass, where he lay, exhausted. He was covered in black mire from head to toe.

"Let's not do that again," he panted. "What in God's name was that?"

"I think we may have been seeing will-o'-the-wisps," Giovanni replied. "The spirits of those who died here in the swamp. It's said that they like to lure the living down into the bog. Most of them are people who died violent deaths."

"Thousands of people died violent deaths around here, so I'm sure there's plenty happening in these swamps." Gwendolyn furrowed her brow. "Strange that I've never heard of will-o'-the-wisps around here. Maybe they have something to do with the ominous stars tonight."

Paulus shuddered violently. "I felt slimy hands dragging me down. And then that rusty sword! Let's leave here as soon as possible. I promise I'll be good and stay behind our leader Gwendolyn from now on."

"Our leader Gwendolyn!" She winked at Paulus. "Those words from your mouth, fat man? I never thought I'd see the day!"

"I swear, if you call me fat one more time, I'll push you into the moor," Paulus said. "Ghosts or no ghosts."

"Stop fighting," Lukas warned. "We need to focus on finding Elsa. If the marquis is right, she and Schönborn must be somewhere nearby."

If not, I've probably lost my sister once again, he added to himself.

Then he trudged after Gwendolyn.

They stuck to drier patches of meadow. Gwendolyn took the lead again, hopping from one patch of grass to the next. Occasionally she turned around, backtracking and then pointing the others in a different direction.

Lukas couldn't figure out how Gwendolyn managed to orient herself so well in the darkness, but her family's sobriquet of "Falcon Eye" had obviously come from somewhere, as she'd demonstrated at the Prague Castle wall.

They were finding more rusted weapons and armor now. Rotten wood, likely from old wagon wheels, lances, and arrows, gave off an eerie green glow.

Once, the point of Lukas's boot caught on a broken rapier, and he fell on his face. Later, he passed a helmet with some sort of rotten swamp grass growing out of it. Bones were scattered here and there, many with scraps of clothing still clinging to them. A skull grinned at him from a rock, almost as though someone had placed it there as a landmark. Lukas couldn't help thinking of the skulls placed along the Vltava Bridge as a reminder of the Bohemian uprising.

"*Merde,* we've been wandering around this battlefield for an eternity," Jerome grumbled. "Where can Schönborn be? How are we supposed to find him here in the darkness? Maybe the marquis was lying to us before and sent us on a wild-goose chase."

Lukas shook his head. "I doubt he was lying. Anyway, I sense that Elsa is somewhere nearby. This place is practically made for dark magic."

"Best if we climb the hill so we can get a better view," Gwendolyn suggested. "It's light enough out tonight."

After rounding several additional swamp fields, they finally reached the foot of the hill. White Mountain didn't strike Lukas as particularly tall, but it was the highest elevation in the area. Blackberry bushes and low shrubs covered the ground like weeds. As they trudged up the hill, Lukas kept getting caught on thorns. Once again, it felt like something was trying to prevent their progress.

All of a sudden, fog rolled in again, as though out of nowhere, billowing white just around knee height. Then it changed, drifting back and forth, taking on the forms of human beings. More and more of them were appearing around them now! Lukas saw soldiers fighting to the death, and the outlines of bodies with spears, arrows, and swords sticking out of them. A man in ghostly white, wrapped in a torn leather doublet, came straight at Lukas. The specter's eyes were wide with fear, his hands outstretched; a large, bloody wound gaped in his side. Lukas stepped back in horror, but the man followed him, staggering toward Lukas and . . .

. . . passed right through him.

A cold chill, like a draft of wintry air, was all Lukas felt. Then the man disappeared.

The Battle of White Mountain! Lukas thought. *It's happening again! With the ghosts of the soldiers who died in it!*

Fear ate at him now, making him hasten up the mountain faster and faster, until he was completely out of breath. Horrible crying and shrieking sounds echoed all around, and an entire army seemed to be climbing the hill behind him. Lukas grew increasingly afraid—the ghost soldiers would soon catch up to them. He could already feel their cold breath on his neck.

Lukas hurried onward. Now the fog was so thick that he couldn't see any of his friends. The tendrils of mist before him came together to form a cannon, and then a blast rang out. The ground seemed to burst beneath his feet, and Lukas somersaulted out of the way.

None of this is real! he thought. *Please, God, let this not be real!*

Men waving standards hurried past him down the hill to meet the enemy soldiers. The sounds of battle rang out: thundering cannon fire, shouted orders, screams of mortal agony. Another shout joined theirs now, growing louder and louder.

"Lukas! Hey, Lukas! Do you hear me?"

Someone shook him, and the ghostly figures around him disappeared as quickly as they had come. Lukas found himself staring at Jerome's face.

"Everything all right with you?" his friend asked him.

Lukas shook himself as though waking up from a nightmare. "The soldiers, the b-battle . . ." he stammered.

"What are you talking about?" Jerome gave him a light slap on the cheek. "There are no soldiers here. Only bones and rusted weapons."

Lukas glanced around, blinking in confusion. He was near the crest of the hill, which was bathed in moonlight. Fog swirled around beneath them, but the view was clear up here at the top. There were no ghost soldiers, no cannons, no battle cries. The only sound was the howling wind.

"I guess something clouded my mind, as they say," Lukas replied in a flat voice. "Thanks, Jerome. If you hadn't been there, I probably would have gone mad."

Jerome grinned. "You're not the only one being haunted. Giovanni saw a ghost, too—he sprinted away from it like a rabbit. But Paulus caught up to him and calmed him down." He glanced up at the hilltop. "The others are waiting up there."

"To think that you were the one most afraid of ghosts earlier," Lukas remarked, marveling. "And now I'm the one seeing them!"

Jerome shrugged. "Giovanni says I must lack imagination. None of us has ever been as interested in books as he is. Apparently, your imaginations run away with you faster."

Lukas had to laugh. "True. But if I'm seeing ghosts, then I wonder what Elsa . . ." He stopped short. "Come on, let's go," he said, striding off quickly. "Hopefully, from up there we can see where Schönborn's brought Elsa."

They reached the summit a minute or two later. Even though it was summer, the wind up here was unnaturally cold, and it howled so loudly that the friends could barely hear each other.

"Well, Schönborn isn't up here, anyway." Giovanni gestured around the bare mountaintop, looking disappointed. "Damn it! Maybe the marquis *was* lying to us."

Lukas glanced around. The moonlight was bright enough that he could at least make out some of the surrounding area. Below them lay the meadows and bogs; farther on, the dark Vltava River snaked along through the landscape, and then the city lights gleamed on the other side of that. To the north, the hill ended at a small wooded area surrounded by a wall.

Lukas squinted in that direction, blinking. "There's a building over there, on the other side of the wall," he said. "It looks like a church or a chapel."

"That's the Church of Our Lady Victorious, which stands in memory of all those who died," Gwendolyn explained. "The remains of the fallen are buried there. My father took me there a few years ago and told me all about the battle."

Jerome shuddered. "The bones lying around here are more than enough for me."

"Well, at least they stay lying around for you, instead of walking around like they do for me and Lukas," Giovanni countered. "So, what's that over there?" he asked, gesturing into the woods.

Lukas turned to look in the direction Giovanni was pointing. There was a clearing in the forest, with a large building in the center. It had a strange shape, but there wasn't enough light to see more specifically.

Gwendolyn furrowed her brow. "As far as I know, it's Castle Hvězda. It's a summer palace that's been here for a fairly long time. Father and I walked around in that overgrown park there, looking for a deer. The lodge is . . ." She broke off.

"What?" Lukas asked.

"I just remembered what 'hvězda' means," Gwendolyn replied in a shaky voice. "If you look more closely, you'll be able to figure it out for yourself."

Lukas squinted and leaned forward, but all he saw was a black shadow. Gwendolyn simply had better eyes. Frustrated, he asked, "What does it mean?"

"*Hvězda* means 'star.' The lodge down there is shaped like a six-pointed star, like a hexagram."

Giovanni groaned. "A symbol used in invoking demons! I'll bet you all anything that Schönborn and Elsa are somewhere down in that accursed palace. Hopefully it isn't too late!"

XXV

The friends ran down the hill toward the woods as fast as their legs could carry them. Lukas occasionally got snagged on the blackberry bushes, but at least no more ghost soldiers appeared. Here on the north side of the hill, a cold, wet breeze had blown the fog away. The closer they came to the woods, the more clearly they could see the outline of the palace towering behind the low trees. It really was shaped like a six-pointed star.

Lukas regarded the symbol more closely. It looked familiar. It was made up of two triangles—one upright, one upside down. There were smaller symbols inside it, but Lukas couldn't make sense of them.

"We've seen this star before," Lukas told Giovanni, panting. "At the synagogue, in the Jewish quarter. Remember?"

"The Star of David," Giovanni replied. "Also called the Seal of Solomon. It's an important symbol of Judaism, but alchemists use it a lot, too, and so do sorcerers when performing rituals."

"A giant hexagram." Lukas shook his head. "Schönborn couldn't have picked a better place for an invocation."

They reached the foot of White Mountain. The woods lay before them, surrounded by a crumbling wall about as tall as Lukas. A few paces away, there was a rusty iron gate hanging crooked on its hinges. There were hexagrams to either side of it as well.

"These stars on the gate weren't there when I came here with my father," Gwendolyn said thoughtfully. "They must be new."

"During my time as a novice monk, I learned a few things about hexagrams," Giovanni said, pointing to the symbol. The gate squeaked quietly on its hinges. "The two triangles represent unifying the opposites in life: fire and water, man and God, good and evil, black and white."

"Black magic and white magic!" Lukas cried. "My mother was a white witch, and Schönborn is a black magician."

Giovanni nodded contemplatively. "I suppose the hexagram helps that bastard unify the two powers. But what the hell would these letters mean?"

"L-I-L-I-T-H," Jerome read aloud, clockwise. "Hm, sounds like a girl's name."

"A girl you don't know?" Paulus teased. "I didn't think there were any of those left."

"That's a terrible thing to name a girl," Gwendolyn said.

"Why?" Lukas asked.

"Lilith is the mother of all witches, a winged demon who eats children. In my country, we call her the Devil's grandmother."

"Wonderful." Jerome gripped his forehead. "We've found the Devil family's summer residence."

"The name is probably part of some sinister spell," Lukas murmured.

"There's only one way to find out." Paulus pushed the rusty gate open. "Come on, before it's too late."

They all went into the dark forest, which they soon discovered was actually an overgrown park, just as Gwendolyn had claimed. A boulevard flanked by scrubby, stunted oaks led directly north, to the center of the property. They crossed a stone bridge completely carpeted in moss. Black water gurgled beneath it. Statues of old, long-forgotten warriors lined the path, crumbling and covered with ivy.

After a while, Lukas came to a rotting, collapsed arbor, nearly unrecognizable beneath the ferns and other foliage. He tried to picture how beautiful the park must have been once. Dukes, counts, and baronesses had probably hunted and feasted out here. Lukas could practically see the noble lords and ladies galloping along the paths and over the bridges on white stallions, hunting for foxes, does, and bucks. But nature had reclaimed the park in the meantime; the woods were gloomy and impenetrable. Branches and twigs had pushed their way in front of the moon, leaving everything underneath as dark as a grave.

Now Lukas became aware of the noises around him. First only whispering and rustling, then a soft growling sound, the screech of a tawny owl, and the bellowing of a distant buck. Smaller paths and deer passes branched off from the main road. The onetime boulevard was so overgrown with grass and bushes that the friends kept losing their way.

"Jesus, Mary, and Joseph, you can't even see your hand in front of your face here," Paulus complained. "Someone light a couple of those torches the rabbi gave us."

"You might as well wave a flag and shout, 'Here I am,'" Gwendolyn retorted. "Trust me, we're safer in the dark."

"I keep running into trees every ten seconds," Paulus grumbled.

"I suggest we use just one torch," Lukas said to end the argument. "That ought to be enough." He pulled out the tinderbox, and soon the warm glow of a single pine-pitch torch was spreading around them.

They could at least see a few feet in every direction. The eyes of small wild animals gleamed around the edges of the path.

"That's more like it," Paulus declared. "All right, then, let's—"

"Shhh!" Giovanni frantically waved his hand. "Do you hear that?"

There were whistling and hissing noises in the air, and they sounded like they were approaching rapidly. A fluttering sound accompanied them, like the wings of a hundred birds.

"The torch!" Gwendolyn shrieked. "Put out the torch!"

Just as Lukas dropped the torch, a black, hissing cloud descended upon the group. Lukas felt tiny teeth on his face, and leathery wings brushed his cheeks.

"*Merde,* it's those disgusting bat-cats!" Jerome cried. "A whole swarm of them!"

Lukas flailed and boxed wildly in every direction. He managed to grab hold of a few of the beasts and throw them to the ground, but new ones took their places immediately—all cheeping, hissing, and biting. It felt like a thousand needle pricks.

"Put the damn torch out already!" Gwendolyn shouted. "The light is drawing them!"

Indeed, the torch on the ground was still lit. Lukas stomped it out, and immediately the hissing grew quieter. Now Lukas heard the hum of Gwendolyn's bowstring over the infernal noise as she fired off arrows, nearly one a second. Something let out a pitiful squeak, and then every-thing was finally still again. For a long moment, the only sound Lukas heard was his friends' heavy breathing.

"If anyone had any doubts about Polonius being somewhere nearby, I presume they've been put to rest," Giovanni panted. He'd run dozens of the bat-cats through with his blade, as had Paulus and Jerome, but most of the beasts had been brought down by Gwendolyn's arrows. All around them, the forest floor was covered with the winged creatures, some of which were still in their death throes, stretching toward their feet, trying to bite them. Lukas and the others all had bite marks on their faces and arms, but luckily, they were mostly just minor scratches.

"Very likely that Polonius and Schönborn know someone's coming now," Lukas remarked. "The alchemist probably trained the beasts to let him know. We'd better hurry."

They hastened onward through the woods, without a torch this time. Though the path was completely overgrown here, Gwendolyn still had no trouble finding her way, but the others kept bumping into low-hanging branches and tripping over tree stumps. Lukas felt like he was stumbling more than he was walking. Twigs brushed his face, startling him into thinking that those wretched bat-cats had returned.

Lukas's thoughts revolved around Elsa, who was still in the clutches of that hateful alchemist. What in God's name were Polonius and Schönborn plotting to do with his sister?

At the same time, he recalled what his friends said Elsa had managed to do to the Prague guards with a single spell. How had Giovanni put it?

Your sister really is a monster.

Had the book actually made Elsa into a monster, a daughter of Lilith?

The woods abruptly ended, and they stepped into a clearing with a small pond that merged into a canal on either side. The pale moonlight reflected in the water.

Castle Hvězda loomed somberly behind it.

It wasn't a particularly big castle; it had no towers or any of the usual adornments.

From up close, Lukas could see that the building really was shaped like a six-pointed star. It seemed dilapidated. Most of the tiles on the tentlike roof had been blown off, and black holes stared back at Lukas where the windows had once been.

Soft, almost imperceptible singing floated out from the interior.

"The invocation," Lukas whispered. "It's already started." He hurried toward the pond, but Jerome called him back.

"Hey, *un instant!* Surely we're not going to swim in that? God knows what other types of creatures Polonius has created. Pike the size of a ship? Slimy white frogs?" Jerome grimaced. "I wouldn't put anything past those alchemists."

"We don't have to swim," Gwendolyn replied. "There's a bridge over there."

Sure enough, a bridge spanned the narrowest part of the pond, though most of its stone railing had collapsed.

"Oh, great," Jerome groaned. "Is that even going to support you, Paulus?"

"Shut your mouth, or I'll toss you to your white frogs." Paulus strode ahead, and the others followed him.

The bridge didn't exactly inspire their confidence up close, either. Several of the wooden pillars holding it up had rotted through, and there were holes the size of Lukas's head in the planks.

"Don't think about it, just go," Giovanni told them. "The faster we cross, the better."

Just as he was about to step onto the bridge, a large shadow appeared on the other side. The figure slowly approached, finally halting in the exact center of the bridge. A cloud had passed in front of the moon, so that the creature was hard to identify at first, but then a slight breeze picked up, clearing the sky again, and Lukas saw that it was a large buck.

A very, very large buck.

Its antlers were gigantic—it was a sixteen-pointer at least, Lukas thought. He'd only seen a buck like that once before, with his father, deep in Lohenfels Forest.

His father had lowered his crossbow in reverence, allowing the animal to run off unharmed. "The lord of the forest," he'd called the buck.

This buck had an imperial air about him, too. But then he abruptly turned his head in their direction, and Lukas's admiration gave way to sheer horror.

It had the head of an enormous wolf.

The creature opened its toothy maw and let out a loud howl. It was bound to one of the bridge pillars by a long, heavy chain.

"God in heaven!" Giovanni blurted out. "That's the howling we heard when we were at the top of White Mountain! This horned monster here must be keeping watch." He shook his head.

Jerome drew his rapier with a grim expression on his face. *"Alors,"* he said. "The way I see it, either we defeat this monster, or we have to swim. I prefer the monster." He stepped resolutely onto the bridge. Lukas, Paulus, and Giovanni moved in behind him, blades drawn, while Gwendolyn nocked an arrow.

The creature reared up on its hind legs, letting out another spine-chilling howl, and then galloped toward the friends. The chain appeared just long enough to reach the end of the bridge.

Gwendolyn's arrows hissed through the air, but the wolf-buck kept right on running, the sharp, daggerlike tips of its antlers pointed straight at them. Lukas ducked away at the last moment, but he got caught and slipped. He felt something behind him burst, and heard it tumble into the lake with a loud splash. He stumbled, grasped at empty air . . .

. . . and then fell in as well.

The water was warm and stank of rotting algae. Lukas flailed wildly, feeling his feet snag on something slippery. Terrible images of Jerome's giant monster fish and white frogs flashed through his mind. He opened his mouth to scream, but water rushed in and made him cough instead. His fear of the unknown horrors in the murky depths was so great that he couldn't think clearly. He paddled and thrashed around like a drowning man.

"Here, my hand! Take my hand!" It was Gwendolyn, bending over the crumbling railing and reaching for him. The battle with the wolf-buck raged on behind her; Lukas saw Jerome lunging into another attack. Gwendolyn stretched out her hand, and Lukas grabbed it in desperation—but at the same moment, the creature kicked out one of its hind legs and hit Gwendolyn in the back. She let out a short shriek before tumbling into the lukewarm sludge directly beside Lukas.

She clung to him, kicking frantically. Lukas could feel her body underneath her soaked doublet; their lips were only inches apart. A warm feeling flooded through Lukas, making him completely forget his fear of the nightmarish creatures potentially lurking below them.

The feeling lasted for only a second, and then Gwendolyn released him and started swimming toward the shore. He crawl-stroked after her. Together, hand in hand, they climbed out of the water. She nestled against him once more for a moment. "I thought that . . . that some huge, pale frog was under my doublet and . . ." She shook her head, breathing heavily, and made a face as though the mere thought of frogs was worse than hellfire and brimstone.

Lukas couldn't help grinning. For one brief moment, Gwendolyn hadn't been quite as self-assured and arrogant as usual. She'd been genuinely afraid, and he'd been her protector, the person she could hold on to.

"Hah," he said, "trust me, if there had been a frog under there, I would have—"

"Hey, lovebirds! Finished with your swim?" Paulus's voice put an end to their moment alone. Lukas looked up toward the bridge, where his three friends were standing. The dead wolf-buck lay between them. Its long red tongue lolled out of its mouth; its once-glistening eyes were lifeless.

"Jerome hit it right in the throat," Paulus told them, elbowing his friend in the side. "You know how it is—our pretty little Frenchman would rather go berserk than get pond scum in his perfect hair."

"One more word and I'll do it again, *mon ami*," Jerome shot back.

"Save it for the palace." Giovanni pointed to the building, which was now directly in front of them. The massive portal leading inside stood open a crack. Soft singing was still audible from within. "Everyone ready?" he asked.

The others nodded silently, grasping their weapons.

Then they entered the dark castle.

XXVI

The first thing Lukas noticed about the palace was the smell. It stank of sulfur, and of some other scents he couldn't identify. There was no light anywhere, and the windows were shuttered, so they were in absolute darkness. He could hear the quiet singing much more clearly now. It was more of a lament—a language he didn't know, sung in high, sorrowful tones.

Lukas's breath caught in his throat.

"Elsa!" he exclaimed, horrified. "That's Elsa!" He wanted to run toward the sound, but Giovanni held him back.

"We don't know if it really is Elsa," his friend said, trying to calm him down. "It could be a trap, or someone else entirely. In any case, we should be on our guard. And we can't do that if we just dash off blindly into the darkness." Giovanni turned to Gwendolyn. "Do you mind if we light a torch? Hopefully those accursed bat-cats can't fly through walls."

Gwendolyn responded with a reluctant nod, and Giovanni lit one of the torches they'd brought. The room they were standing in was triangular, with the entrance at the point. There was another door in the broad side, across from them.

"We're definitely at the bottom point of the Star Palace," Giovanni mused. He was silent for a moment, listening. "The singing is coming from closer to the center." He began walking to the door, toward the sound, but stopped in his tracks when Jerome let out an astonished cry.

"Hey, look over here!" Jerome pointed to the middle of the chamber, where a symbol was drawn on the floor in black.

Lukas craned his neck to look at it. A large *L* had been smeared hastily onto the stone floor in soot.

"An *L*, just like the hexagram on the garden gate." Giovanni scratched his chin. "If this castle has six corners, each one probably has one of these symbols. This has to be some dark ritual. On your guard, everyone."

They left the chamber, with Lukas hastening out in front. His fear for his sister's safety made him forget all caution. He knew they had to be alert, but he felt like storming on ahead alone. He turned down a dark hallway—and shrank away in alarm when, out of nowhere, a figure appeared across from him in the torchlight. The stranger jumped back as well. When Lukas glanced around the corner, the other person appeared again. Slowly, Lukas reached for his rapier . . .

. . . and the other person did the same thing.

Lukas let out a sigh of relief. "A mirror," he exclaimed. "I thought some new monster was coming out to fight us."

"Would have been an awfully small monster." Gwendolyn grinned, shaking the pond algae out from her red hair. Only then did Lukas realize that he, too, was shivering in his damp doublet. It was far colder inside these stone palace walls than outside in the park. It pained him that Gwendolyn was back to teasing him like he was a little boy, when he'd been her protector just moments ago.

"A hall of mirrors." Giovanni nodded. "I've heard of these. Supposedly counts and barons often have these in their summer palaces. I'll never understand how someone can spend money on such a thing when their own farmers are starving to death."

Lukas walked ahead with the torch, seeing his own frightened face staring back at him. The hallway branched off again and again, often leading around in a circle or coming to an abrupt end.

When Lukas glanced into the many mirrors, he realized how tired and weary he looked. He'd lost his hat somewhere up on White Mountain, and his wet, stringy hair hung into a strangely unfamiliar face—one that was older and more experienced, but also harder and colder. Lukas would be fifteen soon. Just two years ago, he'd been playing with his father in the forest. It felt like an eternity had passed since then.

You've become a fighter, he told himself. *Like Zoltan was.* He wasn't sure he liked this change in himself.

After a while, the friends got used to the mirrors. They felt their way through the labyrinth and finally came to a door. It led into another triangular room, with another symbol on the floor.

"An *I*," Giovanni murmured. "Just as we suspected, one letter in each field."

Lukas listened to the singing that was still emanating from the center of the palace. Suddenly, he wasn't quite so sure that it was Elsa's voice he was hearing. It sounded shriller, spookier, almost not of this world. "We need to keep going," he urged the others. The smell of sulfur was getting stronger now.

"Before we go face our enemies, I need to tell you all something," Gwendolyn announced in a somber voice. She touched the quiver at her side. "I've already shot a lot of arrows. I managed to collect a few in the park, but then that wolf-buck came along, and I fell into the water."

"How many do you have left?" Lukas asked.

Gwendolyn checked inside her quiver. "Three."

"Three arrows?" Giovanni stared at her, aghast. "Well, this is just getting better and better. A demonic ritual including a golem, a sorcerer who can't do magic, and now just three arrows." He let out a pained laugh. "But who ever said the Black Musketeers had it easy? There's no turning back now, anyway."

They returned to the hall of mirrors, which seemed to extend throughout the entire castle. Another room followed, with another symbol on the floor—an *L* again this time. The singing was very loud now, and the stench of sulfur was so strong that it nearly made Lukas gag. A huge portal with tall double-winged doors led into the center of the palace. It was standing slightly ajar, and Lukas thought he saw moonlight on the other side. There was a cool breeze blowing in.

"I think we're nearly there," he whispered. He gave the others one last, resolute look, and then nodded. "One for all and all for one."

"For Elsa," Paulus said quietly, drawing his schiavona from its sheath. "Let's go give that golem and all its henchmen a good, solid kick in the ass."

Cautiously, Lukas pushed against the doors, and they swung open without a sound. The room on the other side was large, with high ceilings—extremely high, in fact. Torches burned in holders on the walls, their flames waving back and forth in the wind. Lukas looked up and realized that there was no roof here at all—only a few old, rotten beams. The stars gleamed brightly above him; together with the torches, they bathed the room in an almost unearthly glow.

They had reached the center of the Star Palace.

Lukas glanced up ahead, and his heart leapt into his throat. Elsa was there, at the center of the room.

But she wasn't alone. Elsa was kneeling inside a hexagram drawn on the floor, rocking back and forth as though in a trance, with the *Grimorium* lying open in front of her. It really had been her singing all this time, and her song still sounded high and eerie, like a chorus from the underworld. She kept her eyes closed; her face was deathly pale.

"NABOR, ULEXIS," she murmured. "AD XANATAS AETERNITAS . . ."

Polonius stood beside her.

The alchemist looked just as he had at their last encounter near Prague Castle: gaunt and hunchbacked, with deep wrinkles and thinning gray hair. But now his frock was red rather than gray, and in the moonlight, it gleamed like blood.

What horrified Lukas the most, however, was the sight of Polonius's thin, gnarled hand resting affectionately on Elsa's shoulder, stroking it gently from time to time. It was a scene of intimate togetherness, and it made Lukas sick to his stomach. Both Polonius and Elsa were so caught up in what they were doing that they hadn't noticed the friends yet.

A wave of fury crashed over Lukas. All he could think about was Elsa. She was in danger! That accursed alchemist was plotting to do something with her. What, exactly, he couldn't say. It almost looked like he was planning to suck her power out of her like a giant, bloodthirsty spider. Lukas dropped his torch. He drew his dagger and stormed toward Polonius without waiting for his friends. Yelling, he thundered toward the hexagram . . .

. . . and bounced off.

He let out a yelp of surprise as he tumbled back, and gripped his bleeding forehead. He was so surprised that he didn't even feel pain. What had just happened?

Only then did Elsa's singing stop. Polonius's laughter rang out in its place, which only enraged Lukas even more. He got to his feet and ran toward the hexagram once more, but again he slammed into some kind of barrier.

He was about to throw himself at the invisible wall a third time when he felt Gwendolyn's hand on his shoulder, pulling him back.

"Don't!" she exclaimed. "You'll only end up with more bruises." She gazed straight into his eyes, speaking in a calming voice. "We can't step inside the hexagram, understand? Not like this. There's some sort of spell protecting it."

Lukas nodded, breathing heavily. The others had stepped up beside the hexagram as well, and now all of them stood there, weapons drawn, staring at the six-pointed star with Polonius and Elsa at its center. The hunchbacked alchemist was still chuckling. Elsa's eyes were open now. She looked in Lukas's direction, but it was as though she was staring right through him.

Unbearable pain shot through Lukas's heart. His sister had never looked at him that way. So cold and indifferent, not like a brother, not even like a human being. More like a thing.

Like an annoying obstacle, he thought. *Like a bug she wants to squash.*

Only now did Lukas have the opportunity to look more closely at the star on the floor. Here, too, he saw letters spelling out the name "Lilith." Three of the shapes also contained flickering candles, along with smoking pots emitting that nauseating sulfur stench. The other three had objects in them. Lukas gave a start. He knew those objects all too well.

The Imperial Regalia!

The scepter, the crown, and the sword.

Lukas knew immediately that these were the real Regalia, not the counterfeits that had been planted for them to find.

Polonius's laughter died abruptly. For a few moments, the hall was completely still; the only noise was the distant rushing of the wind.

"So, you've actually found your way here." The alchemist's voice was sharp and sinister. "Let me guess: that cringing little French sneak of a marquis let it slip, didn't he? And you defeated my guards in the park and in front of the palace, too. My compliments." He clapped sarcastically as he regarded them with his penetrating stare, particularly Lukas. "But you actually thought you could just march in here and kill me? *Me?*" Polonius shook his head as though disappointed in them. "You ought to know me better than that."

"I don't know you, Polonius, and I'm not interested in knowing you, either," Lukas retorted. "I only want my sister back. After that, I promise you, we'll leave you in peace. Regardless of what you're planning to do."

Lukas meant what he'd said. He honestly didn't care what Polonius was plotting. All he wanted was Elsa. His nagging, smart-mouthed, occasionally intolerable sister whom he loved more than anything.

"I'm afraid that's not going to happen." Polonius smiled coldly. "I need your sister. And besides, you do know me, Lukas."

"How would I know you?" Lukas asked, shrugging. "And I'm still not interested in knowing you."

"Ohh, but *yes*, Lukas. Yes, you *do* know me. And yes, you *are* interested in who I am." An insane grin flitted over the alchemist's face. "Just look more closely. *You . . . know . . . me!*"

Suddenly Polonius's voice sounded different, strangely familiar. At the same moment, he began to change. The hunched old man seemed to stretch out; his features transformed, and his entire body twitched and trembled. Polonius straightened up, and his frock tore in several places where it was now too small.

Then another man was standing in the center of the star.

"Schönborn," Lukas whispered. "I should have known!"

XXVII

The laughter ringing out now was only too familiar to Lukas. The inquisitor had hardly changed. At most, the pale-blond hair beneath his silk cardinal's cap had thinned out slightly, and his face had grown more angular, which made his aquiline nose stand out even more. Schönborn was tall and gaunt, much taller than Polonius had been. Only the eyes were the same. Lukas thought back to their first encounter at the White Tower. Polonius's eyes had seemed strange to him then. Now he knew why.

I should have recognized him by his eyes, Lukas thought. *Polonius is Schönborn.*

Elsa turned away and paged through the *Grimorium,* as though her brother wasn't worth thinking about any longer. Her lips moved silently as she read.

"Yes, I'm Polonius," the inquisitor told them from the center of the hexagram. "That old fool. We used to work so well together. His animal experiments were practically flawless—we were moving in an excellent direction—but he had scruples about experimenting on humans." Schönborn shook his head. "What a waste of talent. You saw for yourselves what my bear-man was capable of. A deadly beast, almost as perfect as my frozen ones."

Lukas thought back to the sad creature in the White Tower, the monster that had once been a person like himself. "You're the beast, not that poor creature," he spat contemptuously. "You killed Polonius so that you could take his form, didn't you?"

"Killed? It was more an act of mercy." Schönborn shrugged. "Polonius was ancient and useless anyway. The Kaiser was planning on throwing him out like a rabid cur because he wasn't making any progress on creating gold. Really, I was only doing the old man a favor," he said with an evil smile. "Besides, I had to keep you all from recognizing me."

"I liked him a good deal better as Polonius," Paulus growled. Like the others, he had stepped up beside Lukas. "Polonius was just an old wretch, but at least he was an old wretch who could be killed." Furiously, he kicked the invisible wall. There was a buzzing sound, almost like a bolt of lightning. Paulus cried out as he flew back several paces, where he lay on the floor, groaning.

"The spell wall is growing stronger!" Schönborn exclaimed. "Lilith's power is flowing through the room. Soon we shall achieve our goal."

"You orchestrated all of this, didn't you?" Giovanni piped up. "You brought us to Prague. You had Matthias bring us those messages, and you hid the fake Regalia around the city." He shook his head in disbelief. "Your friend the Marquis de LaSalle said something about a game. Is that what this is to you? Just a game?"

Waldemar von Schönborn's eyes glinted derisively. "All this effort, just for a game? You ought to know me better than that, clever boy."

"Don't you all understand?" Lukas exclaimed to his friends in despair. "We brought him Elsa! Without those damned Regalia objects as bait, she'd never have left Castle Lohenfels. All he ever wanted was her and the book!"

Gwendolyn furrowed her brow. "But then why didn't he just kidnap her from the castle?" she asked quietly. "If what he says is true, you'd never have been able to stop him. So why go to all this trouble?"

"I hate to agree with a girl," Jerome remarked, "but I'm afraid Gwendolyn has a point. Why do all of this?"

Lukas hesitated. His friends were right. He was missing something here. He glanced back at his little sister, who was still brooding over the *Grimorium*. Elsa lifted her head and smiled at him evilly. Her features were eerily similar to those of Schönborn, her father.

She's becoming more like him every day, Lukas thought sadly. *From one spell to the next . . .*

And then it hit him.

All at once, he understood the devilish plan Schönborn had been following. He recalled all the times Elsa had used her magic here in Prague. And how every spell, every moment spent with the *Grimorium*, had drawn her a little further to the dark side. Every time she'd cast a spell, she'd become a little more like her father.

"The spells!" he exclaimed loudly. "Schönborn just wanted Elsa to use magic! That's why he created all these obstacles and hiding places."

Giovanni shook his head in disbelief. "You mean that the only purpose to this whole game of hide-and-seek was to make Elsa spend more and more time with the *Grimorium*?"

"The more she uses it, the more spells she casts from it, the more she becomes like . . . ," Lukas replied. "Don't you see? The spells have changed her! Schönborn might have been able to kidnap Elsa from Castle Lohenfels, but she'd never have gone with him willingly. He needs her help, because the *Grimorium* has chosen her, not him. He needed her to use magic, to cast large, powerful, evil spells."

Lukas looked over at Schönborn, who remained silent, smiling thinly at Lukas's revelation. He thought back to Elsa's first spell in front of the marquis's palace, where she had made them all invisible. At Castle Prague, she'd used the book to kill the bear-man. Later, she'd slaughtered an entire unit of Prague guardsmen as though they were annoying insects. Her spells had become ever stronger, ever more horrible, and so had she. The book had continued changing her, until finally she'd followed her father, Schönborn, of her own free will.

The inquisitor's plan had worked perfectly.

And we were all just little pawns in his game, Lukas thought. *Zoltan, the Black Musketeers, even Senno.*

"As Polonius, I was always nearby, able to watch you and influence you." Schönborn laid his hand on Elsa's shoulder. "You were so kind as to bring me back the daughter I love above all else, and together, we are invincible!"

Desperately, Lukas turned his attention to his sister. Now he understood that he didn't need to save Elsa from Schönborn, nor from any frozen ones or golems. No, he had to protect her from her worst enemy.

Herself.

"Elsa, do you recognize me?" he pleaded. "It's me, your brother."

Elsa stared at him with eyes full of hate. "Of course I recognize you, you idiot," she sneered. Her voice was strangely distorted, deeper than before, full of contempt. "You're the big brother who always wanted to keep me small, the one who thought of me as just his annoying little sister who liked books and other nonsense. The brother who never believed I was capable of anything. Just like Mother. Yes, you two always got along wonderfully. You were so much *alike!*" She practically spat the last word out.

"Elsa, what are you talking about?" Lukas whispered.

"Haven't you ever wondered why Mother only speaks to you in your dreams?" Elsa asked. "Why she talks to you, but not to me? It's because she knows that I'm stronger than she is! My father promises that I'm going to be the most powerful sorceress in the world. Unlike Mother, who was just a useless herb lady who conjured lizards' tails back on and helped a couple of old fools get some porridge. Such a waste!" Elsa's voice grew louder and shriller as she spoke. Her eyes sparked with fury. "She had so much power, but she didn't use it," she went on. "Ever since the Battle of White Mountain, she had the *Grimorium Nocturnum*, the most powerful magic book humanity has ever seen! But she just kept it hidden away. She failed. All of you failed! But not me. *I'm* on the winning side now!"

"Elsa, think about what you're saying," Lukas begged. "That's not you. This black magician is putting ideas into your head."

"That black magician happens to be my father, in case you've forgotten. You never let me do magic because you were jealous. Thanks to him, I know how much power lies dormant within me."

Lukas shook his head. "That's nonsense. Don't you see that this monster is exploiting you for his purposes?" He feared he'd lost Elsa for good, and it made him feel nearly paralyzed. He cursed himself for not having seen the signs sooner. They'd driven Elsa straight into her father's arms.

Waldemar von Schönborn stroked his daughter's hair. The gesture might have seemed almost loving if it hadn't been for the sinister, calculating look on his face. "Good girl," he cooed. "Now, we shouldn't let these fools disturb us any longer. We have a ritual to finish, so let's continue the incantation."

Elsa nodded eagerly. Then she began singing again in her high voice.

"WALDO . . . IN SUPERIO . . . MADAGASTAN . . ."

"As long as we have to stand here watching you," Giovanni piped up in a loud voice, "at least tell us what it is you're planning."

"What I'm planning?" Schönborn raised an eyebrow. "Elsa and I are going to extend the war."

"Extend the war?" Jerome echoed, gaping at him. "But what do you get out of that? I figured you'd be doing a ritual to conjure yourselves a pile of gold. A couple of pretty girls, maybe—but war? That doesn't benefit anyone."

Schönborn laughed as Elsa went on singing. "You fool!" he said. "The war has plenty of benefits. Influence, money . . . it ensures that the strongest survive, while the others become slaves and subjects. It reorders the world to my advantage! I've invested plenty of ducats in Wallenstein's army, to make sure they will continue to rob and plunder." He shrugged. "There have been troublesome attempts to end the war recently. People are getting tired of it—even Wallenstein is dithering." He gestured to the three articles of Imperial Regalia. "With these powerful objects, we are weaving a dark spell that will keep the fires of war burning for many years, maybe even decades."

"You mean you're going to create an entire army of frozen ones?" Lukas breathed.

Schönborn grinned. "A fine thought! But Elsa and I are not powerful enough for that. Not yet," he added. "Besides, I need to improve my little darlings first. I must make them invincible, fire-resistant. But until then . . ." He shook his head. "We will only need one death spell to extend the war." He winked at the friends. "Aimed at the German Kaiser himself."

Lukas stared at him, thunderstruck. "The Kaiser? You're planning to murder the Kaiser?"

"The Kaiser is well guarded in Vienna," Schönborn explained. "No assassin can get anywhere near him. But thanks to this spell, he'll fall over dead in church tomorrow, right in the middle of morning Mass. Some will blame the Protestants, others the German princes, others the Swedes. The war will continue." He gestured up at the firmament, clearly visible through the open roof. The sky was already taking on a pinkish hue—dawn was approaching.

"The stars are in a unique position tonight," Schönborn continued. "Mars is in Leo! Everything points to death and destruction. When the Kaiser dies today, the astrologers will all moan and lament and prophesy a dark future. The war may well stretch out for decades. Plus, with these three genuine objects of Imperial Regalia, I can blackmail all of Europe.

Without them, there can be no coronation." He giggled. "Perhaps the French king would like to be emperor next, maybe the Russian czar? Or perhaps some sultan? It isn't important who rules, as long as he only rules under *me*."

"And you're using my sister for all these sinister plans of yours! Monster!" In his fury, Lukas was nearly ready to throw himself against the invisible wall again.

Then he heard a humming sound behind him.

Lukas glanced over his shoulder. It was Gwendolyn, loosing an arrow. But she wasn't shooting at Schönborn—she aimed it straight up into the air. The arrow hurtled into the sky until it could no longer be seen, and then finally plummeted back to earth, landing on the floor amid the runes of the hexagram without doing any damage.

"Wonderful," Giovanni sighed. "Now we only have two arrows. Our prospects are looking rosier all the time."

"I'm growing weary of your foolish attempts," Schönborn said in an arrogant tone, kicking the arrow into one corner of the six-pointed star. "I left you all alive for Elsa's sake, but now it's too late." He snapped his fingers. "Time for you to face your last opponent."

Something rumbled. Lukas glanced to his right, where a gigantic creature appeared in the large doorway. Though Lukas had never seen this colossus before, he still recognized it instantly.

It was the golem.

XXVIII

The thing stepping into the hall was absolutely massive. Lukas guessed that it was at least three paces tall. Its chest was broad like an ox; its arms and hands looked like they could smash entire walls into dust. The golem was naked and angular, like some sculptor's experiment gone horribly awry.

It really did appear to be made of clay. Its skin, brown and cracked, looked as hard as the thickest armor. Even so, its movements were anything but ponderous—it moved toward the friends with the grace of a well-trained fighter, shaking the ground with every step it took.

"Kill them!" Schönborn ordered from safe within the hexagram. "All of them!"

The golem raised its fist and sent it flying at Lukas, who jumped aside at the last moment. Immediately, the clay monster wound up for its next attack. This time, it hit the wall behind Lukas with a thundering crash. Lukas felt the wall tremble under the force of the impact; small stones and bits of plaster rained down from overhead, and a large crack appeared in the middle of the wall. The golem was obviously unimaginably strong.

Lukas's three friends hurried to his aid. Paulus threw himself at the golem with a loud yell, but the creature merely smacked him away, flicking the heavy, muscular boy aside like an annoying fly. Paulus flew through the air and smashed against the wall, and then finally landed in one corner of the room, where he remained, motionless.

"Oh, Lord, Paulus!" Lukas dashed over to his friend, knowing that he had to be severely injured from the blow, if not dead. Tears sprang to his eyes as he knelt before Paulus. "I'm . . . I . . . I'm so sorry . . . ," he stammered. "How—"

"Christ almighty, save the drivel for my funeral. We don't have time right now." Paulus sat up with a groan and reached for his schiavona again. His head was bleeding, and his left arm hung lifelessly against his side, but apparently not even a golem could break Paulus's thick skull.

He growled. "Nobody just throws Paulus through the air like that. Not even a damn golem." He got to his feet and went in for another attack.

Meanwhile, Giovanni and Jerome were dancing around the monster, dodging its powerful blows. The golem was standing with its back to Paulus, so he launched an aggressive horizontal strike directly at its middle. The blow was so forceful it would have cut a steer in half.

There was a clattering noise, and the broad, nearly four-foot-long schiavona lay splintered on the floor.

"Damn it, my favorite weapon!" Paulus grunted. He was still clearly reeling from his injury, but he was boiling with rage despite it—or perhaps because of it. He glanced around for a new weapon, and finally chose one of the burning torches on the wall. Roaring, Paulus launched it at the golem, and it landed on the creature's back. Unlike the frozen ones at the Prague cemetery, however, the golem didn't even notice. The torch fell to the ground and went out.

Lukas knew that this was going to be the hardest battle they'd ever fought.

He was about to launch himself into the fray, but Gwendolyn held him back. "That won't help us," she whispered. "The golem is invincible, you can see that. This would really be a perfect time for some of your magic."

"God in heaven, how many times do I have to say it?" Lukas scowled furiously. "I can't do magic!"

"We'll have to go about it another way, then." Gwendolyn gestured to the hexagram, which Schönborn and Elsa were still inside, both singing an ominous chorale. The book lay on the floor in front of them, open.

"If we can grab the *Grimorium* or disrupt the ritual somehow, maybe Schönborn won't be able to control the golem anymore," Gwendolyn suggested.

Lukas laughed bitterly. "You're forgetting the barrier. We can't get through there."

At that moment, Jerome dodged another of the golem's blows, so that its fist crashed into the invisible field. Even the golem's massive powers were no match for the magic wall, which only made another humming sound. The golem hesitated briefly, and then began another attack.

"See what I mean?" Lukas hissed. "Not even that thing can do it."

Gwendolyn nodded. "We can't overpower it from the side, but maybe from above."

"From above?" Lukas asked, astonished.

She winked at him. "Do you really think I shot one of my last three arrows for no reason? I wanted to see what happened when they fell down into the field from above. And did you see what happened?"

"It landed on the floor!" Lukas breathed. "Lord, you're right."

Gwendolyn pointed overhead, to where several of the rotten beams spanned across the hall. "If I can get up there, I may be able to shoot Schönborn. Perhaps I'll even manage to kill him."

"And how are you going to do that?"

"Do you see that window?" Gwendolyn gestured up again, this time at a pair of openings scarcely wider than arrowslits. "There must be some way to get to the upper floors of the palace—probably back through the mirror maze. If I can get up there, we might have a chance! But you all will have to keep fighting the golem until then, or Schönborn may grow suspicious."

"All right." Lukas nodded. "We'll try. It's probably our only chance."

The golem was in the middle of another attack, arcing its fists out silently again and again. Giovanni and Jerome barely managed to dodge its punches. With their rapiers in their hands, they looked like tiny mosquitos circling around a furious ox.

"Wish me luck," Gwendolyn said quietly. Out of nowhere, she embraced Lukas and kissed him on the lips. Then she disappeared through one of the doors.

"Good . . . luck . . ."

Lukas was so dazed that he completely forgot about the fight for a moment. That girl was going to drive him out of his mind.

Reality caught up to him again when the golem stormed directly at him. He jumped to one side, and the colossus slammed into a wall. The building trembled violently once more, but the monster turned around as though nothing had happened. Now, for the first time, Lukas got a proper look at the creature's eyes. They glowed red in its rough, loamy face like two tiny lumps of coal. There was no life in them, and no sympathy, either. The golem had no nose, and its mouth was more of a cracked line.

Lukas thought back to what the rabbi had told them about the note in the golem's mouth, and how it was the key to summoning the creature. What exactly had Rabbi Bushevi said again?

Only when that note has been removed will the golem turn to clay again.

But how were they supposed to do that? How did one reach into a rampaging stone giant's mouth? Lukas could only hope that Gwendolyn's plan had a better chance of succeeding.

Schönborn and Elsa were still singing their sinister song; now and again, the inquisitor cast a suspicious glance at Lukas and his friends, but he didn't seem to have noticed yet that one of them was missing.

Lukas gritted his teeth. Waldemar von Schönborn had said something about the invisible barrier having grown stronger. Perhaps it was impossible to penetrate from above now, too. Or it would be soon. Gwendolyn needed to move quickly.

"Oh, Lilith!" Schönborn droned. "First wife of Adam, mother of all devils and demons! Transform the materials of sword, crown, and scepter into deadly power! ABAJORETH, MALTATUM . . ." He sang along with Elsa in his deep voice.

"Where's Gwendolyn?" Paulus wheezed, stepping next to Lukas. Blood was running from his forehead into his face, and he wiped it away with the back of his hand. "Did she leave or something?"

Lukas shook his head. "No, she's going up to—"

That was as far as he got before the golem rushed at him and Paulus again, whirling through the hall like a clay tornado. Despite its size, it moved with astonishing grace.

The four of them gave up on attacking the golem, and focused on confusing it with sudden movements, so that it kept stomping back and forth, and occasionally even stumbled a little. They were hoping they could trip it up—dried clay could break, so maybe a golem would, too. At any rate, it seemed easier than reaching straight into the monster's mouth and pulling out a note.

Despite all their efforts, however, the golem remained on its feet.

"We won't be able to keep this up much longer," Jerome whispered to Lukas, wiping the sweat from his brow with his free hand. "Whatever Gwendolyn is doing, she should be quick about it."

Desperately, Lukas glanced up at the roof beams, but Gwendolyn was still nowhere to be seen. Perhaps there was no way upstairs after all.

A shadow approached from the right. Lukas ducked, but it was too late—the golem used his brief moment of inattention to smash him straight against the barrier. Lukas felt a stabbing pain in his back, like a sting from a giant hornet. He bounced off the invisible wall with a shriek and landed on the floor, where he remained, groaning. The golem stomped over to him and raised its fist once more.

At that moment, Lukas saw movement directly above the hexagram. It was Gwendolyn! She had climbed out through one of the tiny windows and was now crawling to the middle of the roof beam. Waldemar von Schönborn had not yet noticed her—his attention was completely focused on helping Elsa continue the invocation.

"Lukas, look out!" Jerome cried.

The golem's fist passed just inches from Lukas's head. Jerome had thrown himself onto the monster. Although it didn't move away, Jerome had at least managed to distract it for a moment. He was clinging to the golem's back, and the creature was shaking him around wildly, like a horse trying to buck a rider.

Now Paulus and Giovanni noticed Gwendolyn up on the roof beam as well. Immediately they glanced away, not wanting to make Waldemar von Schönborn suspicious. "Hey, magician!" Giovanni called to Schönborn. "Look what Jerome's doing with your stupid block of clay. He's teaching it manners!"

"You won't be laughing for much longer!" the inquisitor screeched, visibly enraged. "You could have fled, but now it's too late for that!" He made a motion with his hand, and all the doors slammed shut and locked.

"You're not getting out of here," Schönborn said in a taunting voice. "Eventually, your strength will give out, and then the golem will smash you like annoying insects."

Sure enough, the golem was moving backward now, hoping to crush Jerome against the wall. At the last moment, Jerome leapt off its back.

My God, Gwendolyn, hurry! Lukas thought. *Before it's too late for all of us!*

Gwendolyn was in the center of the beam. Cautiously, she rose to her feet until she was standing, broad-legged, bow in hand. She slowly drew the next-to-last arrow from her quiver, nocked it, aimed carefully . . .

. . . and fired.

XXIX

The arrow hit Waldemar von Schönborn directly in the chest. More confused than frightened, the inquisitor stopped singing and regarded the feathered shaft protruding from between the folds of his frock. Only then did his gaze shift upward to Gwendolyn.

"How dare you," he barked. "You're nothing! Nobody!" His face turned red with fury. He reached out and balled his hand into a fist, as though trying to crush Gwendolyn from a distance. For a moment, it seemed like the arrow hadn't done a thing to him, but then his expression changed. Clutching the shaft in his chest, he gasped, stumbled, and finally toppled forward like a tree.

Elsa stopped singing. The horror shimmering in her eyes pained Lukas more than all of the golem's blows put together. Elsa was afraid for Schönborn—that monster was the one she was worried about.

"Father!" she cried, hurrying over to the inquisitor, who lay twitching on the floor. Lukas recalled that Schönborn had once given the order to have his father, Count von Lohenfels, shot. Now he himself lay in the dust with an arrow in his chest—proper retribution for his malicious murder of Friedrich von Lohenfels. But Elsa didn't seem to care about that. Weeping, she shook her father. A large bloodstain was spreading across Schönborn's frock, turning the cloth even redder than it already was. He looked dead.

"Father, you can't go!" she shrieked hysterically. "The power, you hear me? The power! Damn it, you're my mentor! What will I do without you?"

All at once, Elsa stopped crying. She turned and looked up at Gwendolyn, who was still standing on the beam. The red-haired girl now had the last of her arrows nocked and ready. "You killed him!" Elsa hissed. "Murderer! You will suffer a thousand times over for that. FULGUR IGNIFAXIO!"

She raised her hand and clenched it into a fist, the way Schönborn had done before. As she did, some invisible power seemed to grab Gwendolyn by the throat. She was choking and turning red. Even so, she still managed to aim her arrow at Elsa. She drew back the bowstring . . .

The last arrow, Lukas thought. *Gwendolyn is going to kill my sister with her last arrow!*

"Don't!" he shouted.

Then several things happened at once. Lukas ran at the invisible wall. He didn't know whether it was still there, now that the ritual had ended. All he knew was that there were two girls he wanted to protect at the same time, and those two girls were facing off in a battle to the death.

Gwendolyn and Elsa.

In a fraction of a second, it became clear that he loved them both, his sister and Gwendolyn, each in her own way. What was he supposed to do?

Lukas ran toward the invisible wall, expecting to bounce off. But this time there was no humming sound, and nothing blocked his path.

The spell was broken.

Lukas stumbled into the center of the hexagram, where Elsa was still standing over her father with her fist raised. At the same moment, Lukas heard the arrow whizzing overhead.

I'm too late! he thought.

But her arrow missed Elsa by a wide margin.

It was the first time he'd ever seen Gwendolyn miss her mark. Lukas threw himself at Elsa. She still had one of her hands balled into a fist and thrashed around wildly. She managed to free herself for a moment and stretched her fist out overhead once more. Lukas heard a choking gasp, and then out of the corner of his eye, he saw Gwendolyn flailing up on the balcony. She staggered, slipped, and finally plummeted nearly five paces straight down to the floor, where she lay motionless.

"What have you done, Elsa?" Lukas gasped. "Get ahold of yourself! You're not a murderer. You're my little sister."

"Kill her, kill the girl!" Elsa screeched at the golem, ignoring Lukas's words as she struggled to control her hand movements.

The colossus immediately stopped fighting Lukas's three friends and started toward the lifeless Gwendolyn.

Lukas hesitated. If he let go of Elsa now, she would surely use her powers again. She might very well kill him, destroy every one of them. But if he didn't help Gwendolyn, the golem would dash her to pieces.

He hoped desperately that he would hear his mother's voice. But this time, everything remained silent inside him. He would have to fight this battle alone.

The golem raised its fist.

Lukas released Elsa and ran toward Gwendolyn and the golem. A second later, the golem's fist came hurtling down.

"Noooooooooo!" Lukas shouted. He threw himself between Gwendolyn and the golem, who was just about to crush the body beneath him. Lukas shut his eyes tightly, waiting for the pain, the blackness, the inevitable end. He knew he was going to die. He'd given his life for the redheaded Welsh girl he loved.

But nothing happened.

There was only a soft ringing sound.

Lukas lay motionless, still shielding Gwendolyn, feeling her heart beating against his chest.

Still, no deathblow came.

"Ah, I think the golem is broken," Jerome reported. "It's stopped moving."

Cautiously, Lukas rolled over to see. When he looked up, he saw that the clay giant's fist had stopped only a hand's width away from his head. The colossus seemed frozen, as though something had ensnared it midstrike. Its frightening mouth was open in a silent scream.

Giovanni stepped up beside the golem. "That's not all," he said. "Turn around."

Lukas turned toward the hexagram.

It was empty.

The three pieces of Imperial Regalia were still sitting between the smoking sulfur pots, but both Elsa and Waldemar von Schönborn had disappeared.

"Where are they?" Lukas whispered softly. Leaden exhaustion was spreading through him—he was more tired than he'd been in as long as he could remember.

Paulus shrugged. "No idea. When you threw yourself on top of Gwendolyn, there was a bright flash and a thunderclap, and all of a sudden the two of them were gone."

Lukas shook his head. "I don't understand. Where could they have gone?"

Gwendolyn moaned next to him. She was pale and bleeding from the mouth, but at least she was alive. Lukas bent down to her and slid her out from under the golem's fist.

"She needs a doctor," he murmured, wiping the blood from Gwendolyn's cheek. He was crying silently, though he wasn't sure whether it was out of relief that Gwendolyn was still alive, or grief that Elsa had disappeared. "I really thought my sister had killed her," he blurted out. "If I had only known how much the *Grimorium* would change Elsa . . ." He sobbed. "Damn it, we should never have let her have that accursed book!"

"Speaking of books," Giovanni said, laying a hand on Lukas's shoulder. "If you mean the *Grimorium*, Elsa left it here."

"What?" Lukas straightened up and wiped the tears from his face. It was true—the book was lying there on the floor, near the Imperial Regalia. The open pages were even more singed than before, and one bottom corner was burned, but otherwise, the *Grimorium* looked as harmless and innocent as some cheap little prayer book. Looking at it, nobody would ever suspect that it had probably caused many, many deaths.

"I doubt Elsa left the *Grimorium* here deliberately," Giovanni remarked. "She may very well return from wherever she's gone and try to retrieve it. We should leave this place as soon as possible."

"There's another reason we should hurry out of here." Jerome pointed. "I think the clay beast here may not be completely broken."

There was a creaking, cracking sound. Lukas turned his head and saw that the golem was slowly reawakening. "My God!" he exclaimed. "I nearly forgot the monster. Cross your fingers that Rabbi Bushevi was right." In one fluid motion, Lukas leapt up and reached into the golem's loamy mouth. Between its crannied cheeks, he felt a tiny piece of paper, which he grabbed with his fingers. When he withdrew his hand, he was holding a folded note.

Without hesitating, he tore it into pieces.

"Hey!" Jerome protested. "Now we'll never know how to bring a golem to life."

"I don't want to know, either," Lukas replied. "I only want to see whether we can destroy that thing. It was created to *protect* humans, not to kill them. Schönborn misused the creature for his evil purposes. Just like he used my sister," he added bitterly.

He opened his hand, and the last few scraps fluttered to the floor like snowflakes.

There was another cracking sound. Lukas looked back at the golem and saw several fissures in its earthen skin. More and more spread across the creature; its right arm fell off, and then its left; its feet broke out from under it with a crash, and the giant tipped over to the side. The entire colossus was crumbling before their eyes, like a sandcastle in the sun.

Finally, all that was left of the massive golem was a large pile of clay.

"Ashes to ashes, dirt to dirt," Paulus murmured. "Or however that's supposed to go." He winced in pain. "Let's take the genuine Regalia and get back to Prague as quickly as possible. Gwendolyn isn't the only one here who needs a doctor."

Lukas's eyes drifted from the unconscious Gwendolyn back to the hexagram, where his sister had been. The smudged letters spelling out LILITH were still visible. He'd lost Elsa once again. Where might she be? Was she still alive?

The loss pained him like a dagger twisting into his heart. Tears sprang to his eyes again, but he wiped them away.

Unlike his friends, Lukas didn't think that Elsa would ever return to this sinister place. She would surely want the *Grimorium* back, though. The book was his collateral, the guarantee that he would see Elsa again someday.

If she was still alive.

I'll find Elsa again, he told himself. *Someday.*

Lukas bent down to retrieve the book, and tucked it away without looking at it. Then he turned back to his friends. "Let's go," he said. "It's a long way back to Prague."

When they stepped out of the castle, the sun was just coming up. The treetops were bathed in a soft pink glow, and the birds chirped happily as though nothing was wrong. There was no sign of the bat-cats, nor of any of the other horrible hybrid creatures from Polonius's laboratory. Only the dead wolf-buck was still lying on the bridge.

When they reached the other side of the pond, they stopped in the woods to build a stretcher out of branches for Gwendolyn. Paulus carried the Imperial Regalia in a sack on his back. Although he was injured himself, he insisted on helping carry the stretcher, as well. "I didn't think much of that big-mouthed beast at first," he grunted. "Thought girls would never amount to anything as fighters. But by God, I'd consider this girl fit to be a Black Musketeer."

Lukas washed the dirt and blood from his face in the brook flowing through the woods. He still felt strangely wrung out and exhausted, but the cold water did him good and brought back at least a little of his spirit, though his thoughts were still with Elsa.

And Gwendolyn.

As they walked through the woods, Lukas kept casting worried looks at the redheaded girl on the stretcher. Gwendolyn's breathing was even; her eyelids fluttered occasionally, but her eyes remained closed. Lukas recalled how Gwendolyn's arrow had missed Elsa from that short distance. And suddenly it hit him: she *wanted* to miss. She would rather have died than shoot Elsa.

Even if Elsa had turned into an evil witch.

The many stunted oaks, which had seemed so sinister and confused them so much the night before, now seemed peaceful and innocent in the morning light. Rabbits were scampering around near the crumbling pavilion beside the path.

Just as they reached the edge of the park, they saw a solitary figure approaching from White Mountain, hurrying straight toward them. For a moment, Lukas was afraid it might be Schönborn returning. Lukas reached for the *Grimorium* underneath his doublet, as though the magic book might give him some sort of protection. But as the man came closer, his fear turned to astonishment, and finally to joy.

"Senno!" Lukas exclaimed.

The astrologer appeared to have traveled a long way. His once-beautiful blue frock was torn and filthy, his otherwise-manicured beard unkempt. He was limping, supporting himself on a stick. When he saw Lukas and his friends, he waved and sat down to wait for them on a stone, a short distance below White Mountain.

Lukas ran up excitedly to meet the astrologer. "Senno!" he exclaimed. "We thought you were dead. Drowned in the ocean, or buried somewhere deep underground."

"Ah, well, let's say it wasn't quite that bad, but nearly so." Senno stroked his beard. "That terrible spell tossed me straight into the Bohemian Forest, a hundred dusty miles from here. I had to flee from a band of superstitious goatherds, after I appeared in their stinking hut. Then I rode like the Devil, got mixed up with a couple of robbers, and—"

"Why weren't you transported to Prague, like we were?" Giovanni broke in. The others had joined them now, and regarded the astrologer with a mixture of curiosity and suspicion.

Senno shrugged. "I'm afraid Schönborn must have made that happen. Under the sole of my shoe, I found a piece of crossed lead, which disrupts magic of all sorts. That dog must have slipped it to me somehow, presumably through a messenger." The astrologer glanced around at the four friends, and at the stretcher Gwendolyn was lying on. "At any rate, I'm delighted to find you all here alive," he said, clapping the dust from his robe. "I really thought I was too late."

"And we were a hair's breadth from leaving you nothing but our corpses to bury," Jerome piped up. "Next time you want to help us defeat Schönborn, perhaps you should hurry a little."

"You certainly did show up at exactly the right moment to miss all the action," Giovanni murmured. "One might almost think you waited until you were sure you wouldn't get your hands dirty."

"When I was in the Bohemian Forest, I realized that all of this was just a trap of Schönborn's. I saw the ominous constellation of stars that appeared in the firmament." He pointed up to the morning sky, where the last few stars were just fading away. "When I figured out that it would be centered directly over White Mountain in a day or two, I feared the worst, so I hurried out here as fast as I could."

"Yes, yes, Mars in Leo," Paulus muttered. "Thanks very much, Mister Astro-Driveler. We already know."

Senno sighed. "I'm afraid you've learned far more than that, right?" He glanced furtively at the handle of the imperial sword, which was poking out of the sack Paulus was holding. "Hm, I see you've actually found the Imperial Regalia."

"Only after we were duped by cheap counterfeits first," Giovanni replied, grinning.

"Counterfeits?" Senno tilted his head. "And who's this little red-head?" He pounded the end of his hiking stick on the ground. "How about you start by telling me exactly what happened this past week?"

"First, we're going to bring this girl to a doctor," Lukas replied, gesturing to Gwendolyn. "Then we'll see." He gave Senno a thin smile. "We spent days waiting for you in vain. You can be patient with us for an hour or two."

"One point for you, little warrior." Senno lowered his head humbly, though Lukas suspected that he was grinning to himself. "Perhaps you all know an inn in Prague where we could have a tankard or two of ale," he said. "All this traveling has made me murderously thirsty."

"Oh, yes, we know a tavern like that," Paulus replied happily. Then he flinched and touched the lump on his forehead. "Ah, damn! Well, at least this time I know my headache won't be from drinking too much."

A couple of hours later, they sat down together in the tavern of the Black Boar Inn, where their Prague adventure had begun scarcely a week ago. To Lukas, it seemed like a thousand years had passed since that day. The stuffed head of the wild boar stared down at them from its position above the bar, and the bearskins on the walls still smelled unpleasantly musty—but Lukas now felt somewhat at home here.

The three pieces of Imperial Regalia lay on the table in front of them, between the tankards of dark ale Paulus had drained and a large platter of bread, sausage, and cheese. The crown had a slight dent, and there were a couple of new scratches on the sword handle, but besides that, nothing about the trio of sacred objects suggested that the friends had just wrenched them from the hands of a dark sorcerer.

They'd told Senno everything that had happened to them over the past several days.

"Hm, so we can be sure that these are real Regalia?" Senno asked with his mouth full, popping a piece of cheese into his mouth. His blue frock was still torn, but at least it was free of dust and dirt now, and his freshly oiled beard gleamed.

"Our thief confirmed it earlier," Giovanni replied, grinning. "They're the originals. If anyone here can tell real diamonds from fakes, it's Gwendolyn."

"Who's doing better, by the way," Paulus said, reaching for his tankard again. His head was bandaged, and his left arm was in a sling. "The doctor our astro-driveler so kindly paid for said he'd never seen anyone so cheerful after falling from a height of nearly five paces," Paulus went on, grinning. "She hadn't even broken anything. Good doctor, by the way. He actually thinks that beer has exceptional medicinal benefits—in small doses, of course."

"He probably didn't know that you considered three tankards a small dose," Lukas kidded him as his friend took another drink. He smiled, happy to hear Gwendolyn was going to be all right—but then he grew serious again. "If that golem hadn't suddenly frozen in place, we probably all would have been done for. I still don't understand why it just stopped moving. It was like a miracle."

"Hm . . ." Senno stroked his beard thoughtfully. "I don't actually believe in miracles. I'm more inclined to say it was a spell." He winked at Lukas. "Isn't it possible that, in the end, magic was involved after all?"

"Magic!" Giovanni smacked his forehead. "Of course. That's the answer to this mystery. Lukas cast a spell. That's why the golem froze, and why Schönborn and Elsa disappeared."

"What nonsense are you talking?" Lukas snapped at him. "I've told you I can't do magic . . ." But then he trailed off, thinking about that soft ringing sound in his ears, and about how exhausted he'd suddenly felt back at the palace. He'd felt a similar exhaustion several times here in Prague, always just after some magical occurrence. Perhaps he really had cast a spell? But how? And why had it worked that time? He hadn't done anything.

Had he?

Lukas remembered how Gwendolyn had been lying on the floor of the palace hall, deathly pale. Her red hair had formed a halo around her head, beautiful as an angel, the way it had back at the rose garden when he'd healed her magically. Both times he'd been endlessly sad, but he'd also felt something more.

Something more than affection.

"Love!" Lukas exclaimed, finally understanding.

The others at the table stared at him in confusion.

"Perhaps the golem whacked him in the head after all," Paulus quipped.

Lukas let out a relieved laugh. "No, you don't understand. I finally realized how I'm able to do magic. It's love." He hesitated. The whole thing suddenly struck him as a little embarrassing.

Jerome raised an eyebrow. "How do you mean?"

"I think Lukas is right," Senno piped up. "If I heard you correctly before, Lukas has done magic four times now." He counted on his fingers. "The first time, his love for his mother gave him the strength to heal himself. At Polonius's lab, it was his love for his sister, and in the rose garden and at the palace, it was his love for Gwendolyn."

"But how does that make sense?" Giovanni asked. "Why does Lukas only have magic powers when he loves someone?"

"Love is a very powerful force," Senno explained. "Some people say it's stronger than hate, stronger than anger, stronger than anything else in the world, in fact."

"My mother always said that," Lukas murmured, more to himself. "I should have known."

Senno sighed. "Schönborn is a wizard of black magic, so he draws his power from hate. I'm afraid Elsa is just like her father. Lukas, on the other hand, inherited the gift from his mother, who was a white witch—one of the last in existence. That was why Schönborn wanted to join with her: he thought that their powers combined would be invincible. But the plan went awry. In the end, love triumphed over hate, just as it has today."

"Oho!" Paulus smacked the table, laughing. "Didn't I tell you? Our little Lukas is traveling Cupid's path!" He gave Lukas a teasing bow. "Can we be groomsmen at your wedding, at least?"

"You dimwit." Lukas wound up to give Paulus a fat smack upside the head, but then he stopped, grinning. "Ah, what does it matter? Yes, I like Gwendolyn," he admitted with a shrug. "Whether she's the love of my life, I don't know. I'm not very experienced in such things. But it's a strong feeling, different from anything I've ever felt in my life."

"These strong emotions are what give you the power to do magic," Senno said. "But I'm afraid you won't be able to create them deliberately, the way you build a fire or light a lamp. They come and go without your help. That was how it was with Gwendolyn."

"She *is* pretty, though, with that red hair of hers," Jerome pointed out, grinning. *"Oh là là!"*

"And she can fight, too," Paulus agreed.

"A good match," Giovanni added.

"Oh, stop already, you idiots," Lukas said. "What's the big deal? Why is it so hard for boys to admit that they like someone? Can anyone tell me that?"

Giovanni smiled and gave him a friendly clap on the shoulder. "You're right, we're sorry. We don't mean anything by it."

"And besides, Gwendolyn is too old for Lukas anyway," Jerome pointed out. "Now, my humble self, on the other hand—"

"Ah, if I could just interrupt you young gentlemen for a moment," Senno broke in. "I'm less interested in this girl than in what became of Schönborn and Elsa."

Paulus snorted. "Well, we know that Schönborn is most likely burning in hell. Gwendolyn's arrow hit him right in the chest."

"Don't be so certain about that," Senno countered. "Schönborn and Elsa invoked the demon Lilith; perhaps she helped him. Even without the *Grimorium*, that man is extremely powerful. Which brings me to my next question." Senno's eyes twinkled as he turned to Lukas. "The *Grimorium Nocturnum*. You have it with you, don't you?"

Lukas nodded hesitantly. His hand went to his doublet, where he had the magic book safely against his chest. "Elsa must have lost it when she and Schönborn disappeared so suddenly," he said quietly. "I'm just holding it for her, hoping that she'll return to me because she wants it back. The book changed Elsa; without the *Grimorium*, she might well go back to being the little sister I knew and loved."

"Have you considered that perhaps the book didn't want to stay with Elsa any longer?" Senno asked. "Perhaps that was why it didn't disappear with her. Maybe you're the chosen one?"

Lukas gave a start and scooted away from Senno involuntarily. "How can you say such a thing? The *Grimorium* chose Elsa, not me. I never disputed that, even if she claimed otherwise."

"That's not what I meant." Senno raised a hand in a placating gesture. "I'm only saying that you have great magical powers within you as well. Maybe the *Grimorium* wants to show you how to use them more effectively. Thus far, they've emerged purely by coincidence, as an emotional response—you've never been able to control them. But perhaps the book would help you with that. For the benefit of humanity, of course," he added.

"Or for *your* own gain?" Lukas shot back. "Don't take this personally, Senno, but I don't think I'm going to use the book. I don't even want to open it. It changes people, makes them evil. I saw it happen to Elsa."

"Your sister is young and weak," Senno replied, giving Lukas a penetrating look. "The weak are always led astray quickly. But you are stronger, Lukas. I can sense it."

"My sister isn't weak! And I don't want to hear any more of this nonsense." Lukas stood up. "I'm going to go check on Gwendolyn," he said curtly. "She might be hungry."

Lukas fetched a jug of water and a few slices of bread, and carried them upstairs to Gwendolyn's chamber. He was still confused. He had no idea how to use his powers, nor if they would ever emerge again. He could only hope that he would see everything more clearly in the future.

He also decided he didn't trust Senno. Lukas suspected that the astrologer would be all too happy to use the *Grimorium* for his own purposes. But the book clearly hadn't chosen Senno—that dubious honor had fallen to two children.

Him and Elsa.

Tentatively, Lukas knocked on the door to Gwendolyn's room. There was so much he wanted to talk to her about, but already he felt a lump in his throat. No response came from inside; Lukas heard only a creaking sound. He went in.

Fully dressed in her leather doublet, trousers, and boots, with her bow slung over one shoulder, Gwendolyn was standing at the open window with one leg already over the sill. The shutters were swaying in the breeze, squeaking. Her red hair spilled out from underneath the bandage around her head.

"What are you doing?" Lukas blinked in confusion.

"Isn't that obvious? I'm departing this lovely inn." Gwendolyn bowed with a thin smile. "Sorry that I can't pay for the lodging and the medical care, but in exchange I won't ask payment for my invaluable services on this adventure. Agreed?"

"But you can't just leave," Lukas blurted out. "I mean . . . you're injured! And we still have to bring the Imperial Regalia back to the Kaiser and . . ." Lukas tried to find more reasons to protest.

"I think others are better suited to that task than I am," she replied. "My work is done here. You have your younger sister to find, and I have a younger brother who needs my help." She furrowed her brow, as though she had just come to a decision. "I think Jussi and I will be leaving. Perhaps we'll go back to Wales. Now that Father is dead, there's no reason for us to stay in this city."

"But what will you live on?" Lukas asked, making one last desperate attempt.

Gwendolyn gave him an impish smile. "Oh, don't worry about that. Welsh girls always find a way to get by."

"But you can't go, because . . . because . . ." Lukas hesitated.

"Because what?" Gwendolyn asked, tilting her head to one side.

"Because . . . because I love you!"

Now it was finally out. Lukas felt strangely relieved.

Gwendolyn stared at him in astonishment, and then smiled. Lukas thought he saw a flicker of uncertainty in her eyes. "No boy has ever said that to me," she said with a soft laugh. "Especially not such a good-looking, courageous one who wields a rapier better than anyone I've ever seen. That's very nice of you to say."

"You mean you feel the same?" Lukas asked, hopeful.

"Love?" Gwendolyn shut her eyes for a second. "What a big word! I like you, Lukas. A lot. And I admit that I've been thinking about you. But love?" She shrugged. "Maybe in another life, or in a couple of years."

"Just go ahead and say it. You think I'm too young." It came out sounding more defiant and childish than he'd intended.

"We're both young, Lukas. And there's still so much to experience out there. So many adventures to be had." She winked at him. "Come visit me in Wales. There are lonely moors and deep, shadowy valleys we can roam through. And when it rains, we can slip under a blanket together. Trust me, it rains a lot in Wales. *Hwyl fawr!*"

With that, she jumped.

All that remained of her was the soft echo of her laugh. Lukas hurried to the window and saw her red hair one last time before she slipped around a corner.

Gwendolyn had disappeared from his life.

Lukas sat down on the bed and ran a hand through his hair. He'd acted like such a fool! Like a little boy, not like the proud fighter he wanted to be for Gwendolyn. But then he thought about that brief flicker of uncertainty in her eyes when he'd confessed his love to her, and he was sure that she felt something more for him, too. Maybe they'd run into one another again someday. Until then, he'd have his memories of her red hair, her clever retorts, and more than anything, her unmatched archery skills.

Still slightly dazed, he went back down to the tavern, where Senno and his friends were waiting for him expectantly.

"Well?" Giovanni asked. "How is she?"

Lukas shrugged. "She's gone."

"Gone?" Paulus leapt up. "You just let her leave?"

"There's no stopping someone like Gwendolyn. We should have known as much." Lukas smiled, thinking back to Gwendolyn's parting words.

"Just as well," Senno sniffed. "Women only lead to unhappiness anyway. I can already think of several potential adventures where the *Grimorium* could help us quite a bit."

"I believe I said this already," Lukas interrupted. "I'm never going to use that damned book."

"Not even to defend your homeland?" Senno asked in a sly tone.

Lukas knitted his brow. "How do you mean?"

"I've received word that hostile mercenaries are threatening the Palatinate again. They may very well be at the Lohenfels gates before long."

"Then we'll ride like the Devil and stand in their way," Lukas said. "We've managed this long without the *Grimorium*; we will continue to do so. Besides, you don't use books and love to defeat hostile mercenaries, you use swords."

Senno laughed his high, crystalline laugh. "Well spoken, young warrior. And what about your sister?"

"If Elsa *does* want the book back, she'll come to me," Lukas replied resolutely. "I have a feeling this isn't the end. And when the time comes, I'll fight for my sister."

Senno nodded. "All right, as you wish. I'll depart for Vienna tomorrow, to return the Imperial Regalia. The Kaiser will be pleased to hear that—"

"Ah, speaking of the Regalia . . ." Jerome raised the crown hesitantly. "I didn't mean to break it, *je le jure*! I only wanted to put it on for a moment, to see how it looked on me."

Senno leapt to his feet. "You fool! What have you done?"

Jerome pointed to several empty settings on the crown—the gleaming, colorful gems had fallen onto the table. "They just tumbled out," Jerome complained. "There was nothing I could do."

"Just tumbled out?" Senno lifted one of the stones gingerly and gave it a long, scrutinizing look. Then he picked up another, and then a third. Finally, he cursed and threw them all to the floor, where they shattered. "These stones are fakes!" he exclaimed. "Someone stole the real jewels and put these cheap bits of glass in the crown!"

"I think we all know who that was," Giovanni groaned. "What did I say before? If anyone can tell real diamonds from fakes, it's Gwendolyn. I fear she must have swapped them and taken the real ones."

"But how is that possible?" Paulus asked. "She was lying upstairs in bed injured the entire time."

Giovanni shrugged, grinning. "Don't forget that she's a thief. A fairly good one, too."

Senno stamped his foot furiously. "How am I supposed to explain this to the Kaiser?"

"I suggest you don't say anything to him," Giovanni replied, peering at the empty settings. "Stick a few glass stones in there with wax and keep silent. Only a few of the diamonds are missing—not all of them. If you're lucky, the Kaiser won't notice a thing."

"And if I'm not, I'll end up a head shorter," Senno growled. "And all because of that devil-woman!"

Lukas smiled quietly to himself, picturing Gwendolyn with a pouch full of gems, her bow over her shoulder and her brother beside her—leaving Prague in search of new adventures.

Wherever her path took her, he wished her luck.

EPILOGUE

Eight Weeks Later, at Castle Lohenfels in the Palatinate

Lukas stood in the center of the courtyard, watching the local farmer boys arm themselves and suit up in stained chain mail and rusty helmets. Autumn had announced its arrival with an icy wind that blew cold, misty rain into the boys' eyes, but none of them complained. Their faces were full of grim determination; their hands gripped swords, rapiers, pikes, and lances. Those who had no other weapons resorted to scythes and cudgels. They were all afraid, but they also knew that fear made a poor companion in war.

With dark expressions and anxious hearts, the boys waited for the enemy's arrival.

It had taken Lukas and his friends more than a month to return to the Palatinate from Prague. Senno had found them horses to make their trip slightly less arduous, but the countryside they'd ridden through had still been desolate, ravaged by war. The four friends had passed through destroyed villages and ruined fields where not a single blade of grass grew. They'd seen entire cities burning, their towers and churches reaching to the skies like fiery torches.

Senno had been right. The war had returned to the Palatinate.

Rather than organized armies, there were predatory robbers, small groups and battalions roaming through villages and vineyards, plundering and pillaging. Their sheer numbers were enough to make the Palatinate a living hell. Riders had reported a larger troop advancing from Heidelberg through the Odenwald Forest, toward Castle Lohenfels. Farmhouses and stalls were already burning on the outskirts of the castle woodlands.

They would reach the castle any day now.

"Spread out along the wall!" Lukas called to the boys. "A dozen of you on each side. Look for Paulus, Giovanni, and Jerome—they're your officers! Follow their orders!"

The boys did as commanded, climbing ladders made of woven willow branches up to the wall-walk, where Lukas's friends were already waiting for them. Paulus, in particular, had worked hard over the past two weeks to teach the farmhands and servant boys the art of war. Now they would see whether all their hard work, sweat, and bruises had been worth it.

Lukas glanced briefly toward the castle keep. He'd locked the *Grimorium* away in the cellar there, inside a large chest reinforced with bands of iron. Sometimes, late at night, he thought he heard it calling out to him softly.

It was a high, delicate voice that whispered to him, telling him everything he could accomplish with the book. A rain of gold ducats for new weapons? Impenetrable castle gates? An army of enemy mercenaries going up in flames? In Lukas's dreams, anything was possible. All he had to do was take the *Grimorium* out of the chest and look through it.

Surely it would soon reveal its secrets to him. The way it had done for Elsa . . .

And then it would gradually take control of me, just like it did Elsa, Lukas thought. *Until I end up like Schönborn. An evil black sorcerer.*

He'd managed to resist the temptation thus far. That was partly thanks to his friends, who looked after him, took him out hunting, argued with him, fenced with him, joked around with him, did what was needed to drive his dark thoughts away.

Including his thoughts of Elsa.

"Raise the drawbridge!" Paulus shouted. "Think you can manage that soon? Or are you planning to invite the enemy in to play dice?"

The drawbridge squeaked and groaned as two of the young boys turned the iron wheels to raise it. The four friends had had it reinforced just a few days ago. Now it was time to find out whether it would hold.

There were moments when Lukas missed his little sister so much that he thought his heart would burst. But the girl standing beside Waldemar von Schönborn in that hexagram hadn't been his Elsa any longer. The book had had complete control over her by then. Lukas hoped he would see his real sister again someday, the Elsa he knew from before. That was why he kept the *Grimorium* safe, so that she would come back to him and he could talk to her.

Even though he knew it might cost him his life.

He'd considered destroying the book, simply burning it or throwing it into the river. But Senno had warned him that the *Grimorium Nocturnum* would defend itself, and that it would release forces powerful enough to destroy all of Lohenfels.

So the *Grimorium* remained in the chest.

"Enemy sighted!" called Giovanni, who had the best eyes of any of them. "Everyone to their posts!"

Lukas shook himself, clearing his head, and buckled his rapier on. He didn't have time to worry about that damnable book. He had to defend his homeland and his father's castle, and he had to protect the lives of these young boys.

He climbed up to the wall-walk, where a row of youths were crouched behind the arrowslits, holding longbows and crossbows. Among them was the boy Lukas himself had trained in fencing just before they'd left for Prague. The boy already seemed a great deal older and more mature. His name was Jonathan, and Lukas was going to make a good fencer out of him.

"Are you ready?" Lukas asked.

Jonathan nodded.

Lukas could tell he was afraid, but his gaze was determined—not a twelve-year-old boy's eyes, but those of a soldier defending his land.

"Yes, my lord," Jonathan replied.

Lukas sighed. "How many times do I have to tell you that I'm not a lord. I'm a boy like you, and . . ."

He stopped short, seeing dark points on the horizon. They quickly came together to form a line, and that line was approaching fast. Soon he could make out individual horses and riders. The distant sounds of whoops and shouts reached his ears.

The enemy had arrived.

"Together against death and the Devil!" Lukas shouted, just as Zoltan had once done to drown out all their fears. He raised his rapier, and the other boys followed his lead.

"To hell and beyond!" they cried in chorus.

Lukas smiled ruefully. They weren't Black Musketeers yet, but they could shout their fear into the wind and stand tall when it mattered most.

ACKNOWLEDGMENTS

My children, Niklas (15) and Lily (12), acted as my test readers and editors for this book, too. Thanks for your wonderful suggestions and your severe but constructive criticism! I know I really got on your nerves with all my questions, especially while we were on vacation on Mallorca. It's not always easy being a writer's kids . . . But I'll pay you back by taking you with me on my next research trip up to Wales. Promise!

ABOUT THE AUTHOR

 Oliver Pötzsch spent years working for Bavarian Broadcasting and now devotes his time entirely to writing. His historical novels for adults have made him internationally famous. He is the author of the books in the Hangman's Daughter series, the children's novel *Knight Kyle and the Magic Silver Lance*, and the Black Musketeers series, including *Book of the Night* and *Sword of Power*. He lives in Munich with his family.

ABOUT THE TRANSLATOR

Jaime McGill is originally from Omaha, Nebraska, and recently returned to the States after eleven wonderful years in Berlin. She has translated more than a dozen novels, including works by best-selling German authors like Jessica Koch and Emily Bold. She also holds a master's degree in music, and when not translating, she can often be found holding a bass clarinet, surrounded by effects pedals.